Isabel

Families of Dorset Book 2

MARTHA KEYES

This book is a work of fiction. Names, characters, places, and incidents are either
products of the author's imagination or are used fictitiously. Any resemblance to actual
persons, living or dead, events, or locales, is entirely coincidental.
Martha Keyes
http://www.marthakeyes.com
First Printing: August 2019

❧ I ❧

LONDON, ENGLAND 1813

Isabel Cosgrove fanned herself rapidly, lending only half an ear to the gossip being relayed by her friend Mary, who stood at her side.

A long queue of people stood in the entry hall of the Rodwell's London town home, waiting to be announced—waiting to intensify the oppressive heat which made Isabel's gloves cling to her arms.

Her younger sister Cecilia stood at her other side, listening intently to each morsel of hearsay transmitted by Mary.

Whatever her own indifference to *ton* gossip, Isabel could never have avoided it, surrounded as she was by people who thrived on it. She forgave Mary the weakness, as she knew she had acquired the habit from her mother.

Cecilia had less excuse for indulging.

"So, he *did* follow her to town," Mary Holledge said with a self-satisfied smile. "I expected as much."

"Who?" Cecilia said, turning and craning her neck to follow Mary's gaze.

Mary shot a sideways glance at Cecilia and pursed her lips. She clearly hadn't been speaking to Cecilia. But as Isabel rarely paid her gossip any attention, it was unclear to whom she *had* been addressing herself.

Isabel smiled at her friend's reluctance to enlighten Cecilia. In another world, Cecilia and Mary might have gotten along quite well.

But Mary was not fond of Cecilia, despite their shared love of gossip. She tolerated her for Isabel's sake, but Isabel stood in little doubt of her true feelings. Mary often referred to Cecilia as "the minx" when she was not around.

"Charles Galbraith," Mary finally answered in a reluctant tone.

Isabel stilled and her pulse quickened, her eyes moving about the room. They landed on a dark-haired gentleman with an ethereal beauty on his arm.

She hadn't seen him in years, but she had no trouble at all recognizing the brooding countenance—it was more rather than less pronounced than it had been during his childhood. And yet somehow it enhanced his attraction.

She had wondered time and again over the years what it would be like to finally be introduced to Charles Galbraith during her Season; what it would be like to encounter the gentleman rather than the callow youth who had been an infrequent visitor to her family's home in Dorset years ago.

True, Isabel had not then anticipated that he would be absent from every gathering she attended, or that her own Season would be delayed a year in order to bring out Cecilia at the same time. As it was, Isabel had been introduced to the *ton* in the shadow of her sister's unrivaled beauty and charm. And Charles Galbraith was nowhere to be found.

Until now.

"Julia Darling is a vision, isn't she?" Mary sighed. "Effortlessly reminding us all that we stand no chance at all against her in the struggle for Galbraith's hand." She raised her brows and inclined her head. "Not that there ever *was* any chance for the rest of us."

Cecilia made a noncommittal sound. "Mr. Houghton only said the other night that I am the better favored between Miss Darling and myself."

Mary sent a forbearing look at Isabel. "Your humility is affecting, as always, Cecilia."

Cecilia's head whipped around, an affronted look on her face. "Surely it is not prideful to simply relay someone's stated opinion."

"Oh," Mary said with a look of faux-interest, "do you also relay opinions that are less than complimentary? I could enlighten you if you stand in any need."

"Please don't, you two," Isabel said, feeling unaccountably irritable.

Cecilia's chin came up, and her eyes went back to Galbraith. "He is very handsome, isn't he?"

Isabel felt her jaw tighten. Cecilia often spoke of the gentlemen she admired, and she always managed to contrive an introduction not long after. It had never bothered Isabel much. Until now.

What was this silly possessiveness she felt for Charles Galbraith?

"I am determined that he shall ask me to dance tonight," said Cecilia, the self-extended challenge sparkling in her blue eyes. She sent a sideways glance at Mary. "If only to prove you wrong, Mary."

Isabel gripped her lips together. If it was what Cecilia wished for, she would likely find success.

A gentleman approached the three of them, bowing and then requesting a dance with Cecilia.

Mary let out an annoyed sigh once she was gone. "Is it wrong that I very much hope Mr. Houghton treads on her dress during the set?"

Isabel suppressed a smile. "I think it *is* wrong, Mary."

"She is maddening, though, you must admit."

Isabel said nothing, but the way her body felt tight was a testament to Mary's statement.

She had watched Cecilia gain the attention and affection of countless men during the Season. But to think that she might succeed in doing so with the *one* man Isabel had been watching for in vain at each and every social event …it provoked uncharitable thoughts within her that she thought she had succeeded in ridding herself of.

It was all silly, anyway, and she knew it well. To spend years reflecting on a simple interaction that happened when she had been six years old?

Of course, it hadn't felt simple at the time.

IZZY SAT ON THE STAIRWELL, *her arms folded on top of her bent knees, hot tears streaming down her face.*

It wasn't fair, of course. The doll was hers, not Cecy's. It even had brown hair and white lace around the neckline to match Izzy's.

But Cecy's tantrum had been effective—they always were—and Papa had insisted that Izzy give her the doll to play with.

Cecy would likely set the doll down and forget about it within five minutes in favor of some other shiny toy.

But Papa had wanted Cecy's whining to stop, whatever it took. He was busy transacting business with Mr. Galbraith and wanted no further disruptions.

Energetic footsteps sounded on the stone steps behind Izzy, slowing as they came closer and finally stopping altogether.

"What's the matter?" It was Mr. Galbraith's son, Charles, who had accompanied his father on his business at Portsgrove House.

Izzy brushed at the tears on her cheeks with the back of her hand. She didn't want him to see her crying like a silly little girl—no different than Cecy, really.

He was older, after all. At least nine.

"Nothing," she said, trying not to sniff.

He sat down beside her. "I don't believe you."

She looked at him with a sidelong glance. He didn't look very agreeable, with his dark features and caterpillar brows.

"You'll only laugh at me," she said resentfully as another tear escaped.

He put his hand over his heart. "I won't. I swear it."

Her mouth twisted to the side as she regarded him suspiciously. There was no hint of a smile on his face, though.

She related the events of the morning, annoyed to find that she had begun crying again by the end of the tale.

She avoided his eye as she sniffed, wondering when he would begin giggling at her silly reason for weeping.

He scooted closer to her and put his arm around her.

"Well," he said prosaically, "if you can't have your special doll, we shall have to find something else to do, shan't we? Something to make your sister mad with jealousy."

A small smile threatened at the corner of Izzy's mouth. "Like what?"

A mischievous grin spread across his face, and he stood, taking her by the hand. "Follow me."

No, it hadn't felt simple at all then. Charles had made her forget the doll and Cecilia's selfishness. He had taken her outside where they had rolled down the hill, until their stomachs hurt from laughing, and then they had thrown rocks while sitting on the big fallen tree which spanned the width of the stream—all until Izzy's governess had found them and scolded them.

But the scold hadn't dampened her spirits, and she hadn't even minded when she saw Cecy pick up the doll again when Izzy walked into the room.

Did Mr. Galbraith remember his kindness toward the young Isabel? It was unlikely. He hadn't even seemed to notice her on his next visit to Portsgrove, two years later.

But Isabel had never forgotten him.

She looked at Mr. Galbraith across the room, coming down the set with the utterly perfect Miss Darling beside him.

She swallowed and averted her eyes. A six-year old's admiration was a silly reason to feel jealous at the sight of him with another woman, be she ever so beautiful.

If Isabel ever had the chance to repay him for his thoughtful action, she would be grateful. But more likely than not, they would have no reason to cross paths. Whatever their fathers' business had been, it had long since ended.

She would accustom herself to seeing him from time to time, an announcement of his engagement would be forthcoming, no doubt, and that would be the end of a long, silly girlish fancy.

"Your luck is not in, Cosgrove."

There was only a slight slurring of Charles Galbraith's words, despite the various empty glass bottles next to the table. Charles stifled a yawn as the hands of the mahogany clock struck the hour of two.

"Nonsense." The older man grabbed at a piece of paper, hands fumbling.

Charles shook his head, and the crease in his black brow deepened. He tossed what remained in his glass into his mouth. "I won't take any more of your vowels. I have plenty as things stand."

Cosgrove looked up, eyes as alert as his wine-laden lids would allow. "Some other stake then."

Charles blinked lazily as he raised himself from his chair and reached for his coat.

It was a nuisance having to tread carefully around Cosgrove. The man wasn't likable by any means, but as he was somewhat of a lynchpin in the new investments Charles's father was pursuing, Charles had done what had been necessary to avoid offending the capricious old man. He would much rather have continued the night at Brooks's, but here he was, indulging a man who seemed entirely unable to win a hand at cards.

At least Cosgrove's cellar was well-stocked. It hadn't completely distracted Charles from the miserable prelude to the evening, but it had helped.

"Perhaps another time, Cosgrove," he said.

Cosgrove reared his head back in an unsteady motion of displeasure. "Come, Galbraith. The night is still young! Plenty more brandy below stairs. If you'll just sit down a moment—" he made a motion to pull Charles down into his seat again but was forced to steady himself on the table instead "—I'm sure we can agree upon new stakes. Surely there's something you want besides money?" His slurred words held a hint of desperation.

Charles's jaw tightened. "The only thing I want is to forget this night."

"Well you've not drunk near enough for that," Cosgrove said, pouring more brandy and offering the glass to Charles.

Charles looked at it for a moment and then reached past it to the decanter, drinking its contents in a few swift gulps.

Cosgrove's eyes widened, and he blinked rapidly. "Good heavens!" He eyed Charles with misgiving. "I don't grudge a man some drink, but I draw the line at him being sick on my floors, you know."

"Don't give it a thought," Charles replied, setting the bottle down with a small clank. "I am not known for having a weak stomach."

Cosgrove nodded but glanced at the empty bottle of brandy uneasily. "Forget this night, you say? You may well." He moved the glass of brandy he had poured further away from Charles and looked at him warily. "You're put out. I trust I've given you no offense?"

Charles shook his head.

Cosgrove thought for a moment, and then cocked an eyebrow. "Troubles with the fairer sex?"

Charles's jaw shifted back and forth. "Fair is hardly the word I should choose. Fickle seems more apt."

Cosgrove wagged his finger, shaking his head. "Ah! Haven't met the right one, that's all."

Charles's sardonic brow went up. He reached for the glass Cosgrove had moved away from him and swirled it in circles. "And where might I find such a paragon?"

Cosgrove considered for a moment. "Can't say. I never did meet the right one myself. I married for money. But I should've married a beauty. They both run out, but the money runs out faster, you know, and she'll hold it over your head til it's gone." He shuddered.

Charles tossed back the brandy, uninterested in his host's ruminations. Cosgrove was very near the last person whose advice he cared to follow. His father needed Cosgrove's influence and good will, not his pointless counsel.

Cosgrove sat up in his chair. "Take one of mine! That's the ticket. Got more daughters than I know what to do with. And my Cecilia is devilish pretty. Just look!" He got up from his chair and tottered over to a painting on the wall nearest Charles.

Charles breathed in deeply, summoning patience for the old man, and then turned toward the portrait.

It was a family portrait and demonstrated the accuracy of Cosgrove's statement—he had plenty of daughters. He was seated in the middle of the portrait, his tall and sturdy wife looming over him, and six children surrounding them, only one of whom—the oldest— was a boy. Charles had met some of the children in his younger years when he had visited Portsgrove House with his father, but despite that, he couldn't say that any of them looked particularly familiar.

Cosgrove pointed at one of the girls.

"That's my Cecilia. She's something to behold, ain't she?" He cast a knowing glance at Charles.

Charles swallowed, blinked rapidly, and moved closer to the painting.

Cosgrove patted his shoulder appreciatively. "Yes, yes, my boy. And she's yours for the taking. Provided you win! Which is no sure thing, mind you. My luck often turns with the rising sun. But there.

No need for any more IOUs, aye? What do you say we play a hand for her?"

Charles stood transfixed, willing his eyes to focus. What he thought he was seeing was not possible.

"Curse this brandy," he said, squeezing his eyes shut.

The effects of his foolish drinking were finally manifesting, his eyes becoming bleary and his thoughts a muddle. As his eyes focused on the girl, though, it was clear that his first impression had been wrong. The similarities were remarkable, though.

The girl in the portrait was fair, with flaxen hair, a pair of perfectly pink lips formed in a near pout, and a figure wispy enough to suggest the need for protection. But on closer inspection, there were obvious differences. She had eyes that were a paler blue, her cheekbones were not as defined, and her face was slightly thinner. She looked enough like Julia though, that for a moment he wondered: what would it be like to marry someone so like the woman who had spurned him?

He looked at the blue eyes again. The artist had managed to capture a glint of caprice and coyness. It was the same look he had seen on Julia's face earlier that evening. Though the affectation had been completely absent during their years of friendship, London had changed her.

Her teasing smile swam before him again, and her words reverberated in his mind.

"Well, of course I shan't dance with you when you wear such a positively miserable expression!"

Charles didn't want to be forever frowning in Julia's company, but he couldn't help himself. Not when he feared more every day that he was losing her.

"I am not miserable," he said, exhaling in frustration. "I simply don't understand. It seems that you have changed your mind about what you want. I thought that this Season was a mere formality—a means of appeasing your parents. But your attentiveness to other gentlemen—" his muscles tightened as he pictured the small gestures

of intimacy he had witnessed between Julia and a few of the gentlemen in the room "—it tells a different tale."

She tossed her head. "Surely you can't blame me for preferring the company of Mr. Farrow or Lord Nolan. You've become so preachy and dull of late that it is little wonder, I'm sure."

HE PRESSED a fist to his lip, his knuckles white.

No, he couldn't marry Cecilia Cosgrove. He'd never be rid of Julia's face; of the reminder of what he had lost.

Besides, he didn't want a look-alike. He wanted Julia.

But she had made it plain that she preferred Robert Farrow, that Charles had become nothing but a bother and burden. And that was something his pride—and his heart—couldn't countenance. To go from stolen moments and fervent promises to an inconvenient afterthought? No. He couldn't bear it.

The best chance of driving Julia out of his own mind and heart was to replace her with someone who was nothing like her. The more different the better. If he couldn't have Julia, what did it matter whom he married? He wasn't fool enough to believe he would find anyone who could compare to her. Or to his feelings for her, for that matter. He cringed as he remembered the impulse he'd had to beg her.

But he wouldn't let her reject him twice. Nor would he endure watching her leave him in the dust for another man. No, he would show her that she'd made the biggest mistake of her life; that she'd lost him. Irretrievably.

There were plenty of ladies who would be more than happy to take Julia's place at his side. He had danced with any number of them over the past few weeks. But he would rather have someone who hadn't already made an attempt to lure him.

He looked at Cosgrove's daughters. Two looked to be schoolroom misses—too young for the purpose—and another to be about seventeen. Still too young. Only Cecilia and one other daughter remained.

Next to Cecilia's fair perfection, the last of the five daughters looked plain, as if her purpose was to enhance Cecilia's exquisiteness by contrast. He had almost not noticed her. Her hair was a noncommittal shade between blonde and brown, and her nose looked too long next to Cecilia's proportional button nose. Where Cecilia's eyes hinted at flirtation and mystery, her sister's gaze was clear and direct.

"What of her?" He pointed to the plain one.

Cosgrove peered through squinted eyes. "What, Isabel?" He laughed heartily. "No, no, no, dear boy! Ought to have warned you about that particular bottle of brandy. Quite potent. No, you're looking at the wrong one. Look just here. This—" he pointed exaggeratedly and lost his footing for a moment "—is Cecilia."

"No," Charles said flatly, turning from the portrait. "We play for Isabel's hand or not at all."

Cosgrove's jaw hung limp as he looked at Charles and again at the portrait. He met Charles's bloodshot and unyielding gaze and shut his jaw, shrugging his shoulders.

"Never look a gift horse in the mouth, they say." He rubbed his hands together and walked back toward the table.

"What of the stakes?" Charles said, seating himself and taking the cards in hand. "If I lose, you regain your IOUs; if you lose, I gain a wife?"

Cosgrove nodded slowly, the skin under his chin folding and unfolding, his eyes wide.

A servant was summoned to replenish the empty decanters. Cosgrove drank freely, becoming louder and jollier with each drink, and just as he had predicted, his luck seemed to turn.

Charles sighed. He would have to give Cosgrove back all the vowels he possessed. His father would naturally not be pleased to hear how much Charles had lost. Surely it was better than making an enemy of Cosgrove, though? Charles's father had explained in no uncertain terms that the investment scheme was vital.

Either way, it couldn't be helped. An agreement was an agreement.

Very near the end of the hand, though, Cosgrove's eyes glazed over for a moment as he stared into the distance.

"What is it?" Charles said.

There was no indication that he had been heard. "Cosgrove!" Why had he let himself come? The man was a fool.

Cosgrove shook himself out of his stupor. "Nothing, nothing." He rearranged a couple of cards in his hands, an almost frenzied glint appearing in his eyes.

Cosgrove's run of luck was short-lived, and the hand ended decidedly in Charles's favor.

"Ah!" Cosgrove snapped his fingers. "Fleeced again!"

Despite his loss, his eyes looked energetic and victorious.

Charles frowned. "I could have sworn you had that hand."

Cosgrove shook his head and said, "Unaccountable. You know how terrible my luck is. Well, there's that, then. Isabel!" he shouted at the top of his lungs. He smirked and then called the name again, this time singing it at the top of his lungs. "Isabeeeel! Ha! Perhaps I should have pursued a career in the opera."

Charles leaned back in his chair. His arm hung limply over the chair, his legs stretched out in front of him and crossed at the ankles. Whatever energy Cosgrove had gained, Charles seemed to have lost. His eyes were veiled by slow-blinking lids, masking the dangerous, devil-may-care glint which appeared only on the rare occasion when he had been drinking heavily. Unlike his host, he was not a gregarious drunk, and only those who knew him best would have been able to recognize how deeply he had been dipping.

He dispassionately considered his future. So, he would be married then, would he? So much the better. He would have to marry at some point, and it wouldn't be Julia. So why not sooner rather than later?

His father, for one, would be elated to hear of the alliance. And Cosgrove's daughter didn't look like the type who was turning down suitors left and right. Many a more striking young woman would have jumped at the chance to marry Charles, so why not Miss Cosgrove?

                    ❧   3   ❦

Isabel sat up in bed, resting her weight on one arm as she
listened with a frown. The muffled sound of her name being
shouted in unpleasant and exaggerated vibrato rang out again.
    She flipped the bedcovers over, slid out of bed, and opened the
bedroom door. When she peered out, she saw her younger sister
Cecilia's golden head peeking out of the neighboring bedroom.
    "What in the world?" Cecilia said.
    Paxton the footman appeared in the corridor and stopped next to
Isabel's door. He kept his eyes trained on the far wall, a gesture Isabel
was grateful for. She felt very aware of her state of *déshabillement*.
    "Miss Cosgrove, your presence is requested—" he cleared his
throat as her father's voice rang out, cracking mid-note "—in the
drawing room."
    She winced at the sound of her father's singing. "Might you not
tell him I'm asleep?" she implored.
    Paxton shook his head. "I'm afraid it wouldn't serve, Miss. Your
father has informed me that I am to use whatever means necessary to
ensure your immediate presence."
    Isabel's eyes widened in horror, and Cecilia covered a giggle.

14

"Good heavens," Isabel sighed. "I suppose I must go, then. I won't be but a moment." She began closing her bedroom door.

"Miss Cosgrove?" said Paxton.

She looked a question at him.

He hesitated. "I should perhaps warn you that your father is not alone. He is with a gentleman."

Isabel frowned. "Thank you, Paxton."

She closed the door and stared blankly at the floor for a moment. There was no time to do anything more than slip on her dressing gown and slippers. She knew her father's drunken erraticism better than to take more time. If she delayed, she risked the mortifying prospect of being carried downstairs by one of the servants. And apparently it would all be witnessed by a guest.

She took a quick glance at her reflection in a handheld mirror, blowing out a resigned puff of air as she tucked away a strand of hair which had come loose from her braid.

She paused briefly at the doorway of the drawing room, listening to her father's jovial laughter, wondering what reason he could possibly have for summoning her in the middle of the night. Reason, though, seemed to play no part at all in his drinking habits, so anyone's guess was as good as hers. She took a little consolation in knowing that, if her father's guest had been drinking as much as he had been, neither was likely to remember the night's work. She took a deep breath and opened the door.

Her father was standing with his back toward her, humming with both arms up and moving in synchronicity, as if conducting an unseen orchestra.

His guest lounged idly in a chair which faced away from Isabel. Only a loosely hanging arm, the lower half of his outstretched legs, and the top of his head were visible from behind. The locks were not, as Isabel had assumed they would be, dusted with grey like her father's. They were nearly black.

Her father turned around as the door closed.

"Ah, is that you, Izzy?" He stumbled toward her and squinted at her dressing gown. "Not the dress I should have chosen for such an occasion, but oh well. I tried to tell him Cecy would suit better, but he'd have none of it."

He grabbed her hand and pulled her toward the chair occupied by his guest. With his other hand, he made a presentation gesture fit for the King's court and pulled Isabel around to face the gentleman.

"Allow me to introduce you."

The gentleman brought his head up, and Isabel stiffened. The dark, unkempt locks, the deep brown eyes, the angular jawline—why were they so familiar when it had been years since she had seen him?

He looked at her under heavy lids. There was a hint of curiosity and an unsettling glint in them.

"Izzy, it is my great honor," said her father on the verge of laughter, putting a hand on his heart, "to present you to your affianced husband, Mr. Charles Galbraith." He succumbed to a fit of laughter which morphed into a cough.

Feeling that she must be the butt of some inebriated joke and mortified for her father's behavior, Isabel went to his aid, helping him settle into a chair where he could more safely push through the coughing fit.

As she poured a glass of ale, she felt Mr. Galbraith's eyes on her. She kept her eyes trained on her father as she said, "Please excuse my father, sir. He is prone to talking nonsense when he is—how do you gentlemen phrase it?—in his cups? Yes, I believe that's the expression." She glanced at him quickly as she heard him chuckle. He wore a half-smile.

She offered her father more ale, but he waved it off in disgust.

"I suspect," said Mr. Galbraith, "that you are right about that—his talking nonsense when he is—" he thought for a moment with the same half-smile, "—foxed. Another phrase for you. But in this one instance, it is not nonsense."

Isabel's head came up, and she stared at him. There was no trace of teasing in his expression.

"Well it *is* nonsense, my boy," said Cosgrove. "Izzy over Cecy?" He shook his finger at Mr. Galbraith. "But no turning back now, ay?"

Isabel resisted an impulse to look down. Instead she met Mr. Galbraith's gaze, her cheeks warm. She was too accustomed to her father's insults to take affront. It was the audience which brought the blush to her cheeks this time.

Life had been full of comparisons and comments on her sister's superiority. Isabel's intellect, though, was one area where no one doubted that she outshone Cecilia. It was a capacity which made her all too aware whenever someone was disparaging her, even unintentionally.

Armed with such a sharp intellect, she was unaccustomed to finding situations beyond her comprehension. But this situation was taxing her understanding. Perhaps it was their idea of a practical joke. If so, it was cruel enough that only two drunk people could conceive such a prank.

But what reaction had they expected to such a jest if a jest it was? And if it wasn't a jest, what was the meaning of it?

She pulled her dressing gown tighter around her. "I'm afraid I must be very slow." She stared at Mr. Galbraith.

"Slow?" Mr. Galbraith's brows snapped together. "I sincerely hope not." He surveyed her.

"Oh no," Cosgrove interjected, having finished conducting an encore number. "Izzy's no slow top. In fact, she's more likely to be called a dashed blue-stocking. You are trading beauty for brains, Galbraith." He shook his head disapprovingly and then made a sudden movement as though he would retch.

Isabel grabbed for the nearest vase, reaching it under her father's mouth just in time to catch the majority of what was expelled.

When it was clear that he was through being sick, Isabel set the vase down and helped him sit back in his chair. His face was pale, and the vivacity of a few minutes before was absent.

She became aware that Mr. Galbraith stood next to her, looking at her father with the furrowed brow which he had worn the entire evening. He held a napkin in one hand and wiped the stray sick which had landed on Isabel's hand.

She looked up at him, surprised by the gesture. He was looking at her father, though, with a poorly-suppressed half-smile.

"Fool," he said. The humorous expression he wore took the sting out of the word. "In the end, it was not me who was sick on your floors, Cosgrove. You seem to be in good hands, so I'll leave you in peace."

Cosgrove let out a feeble laugh. "I feel sick as a cat! You must have a stomach of iron."

Mr. Galbraith chuckled and then looked to Isabel. "Miss Cosgrove," he said.

She glanced at him.

He reached a hand out for hers, his expression unreadable. "I will wait on you soon."

She debated whether to provide him with her hand. She felt a need for him to understand that she put no stock in the events of the night; that she expected no such gestures. In fact, she preferred he simply leave as though nothing unusual had happened.

His hand lingered in the air, though, and, not wishing to snub him, she settled on giving him a hasty and aloof hand before taking it back to wipe her father's brow. Should she see him out, given her father's state and the lack of servants? She had no desire to draw out their time together, to interact with him more than was necessary.

She remained kneeling as she replied, "There is no need to wait on me, sir, I assure you. Let us simply agree to forget the events of this night."

His jaw tensed. "If only that were possible. I bid you both good night."

Isabel continued tending to her father as Mr. Galbraith stalked out of the room, but once the door closed behind him, her hands slowed. Already Mr. Galbraith was regretting the night's work. Well, he needn't regret anything having to do with Isabel. She would assure him of that again and again, if needed.

Isabel consigned her father to the care of his valet not long after Mr. Galbraith's departure and walked back to her room in deep thought. She sincerely hoped that Mr. Galbraith would wake with no memory of the night.

She sighed.

"Izzy!" Cecilia's urgent whisper broke through her thoughts. She motioned Isabel to come talk to her.

Isabel hesitated a moment before walking over. She was in no humor to recount what had happened and even less so to hear Cecilia's take on it. It would likely be seen by her sister as a joke at Isabel's expense. She would pity Isabel and then tease that Mr. Galbraith had intended to pay his addresses to her, instead.

"Well?" Cecilia said in impatience. "Who was there? Was it old Mr. Naughton?" She cringed. "The way he stares is so unsettling." She raised her brows expectantly. "What did Father want? "

"Oh, nothing," Isabel said, convinced that she was being truthful. "Father became sick from too much drink. I think Mrs. Dorrell may have a conniption when she discovers that I let him be sick in the Sèvres vase."

Cecilia covered her mouth with a hand. "You didn't!"

Isabel gripped her lips together to keep from smiling and nodded.

She recounted that part of the evening—leaving out Mr. Galbraith's part in it—and brought Cecilia to giggles.

Isabel smiled and sighed. "Well, I am for bed."

"What did Father want, then?" Cecilia asked, yawning.

Isabel laughed weakly. "It is too ridiculous to even bear recounting. Good night, Cecilia."

Isabel laid awake for quite some time after closing the door to her bedroom. She had hope that her father had drunk enough to forget everything by the time he woke in the morning—or early afternoon, more likely. It wouldn't be the first time he had no memory of his mortifying behavior.

She struggled to unravel her feelings on the subject of Mr. Galbraith. She stared at the slit of moonlight the curtains let in, thinking how strange it was to have finally seen Mr. Galbraith at the Rodwell's rout only to see him yet again in her own home later that same evening.

Finding Mr. Galbraith in the drawing room and learning that she was to be the butt of a drunk prank had been even more painful than the situation merited. When her father had introduced her and referred to Mr. Galbraith as her future husband, there had been a split second when she had felt her heart pound with nerves.

It was uncomfortably clear to her that such a thing couldn't be true; nor that she would have had any reason to feel excitement even if it had been. She hardly knew Mr. Galbraith. And at her father's introduction, it was evident that the man looking at her was seeing her as if for the first time.

Whatever strange and irrational reasons she had found for feeling a special interest in him were clearly not reciprocated.

She sincerely hoped to be able to put it all behind her. Soon it would be no more than a distant, uncomfortable memory. For now, though, she would have to do what she could to avoid Mr. Galbraith. It shouldn't be too difficult—after all, he had easily forgotten her.

4

When Charles woke, his head seemed to be gripped in a vice. He groaned as he tried to open his eyes, lying for a few minutes with eyes shut, recollections from the night before trickling in.

He had no trouble recalling the disagreement with Julia. Heaven knew how he wished it had been a dream.

And then there had been brandy. So much brandy. He hadn't drunk that much in recent memory—if ever.

He jolted upright and swore softly under his breath, throwing the covers off. There had been an introduction. An engagement.

He rattled his head from side to side, trying to dispel the fog and recapture the extent of his impetuous behavior. Had he truly agreed to a stake for a woman's hand in marriage?

He flipped his legs over the edge of the bed, resting his elbows on his knees and rubbing his forehead. What was he to do with the mess he had created for himself?

His actions could hardly be considered those of a gentleman. What could have possessed him to agree to Cosgrove's mad stakes?

He cursed himself for letting his feelings for Julia lead him to behave in such an uncharacteristic and abominable way.

He explored his options as he sat on the edge of the bed, massaging his temples.

He could blame it on the drink—after all, that had undeniably played a part. He could pretend to have no memory of the night. Many a man could legitimately make such a claim if they had drunk as much as he had. Charles was nearly sure he'd be able to get away with such a charade. After all, Cosgrove was unlikely to remember much. And perhaps the girl—was it Isabel? —had given no credence to anything he or her father had said, knowing how much they'd had to drink. She seemed to be familiar enough with the way of things among drinking gentlemen.

He smiled slightly as he remembered her use of the phrase "in his cups" when referring to her father.

Letting out a long sigh, he put his forehead in his hands. How he wished he could pretend nothing had happened.

But he couldn't engage in such knavish conduct. His conscience wouldn't allow it. The thought of how his mother would have felt to know of his behavior, and then that he had compounded the reproach by trying to escape the consequences? He could imagine the drooping of her features, the sadness in her eyes; he could hear her say in her sweet voice, "You are so much more than this, Charles."

No, he couldn't disgrace himself and his mother's memory with such conduct, no matter how much it appealed to him. He would have to formally offer for Miss Cosgrove and make the best of the mess he had made for himself.

An hour later, he set off for Belport Street, the set of his jaw matching his determined pace. His resolution flagged only twice as he considered just how final and irretrievable a step he was taking; as he wondered how Julia would react when she heard the news of his engagement.

But there was little purpose in hesitating for the sake of Julia, and he knew it did him little credit to factor her reaction into his decision.

Whether he went to Belport Street or not, Julia had moved forward with her life, discarding him for someone else.

Charles didn't know how much of his dislike for Farrow was due to Julia's infatuation with him and how much of it was genuine and unrelated, but dislike him he did. He had heard enough rumors to strongly suspect Farrow of being a rake. It was entirely possible that Julia would come to regret her association with the man.

Charles was anxious to be there for her when she did, and yet equally determined not to be.

THE COSGROVE HOUSEHOLD had been quiet that morning, a circumstance welcomed by Isabel. Her father was laid up feeling the aftereffects of his carousing, and everyone knew better than to suffer his wrath by making noise.

Isabel had hope that the later he stayed abed, the less likely he was to remember the strange night he had passed. If he remembered enough, though, he would undoubtedly wish to speak to her about it.

It was not a conversation she wished to have, particularly when he would be in an irritable humor due to his headache. It might be an inevitable exchange, but she felt no compunction in doing what she could to postpone it.

She dressed for the day and, as the time drew nearer when her father might be expected to come downstairs, took the book from her nightstand. She walked down the stairs with as light a step as possible, reaching the entryway just as the bell rang and one of the footmen opened the front door.

She stopped short, listening to the exchange at the door with alarm. She knew that voice.

"If you'll just step inside, sir," said the footman, "I'll inquire if Miss Cosgrove is at home."

Isabel whirled around, eyeing the nearest doorway for an escape, but it was too late.

"Oh! Miss Cosgrove," the footman said.

Isabel closed her eyes in chagrin, not even turning around.

The footman stumbled awkwardly over his words.

She breathed in deeply then turned to thank and excuse the footman, assuring him that she would handle things from there. She bit her bottom lip and glanced at the stairwell, sincerely hoping Cecilia would not appear and see her with Mr. Galbraith. The day was already going to be unpleasant enough without one of Cecilia's fits of jealousy.

When Isabel turned to Mr. Galbraith, he was watching her with a curious and evaluative eye. He held his hat in his hands, and his jaw had a decisive set about it.

She wondered if he were there to make his excuses for the night before; to inform her that, not only had he made a mistake in implying that he wished to marry her, but that he would in fact be paying his addresses to Cecilia.

She smiled wryly, wondering whether he possessed enough finesse to carry off such an unwieldy conversation. It might be painful to watch, but it might also be satisfying to hear him bumble his way through such an exchange.

His thick brows were, as they often seemed to be, furrowed. She wondered if he was troubled or whether it was simply the shape and size of the brows that gave such an illusion. His dark and brooding features would be even more striking paired with Cecilia's fair and delicate style.

"Miss Cosgrove," he said, clearing his throat. "Forgive me for intruding on your morning, but I wondered if I might have a word?"

Hearing a noise above stairs, Isabel shot another glance at the stairwell. The likelihood of being able to carry out a *tête-à-tête* in the house without the knowledge of Cecilia or her father was next to nothing.

The thought of confronting Mr. Galbraith alone, face-to-face, while he, she could only assume, apologized, made her feel slightly dizzy. It would be better to hear him out in the fresh air where she wouldn't be required to look at him and could ensure that the interview lasted only as long as it took to walk to the church.

If apologize he must, she would let him unburden his conscience, forgive him with as much frankness and nonchalance as she could muster, and say adieu in the sincere hope that she would be able to avoid him for the duration of the Season. She felt confident that she could maintain the façade of casual composure for the time it would be required of her.

"I'm happy to oblige," she said untruthfully, "but I am afraid I am on my way out the door. I'm only walking around the corner to the church, though, if you'd care to accompany me."

Mr. Galbraith hesitated a moment. "Gladly," he said with a civil smile and set jaw. He opened the door for her, and she thanked him with a smile and nod.

They walked a few moments in silence. While she knew an impulse to fill the silence, she bit her tongue. He should set the tone for the conversation. Otherwise, she was likely to say any number of unnecessary things.

She noted his hesitation with a mixture of sympathy and *schadenfreude*. Admitting one was in the wrong was never pleasant, but it gave her some small satisfaction to know that he was embarrassed. It only seemed fair after her own embarrassment the night before.

"Miss Cosgrove," he said. "I owe you an apology."

She said nothing, feeling too much in agreement with the statement to add anything of value, but her grip on the book tightened, and she swallowed. The rectory normally felt like a quick walk, but today the distance warped to feel much too long.

She saw him looking at her out of the corner of her eye and stared ahead, schooling her features into a pleasant gaze forward.

He cleared his throat. "I will not endeavor to excuse my state last night, but I do wish to express regret that you were made to witness it." He glanced at her, and she repressed a small smile.

"Why do you smile?" he asked.

Her head tilted to the side for a moment before she said, "I'm nearly certain that I shouldn't answer that."

Mr. Galbraith looked nonplussed. "So, you leave me to assume the worst."

"Not at all," she replied. "I hesitate because my thoughts were shockingly unfilial."

He frowned and shook his head, still seeming at a loss.

She let out a small laugh. "Shall I let you cajole me into filial impiety? If I confess such iniquitous thoughts to you, how will I face the rector when we reach the church?"

One of his eyebrows went up. "And if I promise not to betray you to him?" he suggested.

Her mouth broke into one of her rare, large smiles. "Very well," she said. "If you break your promise, though, I warn you that I won't hesitate to cast the blame upon you."

"We have an accord," he said with mock gravity.

She pursed her lips before continuing. "You apologized that I was made to witness your state, as you called it. And I found myself thinking of my father—of his conducting imaginary orchestras and, even more to the point, being violently ill. I find myself wondering if perhaps it isn't *I* who should apologize to you for *his* state? You should not expect an apology from him, I can tell you. Compared to my father, your behavior appears almost admirable."

He laughed at her mention of the orchestra. "I had forgotten about the conducting."

"Oh dear," she said. "Well I am afraid that now you must suffer, like me, with the image forever emblazoned on your memory."

His smile fell slightly. The humor left his eyes, and his jaw hardened again.

What had she said to provoke such a change?

"Whether or not you find my apology necessary," he said, "I offer it to you." He cleared his throat. "I also wish to make clear to you that I was in earnest last night."

She stiffened, and her lips parted.

"I refer to my offer of marriage, of course," he clarified. "I would be honored if you would accept me as your husband."

She swallowed and looked at him. He was staring straight ahead, his square jaw even more distinct than usual. She had expected an apology, not an actual marriage offer.

She considered reminding him that he had never actually offered marriage to her the night before. She had simply been informed that he was to be her future husband. But looking at his clenching jaw, his head held high, and the slight flare to his nostrils, she realized that he was simply trying to do the honorable thing.

"Mr. Galbraith," she said. "I thank you for your desire to do what you feel is right. But I was in earnest when I said that we would do well to forget last night altogether."

He looked at her with an arrested expression.

She gave him a small, encouraging smile. "And forgive me," she said in a teasing voice, "but I am prideful enough to hope that, if I find myself in a position to accept an offer of marriage, the person making it won't do so as if bearing news of their own impending death."

"Surely I didn't say it in such fashion," he said in a doubtful voice.

She only raised her brows.

"In any case," he continued, "it is not the way I feel. Since we are unacquainted with one another, naturally I cannot pretend to senti-ment where it does not exist."

She looked at him, smiling slightly as she pictured the young boy who had cheered her up when she desperately needed it.

"What is it?" he said.

"You don't remember at all, do you?"

He turned his head toward her and frowned. "Remember what?"

She laughed lightly and looked ahead. "We knew each other once, years ago."

He reared back. "We did?"

She nodded slowly. "You did me a great kindness once, on a visit with your father to us in Dorsetshire."

He narrowed his eyes, turning his head to look at her, as if he might remember by searching her face. "Remind me."

She sighed. How many times had she thought back on that instance of kindness? And he had likely never thought on it again.

"I was crying," she said, "because Cecilia had taken my favorite doll. You put your arm around me, consoled me, and then took me—"

"—to roll down the hill!" He looked at her, delight in his expression at having remembered. "Until we were severely berated, if I recall correctly."

Isabel laughed and nodded her head. For some reason, she found great comfort in his remembering.

He shook his head, the grin on his face widening again. "I had forgotten entirely. But it only goes to prove my point. I feel that we could get along with one another quite well. I would endeavor to make you comfortable and to seek your contentment, just as I did then."

She pursed her lips to keep from smiling. "A marked improvement," she said with a dignified nod. "Far less like a death pronouncement and more like making a case in front of a magistrate."

He looked torn between laugh and offense.

As they reached the gate to the church, he opened his mouth and shut it lamely.

Isabel's hand holding the book shot out to bar him from moving forward. Her other hand came to her mouth in a shushing gesture, her ear cocked.

The distinct sound of sniffling reached their ears. It was coming from nearby, inside the churchyard which lay around the corner.

Isabel hesitated a moment, not wishing to intrude on the person's privacy. But the crying sounded like that of a child. She walked toward it, conscious that Mr. Galbraith hesitated before following her.

$$ ❦ \quad 5 \quad ❦ $$

A young girl sat on an ivy-strewn stone bench, hunched over and shaking with sobs. Her dark, uncoiffed hair hid her face from view. Her stature was more that of a young woman nearing the end of her schoolroom days than of the child Isabel had pictured. Her clothing was neat, though not perhaps in the first style of elegance.

Isabel observed the girl for a moment with a frown before approaching further. She knelt in front of her, holding her book in one arm and placing a hand softly on the young woman's knee.

The young lady's head came up in surprise. "Oh dear!" she said in a high-pitched, distressed voice as she looked at Isabel and then Mr. Galbraith.

Even in the sad circumstances in which they discovered her, the picture she presented was food for inspiration. Dark chocolate-colored waves of hair made her porcelain skin all the brighter. Teardrops hung on the tips of long black lashes, framing eyes the color of the ivy surrounding her. The color of the girl's pouting lips matched cheeks becomingly tinged with the double blush of emotion and discovery.

"Whatever is the matter, my dear?" Isabel asked in a soft voice.

"Oh, only everything!" the girl replied. "And indeed I'm very sorry to be crying! Mother would be cross if she saw me, but I feel so very lost that I can't help it!"

"There, there." Isabel took a seat next to her. "It will all be all right." She patted the girl's knee. "We can help you find your way back home."

"Oh no!" the girl said, her eyes wide with horror. "Please don't make me! I can't go back!"

Isabel shot a confused look at Mr. Galbraith who raised his brows and shrugged his shoulders.

"To be sure, we won't *make* you do anything," Isabel consoled her. "But I thought you said you were lost?"

"I *feel* lost," the young lady corrected her. "I came to speak with the rector, but I am afraid he will send me to the workhouse. I'm sure I should die!" Her shoulders convulsed as she began to cry again.

Mr. Galbraith approached cautiously, reaching into his pocket for a handkerchief and offering it to the girl. He stepped back gingerly, as if afraid he might inadvertently set off another burst of emotion.

But the girl only smiled gratefully at him through her tears, saying, "Oh, how kind you are!" She blew her nose soundly.

When Isabel inquired her name, the girl donned a wary look and asked first whether they would force her to return to her mother if she told them. Isabel reassured her that they would do no such thing, after which the girl's shoulders relaxed and she sighed.

"It is Hester Helena Robson," she said in a voice of dejection. "But I detest the name Hester, so you may call me Hetty, if you please."

"Hetty it is," said Isabel with a twinkle. "I am Isabel Cosgrove—you may call me Izzy if you like. And this is Mr. Charles Galbraith."

Hetty had been wiping the corner of her eye with the handkerchief, but she looked up on hearing the names. She looked at Isabel and then at Mr. Galbraith.

"But are you not married?"

Isabel avoided the eyes of Mr. Galbraith. "No, no," Isabel said with a tinge of pink in her cheeks. "In fact, we only became acquainted last night."

Hetty's brow furrowed deeply. "Mama says I should always have a chaperone in the presence of an unmarried gentleman, unless she expressly permits it."

Isabel glanced at Mr. Galbraith to see how he would handle such implied censure. He repressed a smile and shook his head at Isabel with a look of feigned disapproval.

"Your mother is quite right, of course," he said to Hetty. "And how often *does* she expressly permit forgoing the chaperone?" His tone was mildly curious.

The same question had occurred to Isabel. Given the patent fear of home which Hetty had expressed earlier and the naive comment on her mother's blend of strictness and permissiveness, Isabel felt she knew what type of woman Mrs. Robson probably was.

"Oh," Hetty said in a reassuring voice. "Only with three or four gentlemen."

Mr. Galbraith nodded as though his assumptions had been confirmed.

Isabel looked at him with her mouth twisted to the side. The protection offered by Hetty's mother seemed the type that conveniently disappeared when an eligible gentleman was nearby. With such beauty as the girl possessed, it was hardly to be wondered at that she should attract much attention, despite coming from a family who seemed not to belong to the *haut ton*.

"Indeed," Isabel said, unsure what else she could offer. "Perhaps we should go find Mr. Safford. Were you not wishful to speak with him?"

Why Hetty had come to speak to the rector, Isabel didn't know, but perhaps he would be able to help sort out whatever difficulty Hetty was in. It took some coaxing before Hetty would agree to enter the church, but Isabel was able to convince her that Mr. Safford was a kind soul who would do whatever he could to help.

"But will he not rebuke me? I think I have been very wicked. But I didn't mean to be! I promise!" She began to cry again.

"I am sure," said Isabel consolingly, wondering how such an innocent girl as Hetty obviously was could be wicked, "that you have not been so wicked as you think, my dear. Mr. Safford is my friend, and he only ever rebukes me when I forget that the Lord can forgive my sins."

Hetty looked hopeful and wiped at the tear streaming down her cheek. "I am sure I may trust you. You are so kind." She looked up at Isabel. "And very pretty."

Isabel opened her mouth only to shut it again. She couldn't remember ever being told she was pretty, much less ever thinking it. She cleared her throat and stood from the bench, extending a hand to Hetty, and the three of them walked into the church together.

Mr. Safford was walking down the aisle in between the pews, and he turned as he heard the group enter. He was nearing the end of his middle age, and the grey which had peppered his hair for the last few years had become widespread and was itself peppered with white now. His full cheeks always had a red tinge to them, and the lines around his eyes and mouth were evidence of the pleasant smile he generally wore. That smile widened significantly when he saw Isabel.

"My dear," he said, taking one of her hands within his. "You always brighten up the church when you come."

She returned his smile and handed him the book, thanking him for it and expressing a desire to discuss it with him sometime.

She turned toward Mr. Galbraith and Hetty to perform the necessary introductions. Mr. Galbraith and Mr. Safford were already acquainted with one another. Hetty, however, had become reserved when brought into the presence of Mr. Safford. When he put a hand out to invite hers, she looked at him with fearful eyes which began to overflow with tears.

"Forgive me," she sobbed.

Mr. Safford looked at Isabel, who grimaced to convey that she had no information to offer. Mr. Safford put an arm around Hetty and guided her to the pew just behind him.

Feeling that it was perhaps time to leave things in Mr. Safford's hands, Isabel met Mr. Galbraith's eyes. He nodded his understanding. But as they turned to leave, Hetty stopped them.

"Oh no!" she cried out. "Please don't leave! You are my only friends." Her eyes were red, wet, and full of desperation.

Isabel looked over her shoulder at Mr. Galbraith. He looked pained by Hetty's plea and made his way to the pew nearest Hetty and the rector. Isabel followed suit, patting Hetty's hand reassuringly and then seating herself in the pew behind Mr. Galbraith.

Mr. Safford allowed Hetty a few moments to compose herself before inquiring what the matter was. Before Hetty would answer, though, she begged him not to send her back to her mother. Mr. Safford agreed, but his brows drew together.

She lowered her eyes. "I am—" she said in such a low whisper that they were all obliged to lean in to hear "—in a delicate condition." She quite unnecessarily placed a cupped hand on her stomach as if to make her meaning clear.

Though Isabel tried to stifle any response to the pronouncement, her eyes grew round. Hetty hardly seemed old enough to be in the family way.

Mr. Safford grimaced and then placed a comforting hand on Hetty's shoulder. "And the father?"

"Does not acknowledge us," she whispered on a sob, still holding a hand to her stomach. "And I know he won't. No matter what Mama says. He is not a man who can be threatened. I tried. But I see now that he is not at all kind or considerate. He is quite awful, and I don't *want* to marry him. I won't!"

She became frantic, and Isabel rushed over to sit beside her, wrapping a comforting arm around Hetty's shoulders and saying, "Calm yourself, Hetty. It will all be all right."

She looked up at Mr. Safford as if hoping to receive her own reassurance from him.

He let out a large sigh and grimaced. "Who *is* the father, my dear?" he asked gently. Seeing her become agitated at the question, he put a hand up to gently silence her, saying, "Even if you do not wish to marry him, he is legally bound to offer a certain amount of support."

Hetty looked up with painful hope in her eyes. "Is that true? Mama said that we won't get a farthing from him unless he marries me."

The rector clenched his lips together, and Mr. Galbraith rolled his eyes.

"Your mother is mistaken," said the rector. "Until the child is seven, he must provide support. And though I don't wish to alarm you, the law also requires you to name the father."

Hetty looked nervous, her eyes darting from Isabel to the rector to Mr. Galbraith. "Robert Farrow," she said with a nervous glance at them.

A small clanging sound interrupted the conversation. Mr. Galbraith stooped down and emerged holding his pocket watch which he seemed to have dropped on the floor. His color was heightened, and his expression stunned.

Isabel had never heard the name, and she looked back and forth between Mr. Galbraith and the rector, hoping to glean information.

Mr. Safford was frowning heavily. "I see," he said, bringing his hands together palm-to-palm and resting them against his mouth. A few moments in thought seemed to recompose him, though the sides of his mouth were turned down in a grim expression. He asked Hetty a few more questions and then said to Isabel and Mr. Galbraith, "May I have a word with you both?"

The three of them walked a short distance from Hetty where Mr. Safford shook his head and interlocked his fingers.

"It is a very unfortunate situation," he said, shaking his head. "Her family is only recently moved to town—new money, I understand— and their manners fairly coarse, though the girl seems better off in that regard than her parents. They are unused to the ways of higher society. I am also somewhat acquainted with the father of the baby, and I have grave doubts that he can be brought to claim the child. It will likely require intervention from the local justices whom I have found, in similar situations, to be all too willing to accept bribes from fathers of illegitimate children who do not wish to acknowledge their responsibilities. If the girl won't return to her mother, she will become the concern of the parish and most likely end up in a workhouse."

Isabel and Mr. Galbraith's eyes widened simultaneously on hearing this. They looked at one another.

"She wouldn't survive," said Isabel. "I haven't known her more than half an hour, but it's plain that she's just a helpless child."

"Pampered and exploited by her mother," Mr. Galbraith said, shaking his head, "no doubt in hopes of precisely the type of situation she's now in—trapping a wealthy gentleman into marriage. The woman seems entirely reprehensible. And I agree with you, Mr. Safford. I am a little acquainted with Farrow myself. If I know him at all, he will avoid the financial responsibility at all costs, to say nothing of the moral one." His expression was grim, the hard set of his jaw returning.

Isabel chewed on her bottom lip, consumed by the problem before her. She was determined not to leave Hetty exposed to the conditions of a workhouse or to a mother seemingly desperate to turn her daughter's beauty into a financial windfall, no matter the means required.

"Let her come home with me," Isabel said. "Perhaps I can convince my mother to let her stay on in the household. If not, it will at least give me time to see if there isn't perhaps another situation for her among our acquaintances. I will simply say to anyone who might inquire that she is a cousin visiting."

Mr. Safford looked at her with a sort of paternal pride. "You have a heart of gold, Miss Cosgrove."

Isabel felt her cheeks heating up.

"I, too," Mr. Galbraith offered, "will see if I can hear of any situation that might suit her, though I admit that I have difficulty imagining what role she would be suited for."

Isabel had the same thought. Surely the girl must have some skill to recommend her, though. If she had no relation who would take her in, perhaps she could be an abigail or lady's maid? It would not be the sort of life she might have had, to be sure, but her situation seemed somewhat desperate, given the apparent lack of support her family was offering.

It was, at all events, better than the workhouse.

Finding a position for a young woman who would soon be confined for the birth of an illegitimate child, though, was an impediment to be reckoned with. How Isabel could convince her mother to house such a young woman, particularly one whose beauty rivaled that of Cecilia, was a problem Isabel relegated to the future.

"God surely smiles upon your willing and charitable hearts," Mr. Safford said. He turned to Isabel. "But remember that you have no responsibility toward the girl."

Isabel looked at Hetty. She was still seated on the bench, pulling distractedly at a loose thread on her dress. It seemed unthinkable to abandon her to the potential fate she faced.

Isabel smiled bracingly at Mr. Safford and said, "Perhaps I don't have any legal obligation. But a Christian duty, I think."

Mr. Safford took her hands in his. "Bless you, child."

When they returned to Hetty, she looked up at them, fear etched on her face. Her lip trembled. "Am I to be sent home?"

When she learned that she was instead to return home with Isabel, her face lit up. She had taken quickly to "her sweet Izzy," as she called her, and was spilling over with gratitude, overwhelming Isabel with appreciation and praise.

Mr. Galbraith seemed very amused by Hetty's dramatic praise and almost equally so by how uncomfortable it made Isabel. He assured Isabel that he would stay in touch with her as he did his own due diligence in seeking a situation for Hetty, and they parted with a handshake. He seemed to be in much higher spirits leaving

St. James's Church than he had been when he arrived in Belport Street.

Isabel suppressed a sigh after bidding him farewell, aware that his lightened mood was likely due to his relief at her refusal of his marriage offer.

On the walk home, Hetty needed little encouragement to open up to Isabel about her situation. Isabel was able to piece much together from Hetty's often incoherent dialogue. How her youthful naïveté had been preserved was a mystery.

As Isabel had suspected, Hetty's mother had great social ambitions, and fate had gifted her an exquisitely beautiful daughter in Hetty. So, when their financial situation allowed them to move to London, she had jumped at the chance to showcase her daughter to gentlemen of rank and wealth.

Mrs. Robson's aspirations had clearly proven to be well-placed. It was clear to Isabel that Hetty had been too naïve to understand the attention being paid her by gentlemen or to perceive their intentions. Her mother had given her to understand in no uncertain terms which of her suitors' attentions she was to encourage and made her to believe that she was not to naysay those gentlemen on any account.

Piecing together the situation, Isabel hardly wondered at Hetty's current sad circumstances. The girl's guileless nature made her mother's conduct all the more reprehensible, to say nothing of Mr. Farrow himself.

When Hetty spoke of the man it was with awe and some fear.

"He was so kind to me," she said wistfully. "He bought me the loveliest gloves and even an emerald brooch. And though Mrs. Jessop said the gloves were cheaply-made, Mama said it is only because Mrs. Jessop is eaten with jealousy. Mr. Farrow snubbed her daughter Agatha, you know."

Hetty's smile faded, and she began wringing her hands. "But then he stopped coming by the house which made Mama and Papa very cross at me, wondering what I had done to offend him. But indeed, I did nothing! I never upset him or refused him, just as Mama taught me. He even told me he loved me and always would as long as he lived." She began to cry again, and Isabel put an arm around her.

"When he stopped coming, I thought that perhaps he had become ill or even died. He had told me he couldn't stay away from me. 'Not even for a day,' he said. Mama insisted that I go apologize to him for whatever I had done, and she took me to his lodgings and insisted that he see me. But when the footman returned, he said Mr. Farrow knew no one by the name Robson, and he told us to leave immediately."

"Coward," said Isabel with a flare of her nostrils.

"Mama was very cast down by it all until we discovered my delicate situation. She said I must go see Mr. Farrow again, and she sent me with a note which the footman took to him. And then he showed me into a room. And when Mr. Farrow came in, he was furious and insisted he didn't know me and that he wouldn't pay for another man's brat. He told me that if I ever came back to his lodgings, he would have me thrown in Bedlam because my wits were clearly disordered."

She put a hand on her stomach again, crying freely.

"Well," said Isabel, wanting nothing more than to speak a piece of her mind to Mr. Farrow. "You know what I say to Mr. Farrow? And to all men, for I'm convinced they are scoundrels one and all," she added, leaning in toward Hetty. "They may go to the devil!"

Hetty inhaled sharply and then giggled tearfully. "Yes," she cried, emboldened. "Go to the devil, Mr. Farrow!"

Not expecting Hetty to repeat her impulsive words, Isabel's eyes widened. She glanced at the woman walking a few feet away who had turned on hearing Hetty's exclamation, outrage written on her face.

"Oh dear," said Isabel, smiling apologetically at the woman. "I make a very bad role model, Hetty. What is it they say? Ah, yes. Do as I say, not as I do." She made a mental vow to be a more positive influence.

"Well," Hetty replied in a sheepish voice, "I am afraid that I *did do something very wrong, but I was so very upset and hurt that I didn't think it through!"

Isabel felt a pit form in her stomach. "I am sure it was nothing so *very* wrong. But do tell me, for I think it best that I be acquainted with all the particulars of your situation."

Hetty looked up at her hesitantly. "I wrote him a letter." She paused and clenched her teeth. "An angry one."

Isabel tried not to betray any of her unsettling emotions. "Oh, and what did it say?"

"That he was a liar, and that I would tell everyone I met that the baby was his, besides telling them all his other secrets, and that I hoped everyone would know him for the scoundrel he is."

"Oh dear," Isabel said. "He cannot have liked that at all."

"No," she said with a stricken expression, "I am sure he was mad as fire, for he has a terrible temper! Mama, too, was furious when she discovered from Matilda what I had done—she is my younger sister, you know, and she is always spying and telling tales on me." She sighed. "And that is when I ran away."

Isabel took in a deep breath. What had she got herself into? "Well, perhaps it was not the wisest course to write him a letter, though I can surely sympathize with you, as it is precisely what I would have wished to do in your place. We must hope that he was wise enough to realize that you did not mean any of it, and that he will leave you be."

Knowing the little she did about Mr. Farrow, she had some doubts on the subject.

❧ 6 ❧

When they arrived back in Belport Street, Isabel hesitated a moment, debating whether Hetty's interests would be best served if she were present or absent when Isabel explained the situation to her mother. She looked at Hetty who, now that she had cheered up, was a vision to behold.

That decided things.

Though it might not be the most honest or forthcoming of the two options, having Hetty absent was decidedly the more convenient scenario. It would be quite a chore to convince Mrs. Cosgrove to house a girl in Hetty's situation, and Isabel was far from sure she could bring it off successfully. Her mother tended to be jealous when she perceived that any other young woman rivaled Cecilia in beauty, no matter how irrational the jealousy was.

"I hope to be back in a trice," Isabel told Hetty as she showed her into the library, "but please don't be alarmed if it takes a little longer for me to return."

Upon inquiring with the servants, she was informed that she would find her mother in the sitting room.

Isabel sighed and opened the door.

Her mother was sorting through correspondence and didn't look up. She seemed to be engrossed in reading one particular card. Isabel was unsure whether she had even remarked her presence.

"I can't think," Mrs. Cosgrove said aloud, "that the Foxtons would really expect a positive reply to this invitation after the appalling way they treated Cecilia last week. Can you imagine?" She folded the invitation unceremoniously, setting it aside with a sneer.

"What did they do to her?" Isabel asked. Her mother was overly-sensitive when it came to Cecilia.

Mrs. Cosgrove let out a huff. "I have it on good authority that Lady Foxton told her son not to ask Cecilia to dance. Apparently, she said that Cecy would be a waste of his potential. The audacity!" She gave an extra push to the invitation, sending it perilously near the edge of the table.

"Mama, I believe you're mistaken," said Isabel with heightened color and an instinctive straightening of the shoulders. "Lady Foxton did say those things. I heard her myself. But she was referring to me, not Cecilia."

Her mother paused in the act of opening another letter. She looked thoughtful but not convinced.

"I believe," Isabel walked over to the couch and straightened two pillows, "that when people refer to 'Miss Cosgrove,' many who are less acquainted with our family are prone to assume that Cecilia is being spoken of, not realizing I am the elder of the sisters. Whoever told you this must have assumed it was Cecilia rather than me."

Her mother's brow knit for a moment, and then she relaxed into her chair with a sigh. "That does make more sense. Well!" She picked up the discarded invitation, opened it, and smoothed it out again, smiling. "I shall send a response with our plans to attend. I hear that Lady Foxton has ordered three cartloads of orange and yellow tulips for the ball. Tulips! At this season!" She shook her head in awe and began writing a response.

Isabel chewed her bottom lip, hesitant to bring up Hetty. But her mother's preoccupation with social engagements and all things

Cecilia might bode well for Hetty. What did she care whether a young woman needed a home or employment when there were invitations to sort through?

Isabel had underestimated her mother's ability to shift focus, though. And while Isabel had done her best to explain the situation in delicate if somewhat ambiguous terms, her mother swung around in her chair when she realized what her daughter was asking.

"Surely you can't be serious. House a girl of such morals? Or employ her? Out of the question." She turned back to the desk.

Isabel gripped her lips between her teeth and then sighed. "If we cannot employ her, might we not give her a place to stay— temporarily," she rushed to add, seeing her mother turn with wide, appalled eyes. "Just until I can find her a situation? I think it would be the Christian thing to do, Mama."

Her mother scoffed. "Christian? And how Christian would it be to allow her influence in the house? What if, heaven forbid, you or Cecilia were to follow in the girl's footsteps, disgracing our family?"

Isabel shut her eyes to summon patience. The possibility was unlikely in the extreme.

Even if Cecilia found herself in the same situation as Hetty, it wouldn't be a result of naïveté, as it was for Hetty. No, Cecilia was far too wise to the ways of the world. She seemed to find more satisfaction in teasing gentlemen than in giving them what they wanted.

"I should think," Isabel suggested, "that her presence might instead act as a sort of deterrent or cautionary tale?"

Mrs. Cosgrove was prevented from responding by a knock sounding on the door.

"Madam," said the footman. "There is a, uh, female person—" his lips turned down in irrepressible disgust "—demanding an audience with you. She says her name is Theodosia Robson."

Mrs. Cosgrove shot her daughter a censuring glance. "You see? Already we are accosted by the lower classes. Inform her," she said, turning to the servant, "that I am not at home to—"

The door swung open. The footman hopped deftly out of the way to avoid being hit, and a woman entered.

She was short and plump but carried herself with an air of superiority Isabel had never seen in one so clearly out of place in a gentleman's house. The woman looked around the sitting room with a critical eye, letting out an unimpressed "hmph!" while Isabel and her mother looked on in astonishment.

"Madam!" said the servant in outraged accents. "Have the goodness to remove yourself from this house, or I will see to it myself!"

Mrs. Robson ignored him, only saying, "Shabby genteel! Just as I suspicioned."

Isabel's eyes grew wide, and she stifled a laugh, looking at her mother who had been stunned into stillness. On hearing the stranger's verdict regarding the style of her home, though, a gladiatorial light had come into her eyes.

Mrs. Cosgrove dismissed the servant. His surprise was evident, but he looked too much relieved to hesitate more than a moment before bowing himself out.

"I regret that our furnishings are not to your taste, ma'am," Mrs. Cosgrove said with sugary sweetness.

"They hardly compare to Mr. Farrow's grand townhouse. That's for certain." Mrs. Robson looked more closely at an *épergne* and sniffed her disapproval.

Mrs. Cosgrove cocked an eyebrow. "I will have to accept your analysis, being unacquainted with the man."

"Gentleman," corrected Mrs. Robson. "And if you are unacquainted with him, well then, it only goes to show that you ain't fit to house my Hetty."

The martial light in Mrs. Cosgrove's eyes blazed, but she feigned a smile. "Am I to infer from your comparisons that this Mr. Farrow you speak of *does* have an intent to take her in?"

"Well," Mrs. Robson said with a defiant straightening of her neck, "he hasn't made an offer yet, but—" she threw an accusatory glare at Mrs. Cosgrove and rushed on "—I reckon he would have if Hetty hadn't been as good as kidnapped. Torn from the bosom of her mother!" A climactic if somewhat ill-executed sob followed the exclamation.

Hetty may have miraculously escaped home with her naïveté intact, but it was clear from whence her dramatic temperament came.

Mrs. Cosgrove's thin brow went up. "My dear Isabel," she said, not taking her eyes off Mrs. Robson. "Have we, to your knowledge, kidnapped any persons?"

Isabel had been watching the dialogue unfold with great interest. She felt no small degree of apprehension as the women sparred but, along with it, an appreciative awe at her mother's demeanor. She was only too glad that someone else was on the receiving end of her mother's ire. Mrs. Robson seemed not to understand the thin ice on which she stood.

Isabel cleared her throat. "No, Mama. I shouldn't think any of us would dare cause such a scandal."

"You reassure me," said Mrs. Cosgrove urbanely, her eyes still on the uninvited guest. "It appears that you are misinformed, ma'am."

"Do you deny, then," said Mrs. Robson, "that my Hetty is, even now, in this house? Be careful how you respond, Madam. If you deny it, you make a liar out of a man of God, for Mr. Safford himself was the one who told me where to find Hetty."

"Ah," said Mrs. Cosgrove. "And the good rector informed you that we had kidnapped your daughter?"

"He didn't have to." She held her chin high. "I'm quite capable of reading between the lines."

"Indeed?" said Mrs. Cosgrove with the signature single brow raise which made Isabel bite her lip on behalf of Mrs. Robson.

Isabel thought it unlikely that Mr. Safford gave up Hetty's location willingly, but she was unsurprised that he had done so, given the type of threats the woman had likely made.

"Between the lines, you say," continued Mrs. Cosgrove. "I was unclear whether you were able to read at all, but I stand happily, albeit somewhat skeptically, corrected."

Mrs. Robson seemed to be working out this insult, but before she could do so, Mrs. Cosgrove continued.

"You will forgive me, I hope," she said with a smile full of gritted teeth, "for not offering you a seat. I feel certain that it would be distasteful to sully your person by contact with our regrettable furnishings. While we are naturally grateful to have been graced with your presence, I hesitate to assault your fine sensibilities any longer. I will have one of the servants show you out." She walked over and rang the bell, her smile unwavering.

Mrs. Robson stuttered, trying to regain control of the situation. "I insist that Hetty be returned to me."

"Ah, well," said Mrs. Cosgrove, the picture of politeness, "as to that, I feel sure we may depend upon her moving filial affection—torn from your bosom, did you say?—to bring her home. I can only assume that, having been raised by a woman such as yourself and instructed so painstakingly in the recognition of shabby gentility, if she did choose to remain here, only the most extreme need could persuade her to do so. Ah, here is Paxton. Please show Mrs. Robson the door."

Mrs. Robson's confidence seemed to have suffered a blow. She looked as though she was being taken by the tide, unwilling, but powerless against it. Isabel watched with her lips pressed together to keep from smiling as the woman walked out.

When she turned to her mother, though, her desire to smile faded. Mrs. Cosgrove did not look pleased.

"Mama," Isabel said in a pleading voice, "I assure you that Hetty is nothing like the woman you just encountered. She is very engaging, in fact, though I am admittedly astounded that she comes to be so, given what we just witnessed."

Isabel's mother stared at her for a moment. "The girl may stay. Temporarily," Mrs. Cosgrove added with emphasis, as if to quell the gratitude Isabel was prepared to show. "I wish to teach that woman a lesson, but I believe she will do everything in her power to get the girl back, even if she must resort to the law. I have no interest in embroiling myself to that extent, but a week or two will be sufficient to do the trick. She seems to be under the impression that she can force a marriage upon the unfortunate gentleman. Well, I hope for his sake that he is made of stern stuff, or else she is likely to succeed, in which case, heaven help him."

Isabel was grateful to her mother, even if her intentions in housing Hetty were somewhat questionable. How she would find a more permanent solution for the girl in a week or two was a worrisome matter, but any time was better than no time at all. In the meantime, anyone who asked would be informed that Hetty was a relation visiting from the north of England.

Hetty was ecstatic to learn that she would be a relation of Isabel's, even if only an imaginary and temporary one.

It was still with much trepidation that Isabel approached the second obstacle of the day: presenting Hetty to her mother. Had she not been so concerned that her mother would renege on their agreement, she would have found the scene comical.

When the door opened and Isabel ushered in a nervous Hetty, Mrs. Cosgrove's smiling expression transformed to surprise, and her mouth hung open.

"Oh," cried Hetty upon seeing her hostess. "You are even lovelier than I had imagined. I quite see where Isabel has her beauty from."

Mrs. Cosgrove stood speechless, a rare event in the life of the woman whose sharp wit was her best-known trait. She seemed in particular to be perplexed by the reference to Isabel's beauty.

Isabel took hold of her lips between her teeth, entertained to see her mother stunned silent by a naïve, young girl.

"Mama," she said, "this is Miss Hester Helena Robson, affectionately known as Hetty."

Hetty ran over, curtsied, and then, as if losing a fight against an overpowering impetuous urge, wrapped her arms around Mrs. Cosgrove.

Mrs. Cosgrove looked for a moment as though she might recoil but instead settled for an awkward pat on Hetty's back.

Hetty's eyes flew open, and she drew back, looking bashful. "Oh,

I'm quite sure I oughtn't to have done that. Forgive me. Mama is forever scolding me for being impulsive, but I am a slow learner, she says."

A mention of Mrs. Robson seemed to bring Mrs. Cosgrove back down to earth, and she smiled at Hetty.

"Well," she said, clearly determined to encourage anything about Hetty which would provoke her mother, "there is a difference between affectation and genuine feeling that *some* find difficult to discern. But you, my dear, are refreshing."

Hetty's cheeks turned pink with pleasure.

Once Hetty was settled in, Isabel felt that she had passed a successful and more-than-usually eventful morning. With her mind wrapped up in the problem of finding a situation for Hetty, she came face to face with her father in the corridor.

For once, his countenance brightened upon seeing her. His mood was much improved from the morning, a circumstance which significantly dampened Isabel's own mood. She feared what it meant.

"Ah, my little scheming Izzy," he said with a playful tap on her nose. "You have led us a pretty dance. Made us believe you were a shrinking violet. But all the while, you were throwing out subtle lures for a fine catch such as Galbraith. Ha! Well played, my dear. Well played." He clapped his hands three times in slow succession as he laughed merrily.

Isabel chewed her lip. "I am not marrying him, Papa."

"What now?" he said, still smiling.

"I am not going to marry Mr. Galbraith."

His wide grin began to fade, and he stared at her, as if to verify whether she were serious. "Don't be preposterous!"

She shook her head and sighed. "It isn't preposterous, though, Papa. I've already discussed it with him."

"The devil you did!" he hissed through a sneer.

She said nothing.

"You will un-discuss it, then. What made you think you had the right to do such a thing?"

She could think of a number of retorts but said nothing. The thought of trying to "undo" the conversation with Mr. Galbraith made her stomach clench.

"I am honor-bound," he said, "to the terms of our agreement, and I won't let you sully my name because of your missish scruples."

She swallowed. "And if Mr. Galbraith doesn't wish to marry me?"

"He is a man of his word. He will marry you." It was more of a threat than anything.

"You can hardly expect me," Isabel said quietly, "to hold him a hostage to his honor, Papa. I'm certain the two of you can arrange a compromise which will be satisfying to both of you that doesn't require my involvement."

He grabbed her arm and leaned in. "You listen to me," he hissed as his face shook with anger, "I don't give a fig how you go about it, but you will undo what you've done." He leaned back to look at her face.

"And if I can't do what you ask?"

"If," he said, "you disobey me, make no mistake, Isabel—I will speak to him myself. End of discussion."

She turned to look him in the eye. His eyes were fixed on her, angry and desperate. She looked down at his hand which still grasped her arm, shaking with emotion. She knew better than to continue her resistance with him in such a state. If she crossed him, she could easily end up like Aunt Eliza—her name banned from the house forever.

Aunt Eliza's offense had been to fall in love with a man below her station, but Isabel's father would likely view a refusal to marry someone *above* their station with just as much fury.

Whatever reasons he had for desiring a marriage between her and Mr. Galbraith, it would not be abandoned lightly.

Isabel sat in a chair in the parlor, holding the same embroidery hoop she had been working on for months. Whenever she had thoughts to be sorted, she sought out the half-finished piece. Threading the needle and beginning to stitch made order out of the disorder in her mind, and it was never long before her hands stopped moving as she sat in a daze.

The violence of her father's reaction had come as somewhat of a surprise to her. She had expected to meet with resistance, but it had been clear that he would brook no argument on the subject. And while he claimed it was a matter of honor, she knew him better than to believe that.

To those who knew him well, he was a selfish man prone to take shortcuts. His insistence that she marry Mr. Galbraith only made sense if being a man of his word served his interests. Marrying off the daughter he had expected to become a spinster must have been an alluring prospect for him, and to a respected family such as the Galbraiths, no less.

But Isabel couldn't marry Mr. Galbraith. If she'd had no interest in him, perhaps she could have resigned herself to such a future. Two disinterested people marrying one another was feasible. A marriage between two people with unequal levels of attraction and affection— no matter how foolish or unwarranted those emotions might be—that seemed to Isabel a special kind of torture.

Unlike Isabel's father, though, Mr. Galbraith seemed to be an honorable gentleman whose word was his bond, and if he felt that he had led a woman to believe he intended marriage, he would likely consider himself honor-bound to meet such expectations. Their encounter that morning was evidence of it.

What was more, her father had proven himself capable of manipulation in the past. He would not hesitate to pressure, even force Mr. Galbraith into believing that Isabel considered herself jilted.

The thought of Mr. Galbraith believing her such a sad figure was too much for her pride. She could not marry him, but she did not wish him to believe ill of her, either.

But what choice did she have? Her only other option was to throw herself upon the mercy of Mr. Galbraith; to beg him to offer her father an equally-appealing alternative. If Mr. Galbraith didn't wish to marry her—if he'd agreed only under the influence of strong drink—then perhaps he would be glad to come up with a substitute plan together.

Such a conversation would be a blow to her pride—but the alternatives would be worse.

She would have to speak to him. What she would say to him, she had no idea, but she trusted that in the time remaining in the day, she would be able to decide such a thing. Perhaps Mary could help.

❦ 7 ❧

Isabel had been determined not to attend the ball at Almack's that evening. Knowing, though, that Mary would rather lose a limb than miss an Almack's ball and that it was a place where they could have private conversation for a few minutes, she changed her mind. Cecilia would naturally be attending. Mrs. Cosgrove looked surprised when Isabel informed her that she planned to join them, but she accepted the change without a word.

Hetty expressed starry-eyed jealousy that Isabel should be attending a ball at Almack's and watched with great interest as Anaïs prepared her for the ball.

Mary Holledge, aside from being Isabel's closest friend and confidante, was the person to whom she and Cecilia owed their possession of Almack's vouchers in the first place. Mary's mother, Mrs. Holledge, was intimately acquainted with Lady Jersey and, having taken a great liking to Isabel, had put in a good word for her.

She had, conversely, taken Cecilia in dislike almost instantly and would have requested only Isabel's voucher if it hadn't been for Mary. Mary was well-enough acquainted with the Cosgrove familial particulars to know that for Isabel to receive a voucher but not Cecilia would cause an uproar. Isabel would suffer greatly in such circumstances. She would likely be accused of trying to sabotage her sister's matrimonial chances out of jealousy.

Once Mrs. Holledge was brought to understand that excluding Cecilia would be every bit as harmful to Isabel as it would be to Cecilia, she conceded the fight and, good for her word, procured two vouchers.

As a result of her mother's connections, Mary had grown up in a home oozing gossip. If there were information to be had about any member of the *haut-ton*, Mary was as likely as anyone to know it. She also possessed a creative mind, and Isabel stood in no small need of her creative genius—on behalf of Hetty and on behalf of herself.

It had been some time since Isabel had attended Almack's, and Isabel felt a flutter of nerves as the carriage let them down.

In the past, she had never been bothered by being overlooked in favor of Cecilia. But she had disliked the glances of pity she saw in the eyes of some mothers when they saw her without a partner.

She could have perhaps borne the looks, but when their pity moved them to hurriedly find her a dance partner—often a gentleman who was clearly unpleased by the favor being required of him—it had given her a great distaste for Almack's.

She felt quite capable of carrying on engaging conversation, but her experience had shown her that, for those who felt consigned to dance with the less desirable of the Cosgrove sisters, it mattered little what she said.

So, Isabel had absented herself from the weekly assemblies.

As she looked around the sparsely decorated room to see who was present, she noted a number of acquaintances. Mary was not among them, but that was no shock. The Holledges always arrived shortly before the doors closed at 11. Until then, Isabel would have to content herself as best she could with the civil niceties required of her.

Cecilia was soon surrounded by a bevy of people, and Isabel

moved away from the group to stand near her mother. She watched as Lord Brockway approached Cecilia.

Lord Brockway was one of Isabel's few friends. He was a bachelor with a kind heart, a pleasing countenance, and a great regard for Cecilia. With his light brown hair, brown eyes, and Roman nose, he was considered handsome. Agreeable manners, wealth, and title made him one of the most sought-after bachelors in London. But Cecilia had come to expect flattery and conversational fencing in her suitors, and Brockway was not one to engage. This had set him at a great disadvantage.

At times, Isabel found herself wondering how such a decent and genuine man could wish to form an intimate connection with someone as frivolous as Cecilia. Such uncharitable thoughts toward her own sister made her feel guilty, but there was no denying that think them she did.

She watched as Lord Brockway asked Cecilia to dance while two other gentlemen feigned anger at the prospect of being deserted.

Cecilia's cheeks were becomingly flushed—she had never needed rouge to achieve the effect, though she insisted on using it despite that —and Isabel watched as she delightedly handled the situation, leaving the two men laughing and smiling as she stepped onto the floor with Lord Brockway.

They glided apart and then together again and again. Cecilia knew how to please, how to throw the type of arch glances at her admirers which kept them coming back with more and more determination to win her approval. But whatever Cecilia was saying to Lord Brockway in the moments they had for talk, it seemed to frustrate him. Cecilia began to look piqued.

Isabel frowned. Cecilia's attempts to provoke Brockway into showing the spirit displayed by her other admirers was never received well by him. His bow was stiff as the dance ended, and he conveyed Cecilia to her mother with a sober expression. He turned to Isabel and took out his pocket watch.

"Miss Cosgrove," he said. "I believe supper is about to be served. Would you care to accompany me?"

She glanced over at Cecilia who was taking the arm of Lord Roffey, so Isabel smiled at Lord Brockway and agreed.

"Well, my lord," said Isabel gently as they walked. "What is amiss?"

He looked at her, and his mouth turned up into a wry half-smile. "I have never been good at masking my emotions."

"Is it Cecilia?" asked Isabel with frankness.

Lord Brockway frowned and sighed. "Try as I might, I cannot seem to understand her. Perhaps she is simply beyond my abilities to understand—a being on a higher plane than I."

Isabel chuckled. "Cecilia takes pains to appear more complicated than she is. She is like the rest of us, though—in search of approval and admiration."

Lord Brockway doubled back. "Surely that search has long been satisfied? She might have her pick of all the bachelors in this room."

"True," said Isabel, her head tilted to the side. "But that is often the case, is it not? We pursue what we think will make us happy, only to find that happiness eludes us still?"

His gaze was directed at the floor. "I would gladly spend the rest of my life in pursuit of her happiness, you know."

"I believe you would," said Isabel, watching her sister laugh gaily at a comment of Lord Roffey's. She turned back to Lord Brockway. "And it says a great deal about you. You are admirable."

"Would that your sister felt that way," he said. "Sometimes she seems to share your sentiments—she speaks to me candidly and without affectation. There is sincerity in her eyes. But other times—just now, for example—she seems artificial, and at those times it is clear she finds me lacking. But I never know which Cecilia to expect."

He paused for a moment as he handed Isabel into her seat. He sat down beside her and said, "She has given me reason to believe that my suit is not unwelcome, though."

Isabel thought it quite likely. Any man in possession of title, fortune, or a handsome face would be a welcome addition to her entourage. She didn't know just how encouraging to Lord Brockway her sister had been, but she felt that a word of caution might be warranted.

"Cecilia is," she struggled to find the words, "well, she has been cosseted and coddled her whole life, to be quite honest with you. My parents have great expectations of her—they always have had—and I think it has created confusion in her about what will make her happy. Though she has never admitted it, I believe she feels terrified of disappointing my parents.

"Her happiness is tangled up in satisfying their wishes for her future, and it has led her to believe that her primary goal should be to not only meet but to exceed everyone's expectations of her. I don't know that she has truly considered what makes her happy apart from receiving the admiration of others."

"Do you mean to say," Lord Brockway said slowly, "that I am reading too much into her encouragement?"

"I couldn't say that for certain," Isabel said. "I believe at least you are a category unto yourself among her admirers. I don't think she knows what to do with your genuine concern for her—not when she is surrounded by adulation, flirtation, and superficial compliments. It remains to be seen whether she will realize the value of your affection. Only she can decide such a thing."

Lord Brockway was silent for a few moments, and Isabel watched him, hoping her words had not been too harsh. Brockway raised his head, and his eyes searched out Cecilia, seated next to Lord Roffey, one of her boldest suitors.

"I must do what I can to help her understand my earnest regard for her," Lord Brockway said with his jaw set determinedly. "It is my greatest wish."

Isabel smiled bracingly. "I know you would do everything in your power to make Cecilia happy. And if you believe she could make you happy, I wish you every success. For I am concerned with the happiness of you both, you know."

He smiled gratefully.

When supper was finished, Isabel looked to find Mary. Isabel had found her to be a loyal friend with more common sense than she had expected from someone so drawn to gossip.

"Oh," said Mary with an intrigued smile as she came upon Isabel. "You have news."

Isabel cocked her head to the side, and her eyes narrowed. She shook her head and sighed with a smile. "It is uncanny how well you can read people!"

Mary raised her brows mischievously and linked their arms, drawing Isabel toward a nearby window.

As Isabel related the events of the past two days, Mary listened with rapt attention. Her brows went up as Isabel revealed who had been the mysterious man in her father's company. And when it was revealed that her father had wagered her hand in marriage, her hand flew to her mouth, and her eyes widened so much that Isabel broke into laughter. Mr. Galbraith's visit to renew his offer of marriage was met with surprise followed by a nod of approval. Hetty's appearance and the ensuing drama lit the familiar fire of curiosity in Mary's eyes.

But upon hearing of Isabel's conversation with her father, her expression grew grim.

Mary was silent for a few moments after Isabel finished. She looked at Isabel as her jaw moved slightly in thought.

"Never would I have thought these words would pass my lips, but I believe you did right to refuse Mr. Galbraith." She looked at Isabel with a suddenly wary expression. "We are speaking of the same Mr. Galbraith, are we not?"

Isabel closed her eyes to summon her patience. "Do you know another?"

"Yes, in fact," said Mary. "There is that ancient widower who walks around rapping the ankles of young gentlemen he disapproves of with his purple cane. His name is Galbraith, too."

Isabel's eyes widened. "Oh dear! I suppose I should feel more gratitude that he is *not* the Galbraith I'm referring to."

"I believe you should, Izzy. I mean, good heavens! Mr. Galbraith offered for you—twice! Dark, handsome, enigmatically charming Charles Galbraith." Eyes glazed over, Mary gazed forward at nothing in particular.

"Do try to focus, Mary," Isabel said in irritation.

"Right," Mary said, giving her head a little shake. "As I was saying, I suppose you did right to refuse him. Everyone knows he is forever enamored of Julia."

Isabel swallowed before straightening her shoulders and looking back at Mary. "Then why would he offer for me?" she said baldly.

"Pique," said Mary with a shrug of the shoulders. "They're at loggerheads, I hear. Miss Darling's been seen in the company of other gentlemen quite frequently in recent weeks, and Mr. Galbraith has been less than pleased. I believe they had quite a quarrel the other night at the Rodwell's rout."

Isabel chewed the inside of her lip. So they'd had a falling out before Mr. Galbraith had come to her home? The knowledge that she may have been a tool for revenge or retaliation made her stomach drop.

"But it is of no account, really," continued Mary. "The predicament we face is how to satisfy your father's demands." Mary folded her arms, tapping a finger on her upper arm. "Let us reconsider. Would it be a waste of breath to suggest that you contemplate Mr. Galbraith's offer?" She smiled with clenched teeth as if she knew what reaction to expect from her friend.

"An utter waste," said Isabel.

Mary said nothing, but her brows were raised in doubtful hope.

Isabel sighed. "You honestly advise me to marry a man who offered for me—a woman he didn't know from Eve—in a fit of pique, when he is still in love with that angelic creature?" With a raise of the brows she indicated Miss Darling.

"Yes, I see why you might hesitate." Mary's mouth twisted to the side as she considered the problem.

"Besides," said Isabel, "you have only just said that I did right to refuse him."

But Mary wasn't listening. She straightened suddenly. "Izzy, do you think you might persuade your father you have accepted Mr. Galbraith without actually doing so?"

Isabel stared blankly at her.

Mary's mouth turned up into a mischievous half-smile. "Well?"

"Perhaps," Isabel said with an impatient roll of the eyes, "until he spoke with Mr. Galbraith. And even failing that inevitability, to what purpose, Mary? It is ridiculous to even discuss. He would surely discover the hoax."

"How should he?"

Isabel's jaw slackened in disbelief.

Mary said nothing, waiting for an answer, and Isabel put a finger to her cheek in feigned thought. "Well, I should think that the lack of a wedding might be problematic, do you not? Not to mention the absence of settlement talks or the banns being read. But perhaps I am being overly-particular." She dropped her hand and looked at Mary in consternation. "Good gracious, Mary! I had relied on you to help me."

"Well, I think it's a famous idea," Mary said in her own defense.

"Yes, perhaps in one of your outrageous novels, but not in real life, my dear."

"Oh, what are novels but suggestions for how to live our lives in a more thrilling way?" said Mary, undeterred. "Besides, all we need to do is make him think—only temporarily—that you're engaged to be married. Just until we can find a distraction which will bring him not to care the snap of his fingers—" she snapped her fingers with flare, "—for a marriage with Mr. Galbraith."

"Mere child's play, in fact?" Isabel said with a bite to her voice.

"Think, Izzy. Why does your father so wish for this marriage?"

Isabel thought for a moment. "I can't say how much of it is the prospect of being rid of one of his daughters—for I especially am a great trial to him, I can tell you—and how much is due to the connection with Mr. Galbraith. I imagine that my father is uncomfortably in debt, and a familial connection to the respected Galbraith name would give him more credit with his debtors, shouldn't it?"

Mary nodded at the practical reasoning. "Well, then we must find you a husband with a greater connection than Mr. Galbraith. One who is not already in love," she added.

Isabel scoffed at the suggestion, but suddenly her eyes lit up, and she put her hand on Mary's.

"Or," she said, drawing the word out and pausing as she pursued the idea in her head. She turned in her seat to look gravely at her friend. "Not a word must pass your lips, Mary, for this was said to me in strictest confidence."

Mary nodded solemnly, and Isabel wondered for a moment what other secrets Mary housed in her head full of gossip. She could keep a secret when it was warranted.

"Lord Brockway is completely smitten with Cecilia," Isabel said. "He means to offer for her, but fool that she is—" she shook her head "—I don't know that she will accept him."

"Lord Brockway?" Mary said, staring at Isabel with raised brows. Isabel nodded.

"I knew that there was something between them, but I hadn't imagined it to be so serious." She narrowed her eyes at Isabel. "You think she would actually refuse Lord Brockway—the most eligible bachelor in London?"

Isabel's only response was a comprehending grimace.

Mary shrugged her shoulders. "I wash my hands of you Cosgrove women!"

Isabel laughed. "No one would blame you if you did. But please don't. You know Cecilia, Mary. She wants to be worshipped and flattered and flirted with. Lord Brockway loves her too well to appeal to her vanity in such a way, and it puts her off."

"Well I like him all the better for it. Cecilia needs a vase of water to the face," Mary said waspishly, rushing to add, "Figuratively, I mean."

Isabel repressed a smile. "You know I agree with you. But if only we can make her see the value of the match, it might be enough salve for my father's wounds when he discovers that I am not to marry Mr. Galbraith after all."

"It's risky, Izzy." Mary's mouth twisted to the side as she considered the proposal. "I hesitate to make the minx the center of any plan. Selfish, flighty little thing! But it might just serve."

"Well," said Isabel, "I think I must try." After all, what was the alternative?

"Cousin Mary!" Mr. John Burke appeared behind them, smiling and putting out a hand toward Mary.

"Ah, John!" she said. "I can always count on you to ask me for the quadrille." She gave him her hand with a smile and glanced at Isabel. "Let us find a fine gentleman to join Izzy on the floor. We four shall put all the other dancers to shame."

Isabel demurred. "Oh, no, please. Go on. It will give me great pleasure to watch you. In fact, I see my mother just over there—I think I shall join her for some orgeat."

"Orgeat over dancing, Miss Cosgrove?"

Isabel turned toward the voice.

Mr. Galbraith stood just behind her, making his bow. "Might I persuade you to reconsider?" He flashed a teasing smile. "I warn you that I shall take offense if you refuse."

Without even looking, Isabel knew Mary's eyes were on her. Her cheeks tinged with pink.

Mr. Burke laughed. "She hesitates, Mr. Galbraith. Over orgeat, no less. A blow to your ego!"

"No, no," said Isabel with a laugh. "I happen to be one of the dwindling few who likes orgeat. But I would be happy to join you for the quadrille. There is small likelihood of the orgeat running out while we dance, so it can wait." She made a small curtsy to Mr. Galbraith and took his arm, determinedly ignoring her nerves.

They followed Mary and Mr. Burke to the ballroom floor. Isabel swallowed and tried to maintain her smile when she saw who had also joined the set. Opposite them were Miss Darling and her partner, the same man Miss Darling had been laughing with earlier. Mary shot a significant look at Isabel.

Mr. Galbraith was a good dancer and an engaging partner. He was attentive to Isabel and his conversation amusing. The figures of the dance, though, often required them to interchange partners with the couple across from them. When Isabel chanced a quick glance at Mr. Galbraith and Miss Darling, there was a palpable intensity between them. Mr. Galbraith looked grave with his brows drawn together, Miss Darling arch and provoking.

"Do you recall," Mr. Galbraith said to Isabel in a low voice when they were reunited, "Hetty speaking of the gentleman responsible for her situation?"

"Farrow, was it not?" she said.

"Yes," he answered shortly. "He is the man you were just dancing with."

He indicated Miss Darling's partner with his eyes.

Isabel looked at Mr. Farrow and then back at Mr. Galbraith who nodded his confirmation.

Isabel thought back to their time with Hetty at St. James's. When Hetty had revealed the name of the baby's father, both Mr. Safford and Mr. Galbraith had looked shocked. Mr. Galbraith's reaction made much more sense if Farrow happened to also be the new gentleman who had taken his place in Miss Darling's affections.

If the truth came out about Mr. Farrow, though, was Miss Darling likely to continue her romance with him? She might well realize her error in bestowing her charms upon a man like him, and she and Mr. Galbraith might share a happy ending together after all.

If that was the case, it resolved any remaining question in Isabel's mind about her decision to refuse Mr. Galbraith. If she had accepted him only for things to turn sour between Mr. Farrow and Miss Darling, Mr. Galbraith would have sorely regretted it. What a miserable outcome that would have been!

When she was next joined to Mr. Farrow in the dance, Isabel

took the liberty of observing him. He was not watching her. His eyes were on Miss Darling, and there was a victorious air in the way he watched her as she danced with Mr. Galbraith. Every movement he made was charged with self-assurance. And while he adhered to the strict standards of Almack's in his dress, he still managed to set himself apart.

His hair looked windswept, though in a manner too calculated to be natural, and his cravat was tied in a similar mix of haphazard order. It was his confident smirk, though, that completed the persona. She could see how easy it would have been for Hetty to fall victim to him if he had been intent on charming her.

She sensed he might be one of those people who could be very engaging with those they favored while making their dislike felt keenly by anyone not fortunate enough to find themselves in their good graces; someone whose disfavor would be very unpleasant.

When Isabel saw Mr. Galbraith's face, rigid and dark, she hesitated.

"Are you well?" she said softly.

He looked at her and forced a smile. "Never better."

She looked over at Miss Darling, the picture of enjoyment, who seemed to smile all the brighter after whatever had passed between her and Mr. Galbraith. Isabel detected a slightly forced quality to the smile, though, and she frowned.

"Well, I shall pretend to believe you," she said.

Mr. Galbraith's brow lightened slightly, and the hint of a smile appeared.

"I wish to speak to you," she continued, "on some of the matters we were discussing at the church, but I'm sure you'll agree that this is neither the time nor the place."

He nodded. "Shall I call on you tomorrow?"

"Perhaps we could meet at the churchyard again? My friend Mary and I will be there with Hetty in the late morning."

Mr. Galbraith had nothing to say against the plan, and the two soon parted ways, Mr. Galbraith leading her to Mary who was agog with curiosity to hear what had passed between the two.

"For he looked so cross when he danced with Miss Darling and not at all when he danced with you," Mary said once Mr. Galbraith was out of earshot.

"Nonsense," said Isabel, though color crept into her cheeks. "Anyone can see they are in love and only unsure how to manage the muddle they've made of things."

Mary looked skeptical and intent on pursuing the subject, but Isabel successfully distracted her with talk of the plans for the following morning. When Mary discovered the assignation, she was delighted to be informed she would play a part in it and equally so that she would be meeting Hetty.

"For I am exceedingly curious," she declared, "to discover who is to blame for the poor girl's situation. I shouldn't be at all surprised if it were Lord Essop, for he is the most detestable blackguard, and I believe him capable of anything."

Isabel considered staying silent. She didn't like to gossip, nor did she feel it was her place to share the information. However, with a girl as sweet and naive as Hetty, Mary would have whatever information she wanted from her in a matter of minutes.

"It is not Lord Essop," Isabel said.

Mary whirled around to face her. "You know who it is?"

After ensuring that Mary understood she was only relaying the information because she knew it to be an inevitability, Isabel revealed Mr. Farrow's name.

Mary's hand shot to her mouth. "Good heavens!"

Isabel let out a small sigh. "I seem to be the only person who did not share your reaction upon hearing the name."

Mary was still processing the revelation and didn't seem to hear Isabel. Her eyes stared ahead, but they were wide with excitement.

"Izzy," she said in a slow voice infused with energy. "I think that we are in for quite a spectacle to end the Season."

"What do you mean?" asked Isabel, nose and brow wrinkled.

"Just think." Mary placed a hand on Isabel's arm. "Mr. Galbraith loves Miss Darling but offered for you; Miss Darling is torn between Mr. Galbraith and Mr. Farrow; Mr. Farrow having a sordid affair which is sure to come to light now that Hattie has run away from her family."

"Hetty," Isabel patiently corrected.

"He is lucky his father has just died, you know," Mary added as an aside. "Farrow, I mean. I understand his father became extremely strait-laced in his final days—they say he found God again. He would likely have cut Farrow off if he discovered such an affair. But alas, we will have to content ourselves without that part of the drama." She let out a small sigh.

"You are incorrigible, Mary," said Isabel, suppressing a smile. She did not want to encourage her friend's love of scandal.

"Perhaps," Mary replied, "but you must admit that it has been quite flat lately. Now we may really enjoy ourselves!" She clasped her hands and rubbed them together.

Isabel sighed. "If I were not directly involved in the spectacle, as you call it, then it might be more enjoyable. As things stand, though, I am very anxious to wash my hands of it all."

"I would never forgive you," Mary said. "Besides, you haven't the luxury of that option. You have your father to contend with. And what of poor Hetty? You would leave her to fend for herself?"

"Of course not," Isabel said. "I am determined to see her taken care of."

8

Charles Galbraith walked toward the church with a brow slightly drawn and lips pursed. He was reluctant to meet with Miss Cosgrove, knowing that he had nothing helpful to offer for Hetty. He had thought of her situation over the past two days, but his mind had been too consumed with other matters to really pursue anything meaningful.

His reluctance to see Miss Cosgrove also stemmed from a malaise regarding how they had left things before finding Hetty.

He had felt relief that Isabel had refused his offer, but he was unsure how he could convey this to Mr. Cosgrove without giving offense, which could be detrimental to his father's financial prospects.

The fact was that Charles had won, and the terms of his victory had been a marriage to Isabel. If Cosgrove had any sense or any decency as a father, though, he would honor his daughter's wishes. It was she who was unwilling to honor the stakes, and understandably so, since she had no part in deciding them. And her wishes were well out of Charles's control.

Surely Cosgrove would see that.

That Charles was relieved at Isabel's refusal was further evidence of the rashness of his decision. He had been angry with Julia, but he had acted imprudently in accepting Cosgrove's crazed stakes. He couldn't throw in the towel on a future with Julia. Not yet. London had gone to her head; Farrow had exerted a negative influence on her.

But she was going through a phase, nothing more, and Charles was confident she would come to herself if she were removed from their influence.

How could she forget everything they had felt and promised just a few short months ago? If only he were able to spend time with her alone, remind her of the regard they had held each other in, the promises they had made prior to coming to London—she would come around.

How that was to be accomplished, Charles hadn't any notion.

He sighed and turned into the archway leading to the churchyard.

[Image: image1.png]

Isabel, Hetty, and Mary sat on the same bench as Hetty had days before. But this time, Hetty wasn't downcast. She was radiant, speaking animatedly to Mary who listened with wide-eyed attention. The two had taken to one another quite easily, and Isabel sat on the end of the bench, resting her weight on two hands behind her, and looking at her friends with an appreciative half-smile.

She was the first one to notice Mr. Galbraith's presence. Her face fell momentarily on seeing him and her stomach dropped. She couldn't put off the conversation any longer. He was here.

"You've come," she said, rising to greet him.

His eyebrows raised. "Of course," he said. "Did you doubt I would?"

"Yes," she said frankly.

"So little faith in me?" he said with a laugh.

Isabel tilted her head to the side as she considered. "No, it is only that you seemed preoccupied last night, and I couldn't be sure you would remember."

His smile faltered, but only for an instant. "I must have been an atrocious dancing partner."

"Not at all," she said. "You were very civil and executed your duties admirably."

"Good heavens," he said with a look of horror. "A dead bore, in fact."

Isabel laughed and shook her head, turning toward Hetty and Mary. Hetty greeted Mr. Galbraith like an old friend, going so far as to offer him her hand.

He looked at Isabel with a diverted expression as he took it.

Mary was standing back, watching the interchange between the other three. There was a curious light in Mary's eyes as she greeted Mr. Galbraith, and she soon insisted that she needed to speak with Hetty for a moment in private.

Isabel looked a question at her, but Mary avoided her eye and guided Hetty with a firm arm around her waist further into the churchyard.

"They are fast friends, it would appear," said Mr. Galbraith, taking a seat on the bench and motioning for Isabel to join him.

She hesitated a moment but decided that to refuse the seat and stay standing would be unnecessarily rude and awkward. She sat on the edge as far away as possible from him. So far, in fact, that Mr. Galbraith's hand shot out and grabbed her arm to keep her from falling off the bench. Her cheeks burning, she thanked him without meeting his eye.

"You seem to be a bit on edge today," he said.

A smile appeared on her face, and she nodded her approval. "A very good pun." She tilted her head and frowned. "Though somewhat unfeeling perhaps."

Mr. Galbraith chuckled as he realized her meaning. "I'm all thumbs, Miss Cosgrove."

Isabel smiled and looked toward Mary and Hetty. They seemed

to be engrossed in conversation with no immediate intention to return. Feeling Mr. Galbraith's eyes on her, Isabel turned her head to look at him.

His brows were drawn. "I believe you are the one who is preoccupied today."

Isabel sighed. She didn't relish the conversation she needed to have with him. It went against her pride, but she didn't have the luxury of pride in her current situation. And if the conversation were necessary, it was better to face it head on. The sooner she broached the subject, the sooner it would be over.

"I am," she acknowledged. "I need to speak with you on a difficult topic, and I admit that I am reluctant."

He turned toward her, half concern, half caution. "What is it?"

She took her lips between her teeth and took a deep breath. "My father insists that we marry," she said. She tried to ignore the way her stomach clenched as she watched him frown at the revelation. "He maintains that you gave your word, and unfortunately, my own arguments have done nothing to move him from his position."

She waited for Mr. Galbraith to respond, but he said nothing, staring ahead.

She took another breath and, her cheeks infused with color, she continued. "He takes no pains to hide the fact that he is anxious to marry off my sisters and me, but I doubt you can be fully aware how providential he views the opportunity to marry me off. He has long commented that he expected to be responsible for me financially until his death."

Mr. Galbraith turned his head to look at her, and she saw in his eyes a hint of what she had most dreaded: pity.

She smiled wryly. "Don't, please."

His brow furrowed. "Don't what?"

"Pity me," she said, turning her head back to watch Hetty and Mary. "I have long since learned to disregard the things said by my father. But when he threatened to speak to you himself—to attempt to force you to honor the terms of play, I felt it would be much better if you and I could discuss things. Perhaps come up with a plan of our own to appease him."

Mr. Galbraith was looking at her with a curious expression. "And this is more preferable to you than simply honoring the agreement between your father and myself?"

"What, and marry?" She looked at him and raised a brow.

He returned her gaze but remained silent, his lips pursed.

She sighed. "Mr. Galbraith, may I be what I am certain my mother should call 'vulgarly frank' with you?"

His mouth twitched. "Please do."

She looked at him with an intense, calculating gaze, trying to guess how he would respond to her forthrightness. What would he think of her? She couldn't imagine Miss Darling saying what she was about to say, nor Cecilia, nor any one of the ladies she knew.

But she had given up trying to be like them.

"It is obviously none of my business at all," she said, "but I believe that, given the situation we find ourselves in, we must agree to dispose with formality, do you not agree?"

He nodded his agreement, but a smile still tugged at the corners of his mouth.

"Very well," she said, exhaling. "Am I correct in my understanding that you hold Miss Darling in—" she searched for the right words "—shall we say, higher than common regard?"

Mr. Galbraith drew back slightly.

"I did warn you," said Isabel with a defensive note in her voice.

Mr. Galbraith smiled and relaxed. "You did."

Isabel grimaced. "I have shocked you with my vulgarly frank ways."

He laughed. "No. I am not so easily shocked. It was simply unexpected." He was silent for a moment. "To answer your question with equal frankness, yes. Julia and I grew up together and have long intended to wed. Had, I should say. *Had* long intended to wed. Her parents were insistent, though, that she not promise herself to marry before enjoying a Season." His eyebrows went up. "Julia and I both fought them on it, found it to be terribly unjust. They must have been wiser than I. No sooner did Julia arrive in town than she caught the attention and admiration of nearly every eligible bachelor in London. Men far more eligible than I."

Isabel watched his profile, frowning, and said softly, "And she lost sight of things." It wasn't a question but a statement.

Mr. Galbraith looked at her and nodded slowly.

"But you," she said, "remain constant in your regard." Again, it was a statement more than a question.

He hesitated for a moment, as if trying to judge how his response would be received by Isabel, and then nodded again.

It was only what she had expected, but somehow to see him acknowledge it made her stomach clench.

But it was better to be in possession of all the facts than forever hanging on to some ignorant, silly hope. And much better that she help him toward achieving his own desires than to pursue her fruitless ones.

If Miss Darling had loved him, surely that love could be rekindled. It might require some unconventional tactics—ruthless and heavy-handed, even—but only because the tactics employed by the forces at work on Miss Darling were also ruthless and heavy-handed.

If all went according to plan, Miss Darling and Mr. Galbraith could marry happily. Though such an outcome might not appeal to Isabel on first consideration, the practical side of her knew that it was far preferable than for her to marry a man who had no heart to give her in return for her own, one who would secretly be wishing he were with Julia Darling.

"May I now," said Mr. Galbraith, "be what I apprehend your mother would call 'vulgarly frank' with you?"

Isabel couldn't help but smile. "I beg you will be."

"What bearing does my regard for Julia have on our situation? Things between her and myself are at an end."

"Well," said Isabel, "as to that, we shall see. The fact of the matter is that neither of us wishes to be constrained to marry the other, despite my father's insistence that it be so. My first thought was that we offer him something more valuable to him than the marriage of his most ill-favored daughter—" she shot him a look full of humor "—but I believe the only thing which could tempt him would be money, and far more of it than I could ask you to give. It is the most unfortunate circumstance, you know, that he should have won against you for he is unaccountably unlucky in gaming. But that ship has sailed, and we must now make the best—."

Mr. Galbraith put up a hand to stop her. "You are mistaken," he said. "Your father did not win. I won."

Isabel's jaw hung slack, and she looked at him with a blank expression.

"Your father is not, I admit, a paragon of virtue—or of filial affection, it would seem—but he is not so black as to stake his daughter's hand as his reward for winning. It was his loss that brought this about."

Isabel's wry smile appeared again. "I admire your confidence in my father, sir."

She was silent for a moment, digesting the information he had provided. "I don't pretend to be the quickest wit," Isabel said with a wrinkled brow, "but I am normally accounted to have a sound understanding. I fail to see what could have possessed you to agree to such stakes, particularly given your regard for Miss Darling."

Mr. Galbraith gripped his lips together. "My behavior that evening was headstrong and unwise. I am not proud of it, and I am particularly sorry to have involved you. It was abominable of me. I despaired of my success with Julia, and I was angry with her. I wanted to put it all behind me, and your father offered me a way to do that. He had no money left to wager, and he knew I was blue-deviled. He suggested that I marry your sister—Cecilia, is it? Then he had the idea to play for her hand. I think it was in jest at first. But somehow I began seriously considering the idea." He shrugged his shoulders, as if he couldn't account for how it all had happened. "I insisted on you rather than Cecilia, and suddenly we were playing."

Isabel had been listening intently, but she grew suddenly still. No one had ever chosen her over Cecilia. The suggestion would have been laughable to most people.

"Why me? Why not Cecilia?"

Mr. Galbraith shrugged again. "She reminded me too much of Julia. I wanted someone nothing like her; didn't want the constant reminder of her."

Isabel swallowed painfully. She could never escape the comparisons to Cecilia. For a foolish moment, she had felt a flicker of hope that Mr. Galbraith had seen something in her that attracted him. But the only thing which had recommended her to him was how different she was from the woman he loved. It was hardly a compliment.

She had grown to accept that everyone viewed her as inferior to Cecilia. And for a long time, she had seen herself that way. She had once tried to be more like Cecilia—to laugh and flirt, to always be on the cusp of fashion. But her efforts had not left her feeling the confidence she sought. They had only left her feeling like a shadow; a poor imitation of something far superior. And they had left her with animosity toward her sister.

When she had confided such unchristian feelings to the rector, Mr. Safford had taken pains to help her see her own value, to understand that her worth was inherent and not something society bestowed upon her. His kindness and care had had its effect over time, and Isabel had shed much of her resentment. She had gained a quiet confidence, and it was rare that she let a feeling of inferiority weigh on her.

"I see," she said with a feigned smile as she put the thoughts aside. "But if my father lost, what did he stand to gain if he had won?"

"I hold a number of his vowels, and I was to forfeit them if he won."

Isabel pondered for a moment. "So, my father was the de facto winner either way. When you said he had lost, I had a moment's hope that we could simply offer him what he stood to win in place of a marriage between you and me. But I'm afraid there is no question of that."

Mr. Galbraith tilted his head and his brows drew together. "You think he would rather we marry than for me to relinquish his debts? They are substantial."

Isabel grimaced. "I am sure of it. Do you not see? If we marry, he knows he won't be expected to pay his debts to his own son-in-law."

Mr. Galbraith sighed. "How foolish of me not to have seen that. A result of too much drink, no doubt." His eyes went still for a moment as he became lost in thought. He smiled wryly. "I was very sure he was about to take the final hand, but his luck seemed to change suddenly, and he lost."

Isabel grimaced. "He must have realized what losing would mean." She chewed her lip.

"I don't wish to put you in a difficult position," Mr. Galbraith said. His brow was grave, but there was a determined set to his jaw. "But I am a man of my word, and I gave your father my word that I would marry you."

All at once, Isabel felt repulsion and longing. She admired Mr. Galbraith for his desire to keep his word of honor—the strange affinity she felt for him grew at the illumination of his character. She wished, though, that the terms of his martyrdom had not been to marry her.

She could not submit to such a thing, even if it was what she would have wanted under other circumstances.

"I admire you, Mr. Galbraith," she said with a sad smile. "But I can't marry you."

He opened his mouth to speak but she put a hand up to stop him.

"What if I told you that there was another way?' she said. "To appease my father without us sacrificing ourselves to your honor and his selfishness?"

"Go on," he said cautiously.

"Well," she said as she inhaled deeply, "in the spirit of our frank conversation, I have a suggestion to put forward. It will likely be repugnant to you at first, but I ask you to consider it for a day before deciding. I believe it is the best way to preserve both your happiness and mine."

His mouth twisted to the side in a smile. "You terrify me. But let's have it."

Isabel nodded. If he didn't think her a hoyden without a conscience already, he surely would once she laid out her plan.

"My sister Cecilia is, if all goes well, soon to become engaged to a man of great position and substance. If you and I can convince my father that we mean to marry—just until my sister's engagement— then I am convinced he can be brought to give up the notion."

Mr. Galbraith's brows were up, and Isabel colored slightly but continued on. "What's more, I think that we might turn the situation even more to your account with a little care."

Mr. Galbraith's brows went up even further, but his intrigued smile robbed the expression of offense.

"I had the opportunity," Isabel said, "to observe Miss Darling a little last night. You mentioned Cecilia reminding you of her, and I believe that they are both the type of women who enjoy attaining what seems to be just out of their reach."

Mr. Galbraith considered her words and conceded with a nod.

"Perhaps she has come to consider you *too* within reach; to take you for granted."

She waited for her words to sink in, unsure whether he would become defensive of himself or of Miss Darling. But he only pursed his lips as he mulled over what she was saying.

"If my father is to believe that we mean to marry, we will need to act in a convincing manner—or at least keep up appearances enough that he doesn't question things. Might we not use such an imperative to help Miss Darling remember her regard for you? If she believes that your affection and attention is shifting toward another, I think she may come to her senses."

He looked at her through squinted eyes. "This isn't perchance your way of revenging yourself upon me? A plan to jilt me? Teach me a lesson?" He put his hands up in a gesture of surrender. "It would be entirely called for, of course!"

Isabel suppressed a smile. "Very perceptive of you. Nothing motivates me quite like mutually-destructive revenge. I only wish I had thought of it myself."

A responsive laugh escaped him. "But it is a plan to jilt me, is it not?"

Isabel shook her head. "No. We shall tell my father that we plan to marry but that we cannot be formally or publicly engaged because it wouldn't be suitable."

"It wouldn't?" said Mr. Galbraith between a statement and a question.

"Decidedly not." Her voice had a hint of teasing sternness in it. "On account of your uncle's recent death."

Mr. Galbraith stared at her.

"Do you have an uncle who has died recently?" asked Isabel with a hopeful tilt to her brow and voice. "It would be so convenient."

Mr. Galbraith's shoulders shook. "I'm afraid my relatives have never been the type to care about inconveniencing others. My uncles are all wretchedly healthy."

Isabel sighed. "I felicitate them."

"I'm afraid," he said, looking very near laughter, "the only thing I have to offer is an aunt who died nearly a year and a half ago." He bared his teeth in a grimace. "Not very helpful."

Isabel sat up straighter, and she suddenly put a hand over his clasped hands. He looked down at it with laughing eyes.

"On the contrary," she said, taking her hand off his when she realized what she had done. "I believe we may put her to good use—may she rest in peace," she added with soberness. "We will tell my father that you were very close to Aunt—" she paused, looking at him.

"Gertrude," he offered.

"—Aunt Gertrude, yes. She was very jealous in her affections, and never believed any woman could endeavor to deserve you. Thus it came about that you made an especial promise to her on her deathbed

—unwisely perhaps, but one is wont to placate dying people, isn't one? —that you would respect and mourn her death by postponing any engagement or nuptials until she had been gone a full two years. It sounds quite eccentric," she said, seeing Mr. Galbraith's expression, "but Aunt Gertrude was always singular. And since my father believes in nothing so firmly as he believes in the capriciousness and strange whims of females, I think he will not only believe it but will likely expound upon the subject for a number of minutes."

Mr. Galbraith looked torn between amusement and surprise.

Isabel continued. "And as long as he believes we plan to marry, we need not broadcast the information to anyone else—we will simply take pains to be seen more in one another's company. All the while, you will pay less attention to Miss Darling, ensuring that you are cordial but never lingering. We, on the other hand, must be seen to always enjoy one another's company."

"I begin to think that will not be such a task." He was obviously enjoying himself.

Isabel ignored his comment, finishing with, "Following such a plan, I believe we may win on both suits."

Mr. Galbraith looked at her with a mixture of admiration and amusement. "I think that I believe you."

"Well," she said prosaically, "being acquainted as I am with my father and having the advantage of understanding women on account of being one myself, I do think you would be wise to allow yourself to be guided by me in this. Or," she said with a slight sigh, "perhaps you think me only fit for Bedlam, in which case I'm sure there are many who might sympathize with you."

"I admit," he said, "to feeling reluctant. For a number of reasons, not least of which is on your own behalf. If your father discovered the ruse, what would become of you?"

She smiled reassuringly. "Don't let that bother you."

"Don't let it bother me indeed," he exclaimed. "What a rogue you must think me. I am to agree to this plan in which you risk yourself to help me without a thought for what it might mean for you?"

She had considered the possibility that her father might discover the deceit, but she had not allowed herself to dwell on it. She felt she could more easily face her father's ire than marriage to a man in love with another. She had to remain confident that the plan would succeed. Mary would help her see things through.

"I'm afraid you must trust me on that account," she said with a grimace.

He didn't look convinced. "It also seems that much of the plan hinges upon something out of our control: the success of a gentleman's suit with your sister."

"Well not entirely out of our control. I may have some influence there, as well." She sounded more confident than she felt.

He chuckled. "I suppose I should have guessed as much."

Seeing Mary and Hetty making their way back over, Isabel hastened to add, "Only promise me you will think on it. I feel confident that if we work together, we may come about, and you may well have your Miss Darling after all." She smiled at him as confidently as she could manage, while wondering what she might be getting herself into.

Agreeing to spend more time with Mr. Galbraith was the choice of a masochist. To know he would be paying her attention as part of an act and with no one but herself to blame for the farce—well, it would certainly be a test of her charity. But the temporary hurt it might cause would be preferable to a lifetime of pain if they were to marry.

"I apologize," Mary exclaimed as they approached. "I made Hetty promise she should tell me her story—from the beginning—and you know how I ask a thousand questions, Izzy."

"None better," said Isabel with a teasing smile. "I'm very glad that Hetty has told you all. You likely know much more than Mr. Galbraith or I, but it's of no account. What remains is to decide what the best route is for Hetty."

"And I am afraid," Mr. Galbraith confessed, "that I am no help at all. I have been a bit consumed with other matters, but I promise to

reform my ways and see what I can discover from my acquaintances."
He smiled his apology at Hetty, and she looked back at him with
utter confidence.

"And unfortunately," said Isabel, "I am just as little help. But don't
fret, Hetty. We won't leave you to fend for yourself. Mary in particular is very resourceful." She smiled at Mary. "She will undoubtedly
be a powerful ally."

Mary's brows went up and down in a gesture of cunning. "Yes,
indeed."

"What would you like, Hetty?" said Isabel. "I feel that your wishes
should be honored as much as possible, though we can obviously
make no promises."

"Oh," Hetty cried, "I'm sure I could wish nothing better than to
stay for the rest of my life with you, Izzy!"

Mr. Galbraith and Isabel met eyes for a moment, her expression
touched yet flustered, his amused.

"A great tribute to her character," Mr. Galbraith said. "And I'm
sure she shares your sentiments. But I doubt the matter is up to her."
He looked at Isabel with a knowing expression.

Isabel bit the inside of her lip. "It is true, Hetty. I'm very sorry to
say it, but I believe that my mother will not allow it. She will consider
you a threat to Cecilia's prospects. But, come, let us think more on
what type of situation might best suit you. Have you any relations
who might take you in?"

Hetty considered for a moment. "My father's relations all live
near Bradford."

Isabel looked a question at Mr. Galbraith. "Leeds," he said with a
grimace.

They could hardly send her such a distance alone. She was much
too naïve.

"And your mother's family?" Isabel asked, unoptimistic.

Hetty made a look of distaste. "I have never met them, but Mama
has not spoken kindly of them." Her expression softened. "There
may be someone…" She trailed off.

The three others shared hopeful glances. "Who?" Mary said.

Hetty sighed. "Before we moved to town, there was a young man..." She looked shyly up at them. "Until Mama refused to let us see one another. She said that I might marry as high as I pleased and that on no account was I to waste myself on Solomon Abbott. But indeed, he is the best sort of man!"

Isabel could feel Mary's gaze on her, but she avoided her eye. There was little hope that the Mr. Abbott she spoke of would feel any degree of enthusiasm about marrying Hetty in her current situation, whatever his feelings for her had been before.

"Well," Isabel said matter-of-factly, "let us speak more on that later. In the meantime, we must prepare ourselves for the event that it is necessary for you to become employed in some capacity or another. Do you think you should like to be a lady's maid?"

Hetty lit up. "Oh, I should like it very much! My mother says I am skilled with hair."

Isabel was relieved that Hetty had interest in and an apparent aptitude for becoming a lady's maid, though she was unsure that she should accept Mrs. Robson's opinion on Hetty's skill. Isabel would have to judge for herself whether it was accurate or not.

Hetty could certainly be taught how to meet and even exceed the expectations of a mistress more quickly and easily than she could be taught how to arrange hair.

"Well," Isabel said in her practical voice, "perhaps I can persuade Anaïs to take you under her wing for the next few days, to give you a taste for what life as a lady's maid is like. She is the abigail Cecilia and I share," she added as an explanation.

"Splendid idea," Mary said. "That is, if you can understand the girl."

Isabel smiled and placed a reassuring hand on Hetty's arm. "She is very French—strict, but she has a kind heart."

Hetty looked unsure. "But might I not become your very own lady's maid and Anaïs could help your sister?"

Mary sent a knowing glance in Isabel's direction.

Isabel looked at Hetty with a pained expression. "I do wish that were an option, my dear. But..." she wavered as she wondered how to explain the situation without sounding like a victim.

If it had been an option, Isabel would have loved to take Hetty on as her own abigail. But when Anaïs had been hired by her father, it was as maid to both Cosgrove sisters. It was her father's way of economizing without inconveniencing himself. Isabel knew better than to ask for her own abigail, particularly when she was trying not to ruffle her father's feathers. She knew the answer without asking.

Whenever Cecilia and Isabel needed Anaïs at the same time, it was understood that Cecilia took preference, despite being the younger sister. They had shared more than a maid. Isabel had not even enjoyed her own Season. Her father hadn't been able to bear the thought of wasting a Season on Isabel alone when Cecilia's prospects were so much brighter.

"But," Mary piped in unapologetically, "her father is quite odious and will not lift a finger to help Izzy. He is too busy lavishing praise on Cecilia."

Isabel's eyes widened, and she looked at Mary with censure.

Mr. Galbraith, however, was looking hard-pressed not to laugh aloud. "It appears that you are not guilty of filial impiety, Miss Cosgrove, but rather of holding the generally-accepted opinion."

The reproachful look Isabel sent him was sapped of its power by the way she fought off a smile.

"The reasons are of no importance." She glared at Mary and Mr. Galbraith, recomposing her expression as it rested on Hetty. "It is simply not a possibility, despite how much I would welcome your services, Hetty. But don't fret, my dear. I will ensure Anaïs is not unkind to you, and we will do our utmost to find you a favorable situation."

The problem of convincing Anaïs and Cecilia to tolerate the arrangement with Hetty was pushed to the future in Isabel's mind more easily than the nagging problem of who would take on a lady's maid soon to give birth to an illegitimate child. But she hoped that, with Mary's help and connections, they would succeed in finding the right person. The adored Mr. Abbott she regarded not at all. That road would certainly lead to nowhere.

She sighed as she realized how much of her current situation depended upon hope for a positive outcome.

The sound of a closing door followed by rushed footsteps on flagstone broke into her thoughts. She glanced toward the church in time to see the back of a gentleman's coat disappearing from the churchyard.

A small gasp sounded, and Isabel looked at Hetty. Her face was pale, eyes round, and lips parted. Mr. Galbraith's eyes were narrowed, trained on the departed figure.

"Farrow," he said in a curious voice. "A weekday visit with the rector. I had no idea he was so devout."

"Oh no," Hetty cried. "He has come to take me to Bedlam!"

Isabel pulled Hetty in toward her, shushing her softly. "Nonsense, my dear. He didn't even see us."

Mr. Galbraith cleared his throat, and Isabel looked over.

"He did," Mr. Galbraith said, and Isabel felt she could have hit him as Hetty grabbed her desperately. "But—" he emphasized the word "—he merely looked curious at the sight of us. He clearly did not come to throw you in Bedlam. Otherwise why would he have left? And besides, what right could he have to do such a thing?" He shook his head and smiled at her. "You are safe with us."

Hetty looked calmer, and Isabel watched Mr. Galbraith with a small sense of awe. His thick brows made it easy to assume a coarseness or hardness to him, but he was obviously neither. He seemed to handle Hetty's dramatic temperament better than most gentlemen would have. Perhaps he was well-suited to someone like Cecilia or Julia Darling, after all.

A shuffling sound met their ears, and Isabel looked a second time toward the church. Hetty buried her head in Isabel's shoulder, breathing, "It's him, it's him, it's him."

But it was Mr. Safford, standing in the stone doorway of the church. He looked disheveled, one hand bracing the wall for support, the other cupping his head. He was looking with squinted eyes in the direction Mr. Farrow had departed.

"He looks injured," Mary remarked with her brows drawn together.

"Mr. Safford," Isabel called out, leaving Hetty with Mary. "Are you unwell?" She walked briskly toward the rector with Mr. Galbraith following close behind.

Mr. Safford looked over.

"Miss Cosgrove, Mr. Galbraith," he said in surprise, clearing his throat as his voice came out weak and unstable. "What are you doing here? Did you see him?"

"Who? Farrow?" asked Mr. Galbraith.

The rector nodded impatiently.

"He left not two minutes ago," Mr. Galbraith confirmed.

Mr. Safford grabbed Mr. Galbraith's arm, looking at him with round, fearful eyes. "Was he holding anything in his hand?"

Mr. Galbraith looked at the hand intently grasping his arm then at Isabel and back to the rector.

Isabel had never seen him so unhinged.

"I...I...couldn't say," Mr. Galbraith stuttered. "He left too quickly, and I didn't think to look at his hands. I am sorry."

"But did he come into the churchyard?"

Isabel placed a hand on the rector's shoulder, eager to allay his fears. "No. We would have seen him. He left from these same doors."

The rector's hand squeezed Mr. Galbraith's arm even more tightly for a moment before dropping to his side. "Then it is safe," he said, breathing out a sigh of relief.

"What is safe?" Isabel said, confused as ever.

"Nothing," he said softly, shaking his head and then putting a hand to it. "Nothing I can discuss."

"You're injured," said Isabel. A patch of blood stood out among his grey and white hair.

"Surely Farrow's presence has nothing to do with your injury," Mr. Galbraith said with the inflection of a question.

Mr. Safford shook his head. "I must have tripped and fallen. I'm getting old, you know."

Mr. Galbraith looked at him through narrowed, considering eyes, but Mr. Safford excused himself to them, insisting he had matters to attend to.

Mr. Galbraith made his excuses not long after, assuring Isabel that he would think on her suggestion. What could she do if his qualms at her plan remained?

9

The only sound at breakfast was the light clanking of silverware on china. Mr. Cosgrove preferred silence at the breakfast table. Unless, of course, he had something to say. Isabel's conversation with him after her rendezvous with Mr. Galbraith at the churchyard had gone much better than she had expected. He seemed to accept their reasons for keeping the engagement a secret without much resistance, a development for which Isabel was exceedingly grateful.

Of course, she had improvised slightly in conveying the details, insisting that, any effort on Mr. Galbraith's part to cut short his period of mourning would result in him being written out of his widower uncle's will. Isabel had made sure to underline that, because Aunt Gertrude's husband was in town and on close terms with all the gossip-mongers, even a word to Cecilia or Mrs. Cosgrove about the engagement was unsafe.

Her conscience had pricked her at the untruths she was telling, but she tried to ignore the discomfort, rationalizing that it was for the good of both Mr. Galbraith and herself.

"Ah, Cecilia," her father said, taking a gulp of ale.

Both daughters looked up at the unexpected interruption. Isabel found her muscles tensing, hoping desperately that her father would keep his promise not to speak of the engagement. She sipped her tea to distract herself.

"I received a note from Lord Brockway requesting an audience with me." He raised his brows, looking at his favorite daughter with pride and approval.

Isabel's hands paused briefly in the act of bringing her teacup to her mouth. She looked at her sister.

Cecilia smiled and looked down at the roll she held, spreading the preserves in a slow, smooth motion. "Yes, I believed you might be hearing from him soon."

"I think we can expect a very handsome settlement from him," Cosgrove said. "You have done very well, Cecilia. Brockway is every bit the sort of gentleman I hoped you should marry."

"Well," Cecilia said, tugging lightly at the end of her sleeve to straighten it, "as to that, I don't see why we should jump at my very first offer of marriage. Do you?"

Isabel stiffened. She had been hoping that Lord Brockway had been correct in his assumption that Cecilia would accept an offer of marriage from him.

Clearly Cecilia had other plans.

Mr. Cosgrove stared at Cecilia. It was clear that the thought of her refusing such a handsome match had never occurred to him.

Isabel almost hoped that her father would treat Cecilia the same way he had treated her—demanding that she accept the offer. But the thought lasted only a moment. Cecilia was never accorded the same treatment as she was. And even had their father demanded such a thing, Cecilia's tantrums were the one thing which had proven a match for his hard-headedness.

"I, well," he bumbled, "that is to say, do you think you may receive a more advantageous offer?" The warring doubt and hope in his eyes would have been comical to Isabel had she not been fighting the constriction she felt in her throat at hearing Cecilia's plans.

"I don't see why not!" exclaimed Cecilia. "And besides, even if a better offer does not come along, I am confident that I can persuade Lord Brockway to, shall we say, try again?" She gave an upbeat shrug to her shoulders and beamed at her father.

Isabel clenched her teeth, and her cheeks grew warm. Cecilia's arrogance was always maddening, but to hear her claim an ability and willingness to manipulate Lord Brockway was a new low. She felt a strong desire for Lord Brockway to teach Cecilia a lesson until realizing that she depended upon the match for her own situation's resolution.

Cecilia's confidence that she could elicit an offer from someone even more well-positioned than Lord Brockway was as smug as it was questionable. She had many admirers, to be sure, but none that Isabel had seen could be thought to eclipse Lord Brockway—not in wealth, position, or character. Most definitely not in care and concern.

Beauty Cecilia had in spades. But the Cosgroves could not compete with the ancient or titled families with marriageable daughters. If Cecilia didn't take care, she would alienate all her suitors with her overconfidence.

"Well," said Mr. Cosgrove with newfound optimism, "if you are quite sure, then I shall try to put Brockway off awhile."

Cecilia smiled widely at her father, nodding her agreement.

Mr. Cosgrove took a final sip of ale, planted a pleased kiss on Cecilia's golden head, and retreated to his study where, Isabel had no doubt, he hoped to avoid further familial interaction.

Isabel restrained the impulse to speak her mind to Cecilia. If she put up her sister's back, it would only confirm Cecilia in her determination.

If Isabel had not been certain that her sister had kindness concealed under her arrogance, she would likely have tried to dissuade Lord Brockway from pursuing the association with Cecilia. But she knew Cecilia to be confused, overwhelmed, and unsure of herself underneath the picture she presented to the world. Where

Isabel usually sought the counsel of Mr. Safford to sort through her own confusion, Cecilia had looked to society to tell her who she was.

Isabel wondered how it must feel to be valued primarily for her appearance. How long had it been since someone complimented any of Cecilia's other traits?

"I saw your kindness the other day," Isabel remarked. "To the Grenard girl, I mean."

Cecilia's brows scrunched as though she had no idea what Isabel was speaking of.

"The green gloves," Isabel continued. "They were your favorite, weren't they?"

"Oh," Cecilia said dismissively, not even looking at Isabel. "Those old things? They were quite ragged. And besides, they matched her eyes so perfectly."

Isabel watched her with a small smile. It was almost as if Cecilia was embarrassed at anyone having observed her kindness.

"Well, it was very sweet of you. Mrs. Grenard remarked to me the other day how Lydia has mentioned your goodness on three separate occasions since."

Pink tinged Cecilia's cheeks, and she added sugar to her tea, determinedly avoiding Isabel's eyes. "Well, you can't deny she is a silly girl."

"Perhaps," said Isabel. She took a deep breath. "Cecy?"

Cecilia raised her brows to indicate her attention, but she didn't look up. It was rare that Isabel used Cecilia's nickname, and she hoped it would show her sister the benevolent spirit in which she spoke.

"Lord Brockway is as good a man as you'll find. And because of that, he sees you for all your good qualities—many qualities which others overlook in favor of your beauty."

Cecilia still didn't look at her.

"I suppose I just want to say—" Isabel sighed "—do try not to take his regard for granted. He is kind and generous, but he is not a fool."

Cecilia's cheeks went pink again, but whether from embarrassment, anger, or a combination, Isabel didn't know.

"You are very complimentary of him," Cecilia said with an edge to her voice. "Perhaps he should offer for you."

"Cecy." Isabel grimaced, shaking her head. "I consider Lord Brockway a dear friend, nothing more. And you...you are my sister. I want both of you to be happy. Because I hold you both in affection, I would be elated for you to marry. But just as Lord Brockway realizes how much you have to offer beyond a pretty face, I hope you realize what he has to offer beyond fortune and title. That is all I wanted to say."

Cecilia stayed silent, her expression impassive. But Isabel thought she saw the cogs turning in her sister's head, and that was as much as she could hope for.

She raised herself from her chair and moved to pass behind Cecilia toward the door. As she reached Cecilia's chair, she hesitated for an instant before leaning over, placing her hands on the chair back, and dropping a light kiss on her sister's coiffed hair.

"Love you, Cecy," she said softly, pausing another moment before leaving the room.

𝔰𝔢 I O 𝔢𝔰

Isabel took a deep breath as she looked herself over in the mirror. Anaïs had gone to attend to a last-minute demand of Cecilia's, leaving Hetty and Isabel alone.

"You look marvelous," breathed Hetty, standing behind Isabel and adjusting a hair pin.

Isabel smiled at Hetty through the mirror, but her brows were drawn. The note she had received from Mr. Galbraith, agreeing to her suggestion, had been equally welcome and dispiriting. It was no use, though, wasting time or energy wishing that he didn't want to regain Miss Darling's affections. And, since he did, Isabel believed her plan to be the best way forward and the one most sure to achieve the happiness of Mr. Galbraith as well as preventing her own misery.

She had been struggling against her vanity ever since preparations for the ball had begun, though. She wanted to present herself in the best possible light for Mr. Galbraith's sake. If she didn't, she doubted whether the thought of her as competition would even cross Miss Darling's mind.

Even if Isabel did look her best, she couldn't help but feel eclipsed by the woman.

MARTHA KEYES

When such thoughts came upon her, she had to ask herself whether it was really Mr. Galbraith's interests which motivated her to look her best. Or was it perhaps a pesky desire to compete in earnest with Julia Darling for the affections of Mr. Galbraith?

She looked determinedly away from the mirror, turning toward Hetty to redirect such thoughts.

As Mrs. Holledge was indisposed, Mary accompanied the Cosgroves to the ball. The carriage was dark when she climbed in from her family's lodgings, so it wasn't until the party stepped into the light of the ball that she was able to see Isabel.

"Gracious me, Izzy," she exclaimed. "You're a vision! I believe you should always wear that shade of green."

Isabel bit the inside of her lip. "Hetty insisted that I wear it. She and Anaïs very nearly came to blows over the matter. Anaïs believes I should stick to more muted colors."

Mary looked her over again, shaking her head slowly. "Hetty was right, and it bodes well for her desire to become an lady's maid. She clearly has the eye for it. Did she also do your hair? I don't believe I've ever seen you wear it like that. Or anyone, for that matter."

"Yes, it's one of Hetty's creations." Isabel said, bringing a distracted hand to touch the base of her coiffure. "Anaïs was nearly done with my hair when Cecilia called for her again. Hetty was less than admiring of her work and decided to try her own hand at it."

Mary's brows went up. "Well done, Hetty," she said softly, putting a hand on each of Isabel's arms to turn her so that she could admire the coiffure. "But I hope Anaïs doesn't eat her for it."

Isabel laughed, feeling grateful for Mary's lighthearted conversation. She needed a break from her own thoughts and nerves.

Given Cecilia's evident desire to set her sights higher than Lord Brockway, Isabel was having a difficult time remaining optimistic about the rest of her plans. When she conveyed to Mary that her hope for the evening was to help Miss Darling remember her regard for Mr. Galbraith, Mary groaned.

"You are throwing away a perfectly good marriage offer." But before Isabel could answer her, she held up a hand to silence her. "But," she said with a sigh, "I know just how we can assist Miss Darling's memory."

Isabel looked at Mary with misgiving but was prevented from inquiring what sort of methods she planned to use by the arrival of Mr. Galbraith himself.

"Ah, there you are," said Mary with a civil curtsy.

Mr. Galbraith bowed with a smile that faltered for the briefest moment as his eyes came upon Isabel. His eyes flitted up to her hair, and Isabel's cheeks grew warm. Did he think she looked ridiculous? Had Hetty been wrong about the coiffure?

She swallowed, brushing aside her vain thoughts and reminding herself of her objective: help Miss Darling remember her love for Mr. Galbraith.

"I give you fair warning," Isabel said, directing a significant look at him, "that Mary has just informed me that she has *ideas*—" she drew out the word "—for how to handle things this evening."

Mr. Galbraith's brows went up, and he looked at Mary. "Ideas?"

"I'm full of ideas," said Mary, stretching her neck and wagging her eyebrows.

"Heaven help us," said Isabel, sharing an amused glance with Mr. Galbraith.

"We may well require divine help," Mary said with a bite to her voice, "if the two of you intend to stand like that."

Isabel and Mr. Galbraith both looked down at their feet and then at each other, exchanging nonplussed glances.

Mary breathed in slowly and deeply, closing her eyes to summon patience with her pupils. "I mean," she said, "standing as if you're afraid of catching the plague from one another."

She bumped into Isabel who moved to avoid falling. The shift brought her up against Mr. Galbraith, who steadied her with a firm grasp around the arm.

"Pardon!" said Mary with false contrition. "So clumsy of me." She looked at Isabel and Mr. Galbraith with an approving smile. "Much better."

Isabel sent a glance at Mary full of promised future chastisement. "I don't hesitate to tell you that I find your tactics barbaric, Mary."

"And yet very effective," Mary countered.

"Quite," said Mr. Galbraith.

Isabel's head turned, and she looked at him with mock betrayal. "You take her side?"

Mr. Galbraith's eyes twinkled. He leaned closer to Isabel as if to whisper, but when he spoke it was loud enough for Mary to hear. "Only because I am terrified of what she might do to me if I don't."

Mary looked on this exchange with great approval, ignoring the jab at her tactics.

"Traitor," Isabel said without rancor.

"You are already doing much better, you know," said Mary. "But I believe I must still instruct you a bit if we are to carry this off convincingly. Do as I say, and I believe we will live to celebrate this night's work. Stray from what I say, and we will all regret it."

Mr. Galbraith and Isabel looked at one another, controlling with difficulty their mirth at Mary's exaggerated gravity and authority.

"Mr. Galbraith," Mary said in the tone of a commanding officer, and he wiped the smile from his face, replacing it with one of full attention. "On no account must you allow your eyes to wander over to Miss Darling during the evening. She is but an afterthought to you. Izzy is your primary concern."

Isabel's jaw clenched. How long would she be able to keep up the charade? To hear Mary instruct Mr. Galbraith to pay her attention was difficult enough, but she also hadn't missed the small, determined breath Mr. Galbraith had taken before nodding his agreement.

"Very good," Mary said. "You will move as if to pass by Miss Darling without even noticing her. By a chance glance you will suddenly remark her presence. Only then will you speak to her. Briefly." She emphasized the word. "Cheerfully, even. But you will be obliged to cut off the very civil and superficial exchange because you are promised to Izzy for a dance. You must look over toward Izzy when you say this, with all the eagerness of a man in love. Do you understand?"

Isabel swallowed, and Mr. Galbraith nodded again with an appreciative smile at Mary.

"It is all very exact," he said.

"It is." Mary offered no apology. "Lastly, Mr. Galbraith, you must be sure that you ask Izzy to dance more than once. Two sets should be sufficient."

"Surely that's not necessary," Isabel interjected. The thought of spending so much time near Mr. Galbraith was one she was simultaneously intrigued by and anxious to avoid. "Is not one set enough?"

Mary looked at her for a moment before responding. "Decidedly not. The effect it will have on Miss Darling is essential to the plan."

Isabel opened her mouth to protest. She was more worried about the effect on herself than on Miss Darling.

"Izzy, are you dedicated to seeing this through or not?" Mary sounded severe, but Isabel thought she saw a glint of understanding in her friend's eyes.

Mr. Galbraith turned to her, and their eyes met. His were searching and sincere. "Miss Cosgrove, if you are having any hesitations at all, please don't conceal them. I would not have you feel uncomfortable. Despite what Miss Holledge is saying—" he shot Mary a teasing glance "—we don't need to dance. Nor do we need to continue any of this if you are of a different mind. You know I have my own concerns."

His sensitivity made it harder to refuse him what he wanted. Despite her hesitations, she knew she would go through with the plan. She wished to help him achieve what he wanted, so why not make use of their strange situation? It would please her father, too, to see them on the ballroom floor.

And if she was going to do it, she might as well do her very best.

She smiled gratefully at his consideration but shook her head. "No, no. I am of the same mind as before. Let us win back Miss

Darling's heart." She broadened her smile to reassure him, and the one she received in return was its own reward.

Isabel attributed the added warmth in Mr. Galbraith's eyes to the welcome prospect of winning back Miss Darling. He took one of her gloved hands in his, bringing it to his lips.

Her heart skipped at the gesture, but her mind brought her feet back to the ground. It was all part of the act.

On no account could she allow herself to forget that.

✣ 11 ✣

Charles let go of Isabel Cosgrove's hand. He couldn't help but think on the hesitation she had briefly shown. It confused him. The whole thing had been her idea, after all. It was an idea he was still conflicted about. He wanted to recapture Julia's affection, to rekindle what had been lost when the Season had begun. He wished, though, that it had not been necessary.

Furthermore, he wished that he hadn't been obliged to involve Isabel. It seemed unnatural that it should require anyone outside of Julia and himself to arrange their affairs. It was almost like cheating.

When Isabel had broached the idea, he had been equal parts amused and perturbed. Why she should concern herself with his problems when he had only added to hers was a mystery. She was very obviously a kind and generous person. But the fact remained that his arrival in her life had complicated things immensely for her. And yet instead of resenting him, she desired to help him.

But even if the plan did work, would the result be lasting? Or would Julia leave him behind again for the next charming gentleman with greater fortune? And what would she do when she discovered that it had all been a strategy to reignite her feelings for him?

Such questions plagued his mind as he left Miss Holledge and Miss Cosgrove with a promise to return for a set—two in fact—with the latter.

He was ever-aware of Julia's presence in his peripheral vision, but he made sure never to make that fact apparent. He greeted various acquaintances as he walked in the general direction of Julia and Farrow, with no one the wiser about the nerves which made his cravat feel too tight.

Just as he came abreast of Julia and Farrow, he turned his head in a masterfully-unconscious gesture, his eyes falling upon the two. He feigned surprise and smiled, coming toward them.

"Miss Darling," he said with a polite smile and bow. "Mr. Farrow. How do you do?"

He allowed himself a quick look at Julia, thinking how long it had been since he last spent time with her outside a ballroom. She looked as captivating as ever, one escaped blonde ringlet curling around her neck. She flashed him a smile—not the coy smiles she had been wont to give since their first meeting in London, but one of the knowing smiles he thought for so long had been reserved for him.

But she still stood next to Farrow, and smiles were not his goal.

"Well?" said Julia, raising her thin brows at Charles. "Are you going to ask me to dance or not?"

"My deepest apologies," he said with a slight bow, "but I am already engaged for this set." He looked over in Isabel's direction. She stood next to Miss Holledge who was watching Charles. She gave the slightest nudge to Isabel when she saw him look over.

Charles suppressed a smile, hoping that Julia and Farrow hadn't noticed the prod.

Isabel's head turned slowly, searching for Charles. When her gaze landed on him, the corners of her mouth turned up shyly. Her eyes held the knowledge of their conspiracy, and his responded with their own twinkle.

Whatever she had done differently to her hair, Charles found it gave her a very different look than on the other occasions they had met. She looked distinguished, handsome. Where Julia's beauty was impossible to ignore no matter her expression, Isabel's eyes and smile held the transformative keys to her allure. She was direct—sometimes jarringly so—but her eyes danced in the most intriguing way when she found something humorous.

"If you'll excuse me," Charles said, his eyes trained on Isabel except for a brief glance and bow to Julia and Farrow. He left them behind, making his way back toward Isabel and Mary.

Mary was all admiration for Charles's well-executed role.

"I wish I could have captured her expression when you left her to come here," said Mary in delight. "She looked as though she'd swallowed that outrageous feather she is wearing."

Charles was unsure whether this should make him glad or concerned and decided to ignore it. "I believe that you owe me a dance, Miss Cosgrove."

"Oh, for heaven's sake," Mary threw her head back and her arms up. "You must stop being so formal with one another. You are supposed to be engaged, are you not? You must convince your father, Izzy." She turned to Mr. Galbraith— "Call her Isabel—" and then back to Isabel— "Call him Charles."

Isabel opened her mouth to resist, but Mary persisted. "You don't have to do so within earshot of anyone but your father, but I think that it will help you feel more at ease with one another if you do so in private, as well. What do you say, Mr. Galbraith?"

He extended a hand to Isabel. "Isabel, then," he said.

Isabel took in an unsteady breath. "Charles," she said, her tone tentative as she laid her hand in his. A smile tugged at the corner of her mouth. "Yet more evidence of how vulgarly forward I am."

Charles laughed, and his grip on her hand grew more confident, knowing that she wasn't uncomfortable dispensing with formality.

After conveying Miss Holledge to Mrs. Cosgrove, Charles led Isabel onto the ballroom floor for a cotillion. Whatever hesitations she had been having earlier in the evening, there was no trace of them on her face as they danced. Her eyes met his in the same clear, frank way he had first encountered in the family portrait that fateful evening. From time to time, they would gleam with the twinkle he had come to associate with her.

"How do you do that?" he said when he encountered it for a third time.

"Do what?"

"With your eyes," he explained, looking into them with curiosity.

Her smile faltered, and she blinked in quick succession as if something were in her eyes.

He smiled at her reaction, realizing that he had made her feel self-conscious. "It's as if they're laughing."

She laughed on an exhale. "How traitorous of them."

"Yes," he said, "they can be very expressive." He watched a slight blush seep into her cheeks and, not wishing to cause her discomfort, continued, "But I'm not sure whether I'm the object of their amusement or simply an ignorant witness to their mirth."

The dance took them apart before she could answer. He continued watching her, though, as if her eyes might betray the answer. What he knew of her told him that she was far too kind to laugh at him to his face, even if it was only with her eyes.

She turned back toward him, and they interlocked hands, placing the two of them shoulder to shoulder.

"You must promise not to look," she said, holding his eyes, "for I fear Mary will give you a sound thrashing if you do."

"I promise not to look," he vowed in a solemn voice.

"I was thinking," she said in a low voice, "how neglected Miss Darling's partner must feel. I believe she has yet to look at him or speak to him. She seems preoccupied with something—or perhaps someone—over here." Her eyes teased him.

He fought the impulse to look for Julia. In his curiosity over Isabel's behavior, he hadn't noticed that Julia made one of the set.

Was she regretting how she had treated him? He knew that she would certainly not relish believing herself to be replaced in his affections by someone she would no doubt look down upon.

Such sentiments didn't endear Julia to him. Nor did the memory of a similar ballroom scene where, not long ago, he had been the partner she ignored. The memory tainted the possibility that she was perhaps rethinking her actions.

He realized that Isabel was watching him and that he was frowning. He smiled, not wishing her to think that it was her he was displeased with.

"If we are to call one another by our given names," he said, "which I believe is a sensible thing to do—" he leaned his head in closer to her, saying in a lower voice, "—besides feeling terrified of what Miss Holledge might do if we disobey—I think we ought to know more about one another."

Isabel's head tilted to the side. "You are probably right."

"I most often am," he said with a teasing side smile and a wink.

She cocked an eyebrow at him as they shifted dancing positions. "Is that the first thing you would have me know about you, then? That you are always right?"

"Not always," he countered. "Most often. But surely that would not be the first thing you would know about me?"

"No," she said. "Mary is a very good source of information, you know."

He threw his head back and laughed. "How frightening! I am equal parts curious and hesitant to hear you expound on that. What information have you had by her?"

"Almost none, in fact," she replied. "I was only teasing." She tilted her head to the side, considering. "But I imagine she could tell me a whole host of things if I were to ask. Your favorite color, your middle name, your greatest fears. Things of that nature."

He laughed again. Her words sparked a curiosity in him—what assumptions had Miss Cosgrove made about him from the little time they had spent together?

"And what, then, do you feel you already know of me, even without the help of Miss Holledge?"

She looked hesitant, and he half-smiled. "I, for instance," he continued, "know that you are more familiar with cant phrases than most ladies would admit to."

Her mouth twisted to the side in a half-guilty smile. "I have been known to use a cant phrase or two every now and again. All taught to me by my brother Tobias."

His half-smile expanded into a full one. "The mark of a real brother, I think."

She watched him with a strangely soft light in her eyes. One corner of her mouth turned up. "I, on the other hand, have learned that your brows make you look far more threatening than you truly are."

He scowled dramatically and then smiled. "They have proven a useful tool, but I'm sure they have also held back a number of people from seeking my acquaintance."

"Well," Miss Cosgrove said, "surely such pudding-hearts are better kept as strangers."

Charles shot her an impressed look as his mouth twitched. "I hadn't expected to be favored so soon with a demonstration of cant expressions. I am pleasantly surprised. Your father failed to mention such a valuable skill."

Miss Cosgrove laughed aloud. "That is because I am very careful not to demonstrate it in his presence. It would draw an unending string of censure about my multitude of failings."

Charles frowned. His own experience with Mr. Cosgrove had not shown him to be particularly tender-hearted, but hearing how he had spoken of his daughter and how he seemed to treat her shed an even less complimentary light on the man.

"Well," he said, "if that is so, I find that he is much mistaken in his own daughter."

Miss Cosgrove colored up slightly and smiled with a small shrug. "I have learned to accept that how he views me is a reflection upon him rather than upon myself."

Charles's brows shot up.

"What?" Miss Cosgrove said, observing his reaction. "You don't agree?"

"No, it's not that," he said. "Only that I had not expected such wisdom from the lips of someone who had just used the phrase 'pudding-heart.'"

She laughed and shook her head. "Well, I am convinced that a robust knowledge of cant may come in useful. If my father turns me out when this is all over, I take courage in the knowledge that I could successfully impersonate my brother at need. We are very much alike."

Charles smiled. "I should like to meet him, then." And he meant it.

But her words had troubled him. Did she truly worry that her father would impose such a fate on her?

The final figure of the dance completed, he pressed her hand between his just before letting go to bow. Rising from the bow, he looked her in the eye. "I won't let ill befall you, Miss Cosgrove. Even if I must abduct and marry you against your will."

ISABEL LOOKED AT MR. GALBRAITH, her enjoyment at an end. It had been too easy to forget that it was all a charade as they pivoted around the dance floor.

But his words brought her back down to earth with uncomfortable force.

He still felt honor-bound. Nothing she had said had convinced him otherwise. And while she could admire his strong conscience, she loathed that he felt any obligation toward her. She could think of few fates worse than being married to Charles Galbraith while he pined for Miss Darling in secret.

And all because of a night of folly and jealousy.

"That won't be necessary," she said, forcing a smile as she shook her head. She couldn't let her disappointment interfere with their goal.

He offered his arm to her. "And this you know by virtue of some special powers you are possessed of?" He cocked an eyebrow at her as he escorted her off the floor.

"No," she said baldly. "I know it because you are going to marry Miss Darling, of course." His mouth opened, and she rushed on, smiling to relieve any suspicion he might have of the true state of her mind and heart. "And if the frequency of her glances in our direction are any indication, she is fast desiring that outcome as well."

Mr. Galbraith made a motion to turn his head but seemed to catch himself at the last second, his eyelids clenching shut as he grimaced.

Isabel swallowed watching the effort it took him not to look at Miss Darling. The sooner they could arrange things between Mr. Galbraith and Miss Darling, the better. For her own peace of mind and for Mr. Galbraith's. She didn't know how long she could maintain the act. But the better she played her part, the sooner it would all end.

She didn't need to look to know that Miss Darling's eyes were still on them as they arrived at the refreshment table. She took in a quick breath and looked at Mr. Galbraith.

He was watching her with a curious expression as he ate a wafer. He offered her one, and she shook her head with a polite smile. One of his brows went up, but he gave a small shrug and bit into the wafer she had refused. A stray piece stuck to his lip.

At first, she thought he hadn't noticed. But the piece was far too large to remain unnoticed. He paused for a moment and then continued chewing as if nothing were amiss.

She took her lips between her teeth to keep from smiling.

He pursed his lips, but the wafer held on. His brow went up. "What?" he said in a pompous voice. With his thick brows and dark eyes, he could look quite intimidating.

Her lips still firmly between her teeth, she quickly shook her head with eyes wide in feigned innocence. "Nothing."

How long would he leave the wafer?

"Oh," he said. "For a moment you looked at me as though something were amiss." He took a handkerchief from his pocket and dabbed it at the corner of his mouth opposite the wafer. It clung desperately to his lip. He looked at her, his eyebrows up as if in a challenge.

Her mouth twisted to the side, and she took in a slow breath, but she couldn't resist any longer. "Oh, for heaven's sake!" She put up a hand and pulled the wafer from his lip.

He looked at her hand. "Ah, yes, thank you." He took the piece from between her fingers, and then placed it in his pocket, giving it a soft pat. "I was saving that for later. Lady Chadwick's wafers are always the first of the refreshments to go, you know. In fact...." He took two more and slipped them into the same pocket.

She laughed, and his mouth broke into an answering grin, transforming his entire face.

"Ah, there it is."

"What?" she said, her mouth still stretched in enjoyment.

"Your smile." He offered his arm to her. "Come, I believe the next set is forming."

If this was her only opportunity to enjoy time with Mr. Galbraith, then she would make the most of it. She could manage the emotional toll later if it meant spending just one evening being smiled at the way he had just done. After all, she might need the positive memories to get her through whatever would come next.

She took in a deep breath and smiled, placing her arm in his.

❧ 12 ❧

As she walked to the church, a footman following discreetly behind, Isabel wrapped her pelisse more tightly around her as if the constriction might erase the memory her shoulders and waist kept from the night before. Spending so much of the evening with Mr. Galbraith—or Charles as she had agreed to call him —had produced a mélange of conflicting emotions. The close contact was desired—and yet so far from occurring under desirable circumstances.

She had known a small sense of victory as she watched Miss Darling react to his attentions to her. When she had pointed out the triumph to Charles, he hadn't seemed unduly concerned. But perhaps he was simply more adept at carrying out their charade. Or perhaps he couldn't allow himself to hope?

He had seemed to enjoy himself well enough as they had danced together, as had she. But her enjoyment was no counterfeit. It was genuine, tainted only by those nagging moments when she remembered that Charles was putting on a show, just as Mary had ordered him to.

Despite that, Isabel had determined to play her part well—a part that she found far too natural. Conversing with Charles felt instinctual. But over the course of the evening, she was brought back down to earth. Soundly.

She had sincerely hoped that Charles had given up the unfortunate belief of having some sort of duty toward her. But his comment at the end of their first dance had dashed such hopes. *"Even if I must abduct and marry you against your will."*

She couldn't allow it. Cecilia *must* marry Lord Brockway. She must be brought to see reason—for her own sake and for Isabel's.

Isabel picked up her pace, hoping to outrun her dreary thoughts, and soon pulled open the door to St. James's, telling the footman to wait outside. She had made it a practice to attend services twice a week. If ever she needed wisdom and inspiration, it was now.

The pews were not even half full, unlike Sundays where it was sometimes difficult to find a seat. She slipped into an empty pew near the back. As she settled in, Mr. Safford stood to begin his sermon.

She looked around, noting a number of familiar faces. Lord Brockway and his mother sat a few rows ahead. He looked unusually grave.

Mr. Safford's sermon was characteristically inspiring. Isabel had attended church her whole life, but it wasn't until she came to know Mr. Safford that she had come to value her time at church services. Never had a clergyman been so obviously and genuinely devoted to his parishioners. Understanding Mr. Safford's sincerity, seeing the way he lived what he preached—it had brought new value to church attendance for Isabel. That attendance, coupled with the wisdom she had gleaned from him, had sustained her in many ways over the course of the Season.

She watched Mr. Safford read from the Bible and listened as he preached of laying up treasure in heaven. He looked older than she remembered, his face more pulled. And while his words were earnest, they seemed to lack their customary energy. She had never considered what needs or difficulties he might face in his own life. He was anxious to serve others, but who served him?

Midway through the service, two people slid onto the pew beside Isabel. Isabel turned toward the latecomers, and her mouth opened, forming a large smile.

It was Lord Ashworth and Kate Matcham—or Lady Ashworth, rather. Isabel would have to accustom herself to calling her by her new title. Lady Ashworth's cheeks were becomingly flushed, and she seemed to have the glow characteristic of couples newly-returned from their wedding trip.

Lady Ashworth leaned over toward Isabel. "I was sure we would find you here," she whispered. "I am very happy to be proved right."

Isabel squeezed Lady Ashworth's hand with a smile, noting how her other hand was clasped within Lord Ashworth's who turned to Isabel and inclined his head with a broad grin.

She forced away the prick of jealousy she felt seeing them hand-in-hand. What would it feel like to have her own hand clasped within Charles's?

"How was the wedding trip?" she asked softly.

Lady Ashworth took in a drawn-out breath and let it out in a contented sigh. "Spectacular. We spent it all in Dorset, you know, but I think I shall never tire of it, so I was quite content that it be so. William insists that he will take me to the French countryside if the war ever comes to an end." She paused and raised a brow at Isabel. "Perhaps we can all make the journey as part of an extended wedding trip for you?"

Isabel drew back. "For me?" She forced a soft laugh. "You may be obliged to postpone the journey for many years if you insist on waiting for such a thing."

Lady Ashworth shook her head. "It will happen sooner than you think, I'm sure. Who could resist such a kind soul as you are?" She smiled at Isabel with her warm eyes, and Isabel returned with her own weak smile.

Lady Ashworth's words smarted.

A marriage as beautifully-contented as the Ashworths had never felt more desirable to Isabel. And yet never further from reach.

When the service was over, people filtered out of the chapel slowly. Isabel remained in her seat once the Ashworths took their leave. She stared at the stained-glass windows. The sun had peeked through once during the service, and it did so again, casting colorful reflections onto the pews and the stone floors. She could hear the muffled sound of conversation outside.

"Miss Cosgrove." Lord Brockway stood at the edge of the pew.

She stood and walked over to him, greeting him. "And how are you, my lord?"

"I am well enough, thank you." He moved out of the way so that she could exit the pew. He paused a moment and then, as if he couldn't help himself, asked after Cecilia.

"She is well, I believe," Isabel said. They walked toward the exit. "Did you not speak with her at Almack's the other night?"

Lord Brockway's lips pressed together. "No. I believe she was avoiding me. Your father, too, has been putting me off since I asked for an audience with him."

Isabel closed her eyes and grimaced as they passed through the door into the courtyard. The Cosgrove's footman stood near the gate.

Isabel turned to face Lord Brockway. He was correct, of course.

"I'm so very sorry," she said, "Cecilia seems to be going through a particularly headstrong phase. I think all the attention has gone to her head."

Lord Brockway tapped his cane on the ground, looking down at the stones below him. "In your honest opinion, Miss Cosgrove, am I wasting my time? Have I misinterpreted your sister's words?"

Isabel let out a puff of air and then took her lips between her teeth. "I can't speak to what Cecilia has told you—only you can gauge how sincere she has been. As for wasting your time—" she took in a large breath, and let her shoulders drop as she exhaled "—you must do as you feel best, my lord. But, for what it's worth, I haven't given up on Cecilia. I believe she will recognize your value. It is just a matter of whether it will be too late when that occurs."

Lord Brockway was still looking down, running the top of his cane through his fingers. He looked up and attempted a smile. "I have much to think on."

Isabel chewed her lip for a moment. "If you truly desire my advice, my lord, I would advise you to give Cecilia space. Let her sort through this struggle of hers."

He looked skeptical.

"You don't wish to have to *persuade* her into accepting you, do you? You'd like her to have you willingly?"

He nodded slowly, his eyes fixed, unfocused, on some spot behind her.

Isabel nodded her own head in response. "Then let her decision be reached in its own time, absent constant attention from you. Let her miss you. Let her look for you. I think she has come to take you for granted. A reminder that you are not a guaranteed presence in her life will, I think, tip the scales one way or the other. At least you will have an answer."

One of his fingers tapped the knob of his cane. "But what if it is not the answer I want?" He looked up at her.

Isabel felt for him. She knew the bitterness of caring for someone who didn't reciprocate. She heaved a sigh. "Then you must press on, believing you will care for someone else in time—someone who can return your regard the way she should." Her mouth stretched into an understanding grimace. "There is no shortage of young ladies who would do exactly that, you know."

Lord Brockway stood up straight, his gaze scanning upward toward the spire of St. James'. "And yet none of them are Miss Cecilia. What was it Pascal said? *'Le coeur a ses raisons que la raison ne connaît point.'*"

"'The heart has reasons that reason doesn't know.' How shrewd," she said, following his gaze up to the top of the chapel and the cloud-checkered skies above. "My experience, too, has proven the heart to be very stubborn. But cheer up, my friend. We will both come about."

He gripped the knob of his cane and smiled at her. "I will

endeavor to heed your advice and give your sister ample space. Thank you, Miss Cosgrove."

She looked around, noting that all the other churchgoers had departed the courtyard. The footman stood patiently waiting.

Lord Brockway tipped his hat and moved to walk toward the gate but turned back to her instead. "May your heart also attain what it wants and deserves." He walked through the gate and away from the church.

Isabel stared after him for a moment, her eyes unfocused. What did her heart deserve? She had never assumed that the type of happiness she envisioned was within her reach. When she had seen Charles Galbraith again and felt that curious attraction, that desire to know him, she had not truly considered that she would be granted the chance. Nor had she anticipated that to know him more would only whet her appetite for his company.

The more time she spent with him, the more curious and intrigued she became; the more she dreaded no longer spending time in Charles's company; the more she understood Pascal's words.

She smoothed her dress.

"I shall only be a few more minutes, Finch," she said to the footman, who bowed.

She walked toward the garden, hoping for another moment of reflection before returning home. The churchyard of St. James's was her favorite place for sorting through difficult concerns.

Moving past the garden and toward the cemetery, she weaved through the headstones. Whatever Isabel's own situation, Cecilia's chances with Lord Brockway were on shaky ground. Her last caution seemed not to have helped, but she would try one more time to warn Cecilia of what she stood to lose if she didn't change her ways.

She stopped abruptly. "Mr. Safford?"

He was kneeling on the ground, with his hands between two rows of headstones. His head snapped up, and his hands shot away from the space between the graves, his fingers brown with dirt.

"Miss Cosgrove." He looked torn between chagrin and relief.

"What are you doing?" she said, staring at the small box in the shadowed gap between the headstones where the grass grew tall.

Mr. Safford followed her gaze and sighed, hesitating before offering any response.

"It must appear very peculiar."

She said nothing. It *did*, after all.

He regarded her watchfully, and his shoulders settled, as if he had come to a decision.

"May I trust you, Miss Cosgrove?" he said.

She nodded decisively. What a strange question. "Of course you may."

He lifted himself from the ground and brushed his hands together. "You know of Mr. Farrow and his role in Miss Robson's lamentable situation. What you may not know—indeed, no one knows this but myself and some near family—is that Mr. Farrow is, in fact, my nephew."

Isabel's mouth opened wordlessly. "Your nephew?"

Mr. Safford nodded. "My late brother's son." He indicated a headstone just two places away from the one he had been kneeling at before. There was no grass growing on the upturned dirt, and the headstone was new.

"I have long been estranged from my family," he said. "My decision to enter holy orders was unwelcome to my father—he had always been insistent that I study law. But I was stubborn. I had a great sense of purpose." His mouth turned down in a frown, and he scratched his neck pensively. "He could never abide to be disobeyed, though. He told me I was no longer welcome in the family, going so far as to insist that I change my name. I had no communication with them for years. All that I knew of them was what I heard from parishioners who happened to mention them from time to time."

"Good heavens," said Isabel. "How terribly unfair and lonely."

Mr. Safford smiled wryly. "Mrs. Safford has been wonderful company to me, and I chose long ago not to dwell on whatever mistreatment I experienced at my family's hands. I only tell you this so that you may understand what happened next.

She inclined her head, inviting him to continue.

"Months ago, my elder brother Peter sought me out. He had fallen ill and was not expected to make a recovery. Under the circumstances, he felt a desire to make amends and to seek God. His spiritual transformation during his illness was astounding. Such humility had brought him to view his son Robert's somewhat degenerate lifestyle as unsatisfactory and unacceptable; repellant, even. He and Robert came to an agreement—reluctantly on Robert's part, as I understand—that Robert would reform his ways or else face being disinherited of all the unentailed property he stood to inherit. My brother died not long after—but not before he provided me with an alternate will. He was concerned, for various reasons, that Robert was not sincere in his commitment. His final wish was for me to safeguard the will and only to make it known to his executors in the event that Robert refused to reform his lifestyle."

Isabel stared at him, comprehension dawning on her face. "I see. Now that you know Hetty's situation, you must decide whether to make the will known."

He grimaced. "Yes." He shook his head and stared at the leaves above. A slight breeze was rustling the leaves as sun shone through them. "If it had been a 'crime of passion,' if you will, I could look on it with more understanding and leniency. We are all sinners, after all, and often fall short even when we intend to do good.

"But Robert has not taken responsibility. Quite the contrary. He came to visit me last week—the same day Miss Robson arrived. I'm sure you remember it. I'm uncertain how he discovered the existence of the will, but he intended to have it. I refused to hand over the document, after which he threatened my life and then knocked me over the head with his pistol."

"Good gracious," Isabel cried. "I thought you had fallen! He must have taken leave of his senses! Did you inform the magistrate?"

Mr. Safford shook his head. "No. It is a delicate issue, and I have had too much experience with men of the law to entrust them with it. I believe Robert tried to find the will—the vestry was turned upside down when I came to. Thankfully, I had the forethought to hide the document where no one would be likely to look."

"In the box?" Isabel asked.

"Yes. I have placed it in a moleskin pouch which is, in turn, protected by the silver box you see."

Isabel stepped closer to the headstone. The engraving was barely discernable between the moss and lichen filling the worn letters.

"Why are you telling me this?" Isabel asked.

He stooped down to rub a patch of dirt from his brother's headstone and traced the letters of his name with a finger. "If something happens to me, I must be sure that my brother's dying request is honored. Much is at stake for Robert Farrow, and he has already shown his willingness to use violent means to protect his inheritance."

Isabel stared. "You think he might make an attempt on your life?"

Mr. Safford sighed. "I don't know. But I must be prepared. If that time comes, Miss Cosgrove," he said in a grave voice, "the will must be recovered and taken to Mr. John Barratt. He is a solicitor, and I trust him."

"Why not simply give it to him now? You have seen evidence that Mr. Farrow is not reformed, have you not?"

He grimaced and sighed. "I must give him another chance. I have seen even the unrepentant turn to God. My brother is a perfect example of the power of God reaching a seemingly impenetrable heart. I hope to write Robert a letter, encouraging him to reconsider his path."

Isabel swallowed and nodded, glancing at the space between the headstones. She hoped to never be required to set her sights on it again.

She had no idea how much property Mr. Farrow stood to lose if the will was revealed. It seemed unthinkable, though, that a man would seek to kill his own kin. Why not instead reform his ways?

The inheritance was not all he stood to lose, though. If Charles's suit with Miss Darling succeeded, Mr. Farrow stood to lose Miss Darling, as well.

And even if Miss Darling didn't come to her senses and choose Charles—Isabel couldn't dwell on that possibility for the hope it fanned within her—there was a great likelihood that Mr. Farrow's reputation would lead Miss Darling to distance herself from him anyway.

A man with so much to lose could certainly be capable of terrible things.

❧ 13 ❧

Isabel knocked softly on the door.

The door opened only slightly at first, but when Hetty saw who the intruder was, she swung it wide.

Cecilia was seated at the far side of her bedroom, and Anaïs stood behind her, adjusting the pink riband woven through Cecilia's hair.

Hetty followed Isabel's gaze and then sent Isabel a look full of meaning.

Isabel grimaced. Anaïs and Hetty had not taken to one another.

Hetty walked over to Cecilia's chair. "That riband isn't long enough. The pale yellow would go better anyway."

Anaïs didn't even look at Hetty, only muttering something in French, which drew a long-suffering expression from Hetty.

"We speak English here, *mademoiselle.*" Hetty said the last word with sarcasm.

Cecilia applied rouge to her cheeks, paying no heed to the fracas occurring between the two maids. She allowed Anaïs much more license than their mother liked, but Isabel couldn't bother herself with such things at the moment.

"If you are nearly done, Anaïs," Isabel said, "I would like to speak with Cecilia before she leaves."

Anaïs put a final pin into Cecilia's hair and looked over at Hetty, one eyebrow raised in victory. "*Parfait*," she said.

Hetty's nostrils flared as she set down a handheld mirror and moved to leave the room. Anaïs stepped in front of her with a challenging glance and left the room first.

"What is it, Izzy?" Cecilia dabbed perfume on her wrist and then rubbed it on her neck. "I am late. Mama told Lord Roffey to pick us up at eight, and it is already five past. I heard the carriage wheels ten minutes ago."

Isabel placed her hands on the back of the chair her sister sat in, running both hands along the carved wood patterns. "Lord Roffey again. Is he your choice then?"

"My choice?" Cecilia shot her a bewildered glance through the mirror.

"Of your suitors. For a husband, I mean."

Cecilia laughed. "It is a night at the opera, Izzy. Don't be dramatic, for heaven's sake."

Isabel forced a smile. Could Cecilia really be so cavalier about all the gentlemen in her life? Or was there more going on below the surface? The way Cecilia spoke, sometimes it was easy to doubt whether there was a heart behind her caprice.

But Isabel knew better. And that was why she found her sister's affectation all the more aggravating.

"I spoke to Lord Brockway today." She watched Cecilia's face in the mirror, hoping for any hint of a reaction. But there was nothing to signify that she had even heard. It didn't bode well for Lord Brockway.

"I don't know whether your feelings are engaged there, Cecy," she took in a deep breath, "but I think you would do well to reconsider your approach with him."

"My approach?" Cecilia stopped. "Whatever do you mean?"

Isabel pursed her lips. The conversation was shaping up to be every bit as difficult as she had anticipated. Tiptoeing around the matter didn't seem to be helping. Cecilia was determined to be difficult these days.

"I think you are at risk of losing his affection and regard. That is all I wanted to say." Isabel turned toward the door.

"I find it interesting," Cecilia said as Isabel placed a hand on the doorknob, "that you are so well-acquainted with Lord Brockway's sentiments."

Isabel turned to face her, but Cecilia still had her back to her. She was applying some of her Alkanet powder to her cheeks. It matched perfectly with the pink of the riband.

"Perhaps," she said, "you are hoping that his suit with me fails so that you can set your cap at him."

Isabel opened her mouth to reply but was cut off.

"Just like you've set your cap at Mr. Galbraith."

Isabel's mouth clamped shut, and she felt her face warm up. How could she explain to Cecilia what was afoot? Particularly when her own feelings were engaged?

"Is that why you've been so cross with me the past few days? Because of Charles?"

Cecily turned around, her eyebrows raised. "Charles?"

Isabel brought her hands together in front of her mouth and sighed. "It is not what you imagine it to be."

"Then why did you not tell me that it was Mr. Galbraith who was Father's guest that night?"

Isabel took her lips between her teeth, and she brought her shoulders up with a breath. "Because it was nothing."

Cecilia stood. "Don't be ridiculous, Izzy. I've seen the way you look at him. Anyone can see you're half-mad for him. I might have guessed you would try to take him from me. Him and Brockway!"

Isabel stood stunned. "Take him from you?" She put her hands out and then dropped them. "You don't even know him, Cecy, beyond an introduction. How could I—or anyone—take him from you when he's never been yours?"

She put on her glove agitatedly. "You know what I mean, Izzy. You've heard me speak of him, and you couldn't bear to watch me make him fall in love with me."

Isabel rubbed her forehead with a hand. "This is what I mean, Cecy. How can you speak like that? *'Make him fall in love with you?'*" Isabel scoffed, struggling to believe that her sister could sincerely be saying such things. "What a silly thing to say. Besides, he is in love with Julia Darling."

A pugnacious light came into Cecilia's eyes. She folded her arms. "You doubt that I can make him fall in love with me?"

Isabel's brows snapped together, and she swallowed. Did she believe Cecilia could make Charles love her? "I think, Cecy," she said slowly, "that you will have no suitors left if you speak of them so cavalierly. Lord Brockway will only be the first to abandon his suit."

Cecilia's brows flew up. "That sounds like a challenge."

Isabel drew back. There was no talking to Cecilia in this mood. What had happened to bring about such a combative over-confidence, she didn't know. But it troubled her to hear and see.

"I shall prove it to you."

Isabel let out a large breath, closed her eyes, and put her head back. She didn't lose her patience very often, but Cecilia was goading her beyond endurance. "However shall you do that, Cecilia?"

She patted her hair and stared at Isabel. "Quite easily, I think. I'd venture to say that I could do it even in the presence of you or Julia Darling."

"Listen to yourself, Cecilia. Your arrogance is astounding, but more than that, it is distasteful. This is not the sister I know. You do not have to make a conquest of all the gentlemen in London to matter, you know." She shook her head and turned the doorknob.

Cecilia's lids fluttered a few times, the first evidence that any of Isabel's words had struck a chord. But it wasn't enough. Cecilia's jaw seemed to harden, and her smile became brittle. "I have just the plan. We shall all go on an outing together. Then you shall see."

Isabel turned back toward the door, pausing as she opened it. She didn't even turn back toward Cecilia as she said, "You have nothing to prove to anyone, Cecy." She closed the door quietly behind her.

14

Isabel fiddled with the reins in her hands. She had greatly debated whether to join the group on their outing to Mr. Prescott's. In the end, she had decided in the affirmative, if only to be able to inform her father that Charles would accompany her on the outing. He had seemed pleased upon learning of the plans, sending her an impish look and putting a finger to his lips.

"I won't tell a soul," he had said, as if they were complicit in some mischief.

Isabel's frustration with her sister had lightened somewhat after hearing from Mary that no fewer than three of Cecilia's suitors had abandoned her for the newly-arrived Miss Austin. She wished that she could help Cecilia see how little such things mattered. But it was a realization she would have to arrive at in her own time, however painful it was for Isabel to watch.

"Stop fidgeting, for heaven's sake, Izzy," Cecilia said. "You are making Arrow nervous."

Isabel's horse pawed the ground, his ears swiveling from back to front to side. She put a calming hand on his neck. "Oh," she said suddenly, "I meant to tell you that I invited Mary."

"What?" Cecilia frowned. "Why?"

"Cecilia, surely you realize that you invited a group which consists of only five people. And between you and Miss Darling, I anticipate that Lord Brockway and Charles will be rather taken up. So, I invited Mary to make it an even six."

Cecilia made a noncommittal noise. She never liked her plans to be interfered with.

"Did you tell those you invited who else would make up our party?"

Cecilia's eyes grew mischievous. "No, just that it would be a small, intimate group."

"I am surprised anyone agreed to come."

"I am not," Cecilia said, ever confident. "I knew no one would be able to refuse a visit to Mr. Prescott's. Everyone is hoping for a peek at the animals before the grand opening in a few weeks."

Isabel watched her sister with a considering gaze. "How did you manage an invitation? I didn't even know you knew the man."

Cecilia only laughed. "I only met him the other night at the opera." She adjusted one of her gloves. "But he extended the kindest invitation, insisting I should feel free to visit any day this week."

Isabel's eyes narrowed. "Is he expecting our group, then? Or just you?" She had heard enough of Mr. Prescott to know that he had a reputation for being shockingly forward.

Cecilia's hands went still in the act of adjusting her other glove. "Surely you don't believe me so vulgar as to go alone? Besides, Mr. Prescott isn't even there. He is traveling to Algiers. Apparently, there is a panther he is desperate to add to his collection."

Isabel's shoulders lowered, and she let out a small breath of relief. She had been wondering whether Cecilia's recent cavalier attitude was perhaps a precursor to—or even a symptom of—indiscretion.

"Ah," Cecilia said, raising a hand to wave. "Mr. Galbraith and Miss Darling. Arriving together." She said the last word as if she had been extended a challenge.

Isabel felt her throat constrict as she spotted the two approaching on horseback, trailed by a young woman Isabel could only assume was Miss Darling's maid. How they had come to arrive together was a mystery to her. It boded well for Charles, though, surely.

Their plan must be working better even than Isabel had known. Miss Darling threw her head back, and Isabel could hear the musical sound of her laugh even at a distance. Mr. Galbraith's responsive grin made Isabel's stomach feel heavy and yet, somehow, hollow. She turned, unwilling to watch the interaction longer than needed.

She reminded herself of her two objectives for the day: to continue fostering a reconciliation between Miss Darling and Charles, and, as much as it was possible, to protect Cecilia from herself. It was unlikely to be an enjoyable day. But perhaps the silver lining would be seeing the animals Mr. Prescott had acquired.

However the day transpired, she vowed to put on a pleasant face and do her best to enjoy herself. She refused to cut a pathetic figure in front of Charles and Miss Darling, especially.

She sat straighter and smiled as they approached and then came to a halt.

Cecilia greeted them with her wide smile.

"I admit," said Mr. Galbraith, "that I was somewhat perplexed when I received your invitation. I had no idea who to expect. When I happened upon Julia just down the road, we were surprised to discover we shared a destination."

Isabel could only imagine that he would have been surprised. He barely knew Cecilia, after all. For her to have sent him an invitation at all was presumptuous, bordering on brazen. She likely owed his acceptance of the invitation to the assumption that Isabel would at least be present.

"Indeed," Miss Darling said, extending a hand to Cecilia, "thank you for the invitation. I have been waiting very patiently for the menagerie opening, but they seem to put it off time and again."

Cecilia smiled and turned toward Isabel. "You and Mr. Galbraith are already well acquainted, I know."

She shot Isabel a challenging glance, and Isabel met Charles's eyes briefly. He smiled at her, and she swallowed amidst her own smile. Would his smile ever stop affecting her?

"But," continued Cecilia, "I don't believe you and Miss Darling are acquainted. Miss Darling, this is my sister, Miss Isabel Cosgrove."

Miss Darling smiled, but the effect was rendered less amiable by the way she held her head high, looking down her petite nose at Isabel.

"I'm very pleased to make your acquaintance, Miss Darling," Isabel said, curtsying.

Miss Darling inclined her head. Was there a small gleam of malice in her eyes?

"When do we leave?" Miss Darling asked Cecilia, arranging her skirts.

Isabel gripped her lips together, brushing off a feeling of embarrassment at Miss Darling's cool response. Whether she was doing it intentionally or not, Miss Darling had a way of making one feel small. She glanced at Charles. He was looking at Miss Darling, eyes pinched slightly.

Cecilia called attention to Lord Brockway who was approaching. He was acquainted with all members of the group, as was Mary whose arrival followed shortly thereafter, so it was only a matter of minutes before they were on their way toward Prescott Place.

The route passed through the park, crowded with riders and carriages, then continued northwest toward Wesborn Green.

Isabel couldn't help but smile ruefully on behalf of her sister. Mary had managed to address a remark to Cecilia just as the group was departing, leaving Lord Brockway to ride next to Isabel. They were preceded by Miss Darling and Mr. Galbraith, with Mary and Cecilia leading the group. Cecilia shifted in her saddle frequently, glancing back at the other four in the group. How she intended to monopolize both gentlemen would be equally amusing and painful to watch.

Isabel looked at Lord Brockway. "How have you fared since I saw you last, my lord?"

He had been staring at the space between his horse's ears but looked up as she addressed him. He looked to be in much better spirits than when she had seen him at the church. "Quite well, thank you." He lowered his voice and glanced at Cecilia up ahead. "I have been trying to follow your advice."

"And?"

"I don't know, to be honest." He placed a hand on his thigh, leaving the reins in the other hand. "It went against my custom very much, but I refrained from asking her to dance until the very end of the evening last night—a fact which she pointed out as we danced. But I found that there were plenty of ladies in need of partners. In fact, I was able to make the acquaintance of a shy but delightful young woman who only recently moved here from Ireland. I was able to bring her out of her shell by drawing on my own experiences there."

Had Cecilia noticed Lord Brockway's interaction with the young woman he spoke of? If Isabel's own warning to her sister hadn't done the trick, perhaps seeing Lord Brockway pay attention to other young women could. Perhaps that was what had put her out enough to cause the strange and brash behavior in her dressing room the other night.

Lord Brockway recounted some of his experiences in Ireland as they continued riding, and Isabel listened with interest. She had always wished to travel outside of England. She was grateful that Lord Brockway was an interesting riding companion since she only thought to look up at Charles and Miss Darling a few times. Each time, she vowed not to repeat the experience.

Prescott Place was a grand estate, set on sprawling acres of green fields. The building boasted a Tudor-style exterior of red sandstone, punctuated by half-timbering. A number of liveried servants awaited them at the gravel courtyard, one of whom invited them to dismount and leave their horses with the other servants.

"Good day to you, ladies and gentlemen," he said. "Am I correct in assuming that you are Miss Cecilia Cosgrove?" He directed his gaze at Cecilia who inclined her head. "Mr. Prescott informed me that I should be expecting you and your party. My name is John Sweeney, and I will have the pleasure of taking care of you today. Please, if you would, follow me."

The group followed behind him, taking a path around the side of the house. As they turned the corner, a grand building, separate from the main house appeared. Two large wooden doors concealed the interior, and on each side stood a liveried servant. A muffled din could be heard from within.

Sweeney stopped just short of the doors, turning to the group, his hands clasped behind his back. "Welcome to Prescott's Grand Menagerie." He indicated the doors with a sweeping gesture of one hand. "The animals contained in the menagerie come from all corners of the earth."

Miss Darling leaned in toward Charles, whispering something in his ear and coming away laughing. Isabel didn't let her eyes linger to watch Charles's reaction.

Sweeney stood stone-faced. "All the creatures are beautiful, many are fierce, and some are deadly. A few you are permitted to feed. You will find containers with food beside those cages. Do not attempt to feed any of the animals whose cages do not include these containers." He nodded to the two servants, and they turned to grip the large, iron handles.

"Ladies and Gentlemen," Sweeney continued, "prepare yourselves to leave London behind and enter a different world."

The servants threw open the doors, and a cacophony of animal sounds met Isabel's ears. Warm air whooshed past them, along with a pungent odor.

Miss Darling had been speaking with Charles but whipped around at the sound. She wrinkled her nose and then plugged it. "What an awful stench!"

Isabel met eyes with Charles, and his half-smile appeared. "Ahh, the smell of adventure." He took in a deep breath, wafting the air toward his nose, and began coughing.

"You are so strange, Charles," Miss Darling said, leaning away as he coughed.

Charles sent Isabel a teasing glance. Cecilia moved to his side.

"I hope you don't mind," she said to him with what Isabel recognized as false timidity, "but I have heard terrible things about some of the creatures here, and I think it wise to go in with the protection of a strong gentleman."

One of Charles's eyebrows went up, and his mouth fell open only to clamp shut again. He proffered his arm and said, "I don't know that I am a match for any of these animals, but I am happy to oblige if it will help you feel more at ease." He shot a glance at Isabel, and she raised her brows in an enigmatic response. Somehow, she felt sure that Charles would see past Cecilia's excuses. He would not be so easy for the taking as Cecilia had assumed.

The group walked slowly into the building. The interior contained a long walkway, lined by tall, arched cages with bars of iron. Just outside of the cages sat potted trees, and the ceiling had been painted to resemble the sky. Every head turned toward the first cage which appeared on their left: a Bengal tiger sleeping next to a bowl of water. A silver plaque hung next to the cage, and Isabel walked over to it. It contained information about the animal, its name, and its origins.

Miss Darling gasped as Isabel approached it.

Cecilia jumped at the sound. "What is wrong?"

"I can't think it wise to approach so closely," Miss Darling said, looking at Isabel. "It is a wild beast, after all."

"It is not wild right now," Isabel said, her eyes not leaving the plaque. "Only a sleeping beast whose name is Rainier. He is just two years old."

Charles came up beside her, and she felt his arm rest against hers as he read the plaque. Her arm tingled, and she moved to give him more space, trying not to pay attention to the way her arm suddenly felt bare.

"His mother died in the wild," Charles said. "Poor little chap."

A large roar sounded, and Isabel jumped in terror, grabbing onto Charles's arm and burying her face in it. Her heart pummeled her chest. She looked toward the sound's origin. The lion in the next cage over prowled from side to side, watching the group with a baleful glare.

She could hear Charles's breath coming as quickly as her own.

He placed a hand over hers, which were still wrapped tightly around his arm, and pulled her back away from the cage. "I don't think he fancies us."

Isabel laughed shakily and released his arm. She glanced at the imprint her fingers had left on his coat sleeve. "I apologize."

Charles's half-smile appeared as he looked down at her. "I didn't mind," he said softly.

She tried unsuccessfully to slow her heart.

"It seems I was right," Miss Darling's voice broke through. "Wild beasts after all. Aren't they, Miss Cosgrove?"

Isabel rubbed her shaking hands down her dress, hoping to still them. She moved away from Charles toward Mary. "Perhaps so." She glanced at Rainier the tiger. He was still sleeping. "I can't think any of us would be in good spirits, though, if we were taken from our homes and put in cages."

Charles's head tipped to the side, and he stepped over to the plaque in front of the lion's cage.

Cecilia moved toward him. "Well, I don't intend to take any chances. Mr. Galbraith has promised to protect me or else I think I should be tempted to leave." She looked at the lion, which was still prowling, and placed her hand on Charles's arm.

He gave no indication he had noticed, continuing to read the plaque about the lion.

Isabel bit her lip to stop a smile. "You must be very confident in Charles's protection indeed, Cecilia. Now that you've joined him, you are closer than ever to the beast."

Isabel glanced at Lord Brockway. He was standing straighter than usual, and she followed his gaze to Cecilia's arm, interlocked with

Charles's. Cecilia would have to do better at splitting her attention if she meant to win Charles over while keeping Lord Brockway.

Mary stepped up toward the tiger's cage, wrapping her hands around the bars as she stared at the animal. "You know, I have heard it said that the animals can smell fear." She looked over at Cecilia with a provoking arch to her brows.

"Well," Miss Darling said, adjusting the reticule draped over her wrist, "I am not afraid of the beasts. I simply have no desire to return home smelling like them."

Lord Brockway walked ahead, and Isabel followed suit. There were plenty of animals yet to see, and she had no desire to spar with Miss Darling or watch Cecilia make a fool of herself.

"My lord?" she called out.

Lord Brockway stopped and turned toward her. He tapped the top of his cane with his finger, pursing his lips.

"Are you well?"

He offered his arm to her, and she took it. "I am," he said. "Today has already been enlightening."

"How is that?"

He turned them toward a cage, and they approached it. Two foxes stood watching them, ears pricked up.

"Only that I feel I am beginning to better understand your sister." He paused, staring at the foxes as they lowered their heads to drink from their water bowl. "Perhaps I have simply been resisting the truth until now."

Isabel heaved a great sigh. "I can only say that I am sorry. Her behavior recently has been disheartening. I believe that Cecilia will find herself in time. I fear that she will experience a rude awakening which, while it will be painful to observe, may prove a catalyst to change. But I could never counsel you to wait for that to happen. Perhaps losing you will even act as that catalyst."

"Well," he said, lifting his cane and then bringing it down on the floor with a small smack, "in any case, I feel it would be unwise for me to hold out hope at this point. I haven't given up entirely, but I feel free to focus my energies elsewhere in the meantime." He brought up his head, and a smile grew on his face. "Strangely, I feel a weight lifted from my shoulders even as I say that."

Isabel patted his arm lightly and smiled.

Inside, though, she felt a desire to shake sense into her sister. She was happy for Lord Brockway. There was no guarantee that Cecilia would see reason, after all. Particularly if recent history was any indicator.

Lord Brockway deserved to be happy now rather than in some potential future with a changed Cecilia.

But the development had the potential to complicate Isabel's situation significantly. How could she appease her father without marrying Mr. Galbraith when Cecilia seemed bound and determined to sabotage her own chances at a great match?

15

Charles Galbraith turned to locate Isabel and Lord Brockway. They stood together, Isabel's hand on his arm, in front of a cage of foxes.

Julia's head twisted around, following his gaze. "Yes," she said, "those two look quite cozy, don't they?"

He turned his head to look at Julia. What did she mean?

She wagged her brows and then laughed, tucking her arm into his.

He forced a chuckle, shooting another quick glance at Isabel. She was smiling at Lord Brockway.

Had Charles been blind? He hadn't thought a thing of it to see the two of them standing together, but Julia had. It made no sense, though. Hadn't Isabel intended Lord Brockway for Cecilia? Yes, there was no doubt of that. It had been her escape plan—escape from a marriage to Charles.

The fact that she desired to concoct an alternative had been a welcome surprise to Charles at first. But as he came to know Isabel better, anytime she brought up the subject of avoiding their marriage, it rankled. Would it be so awful to be married to him?

Julia's arm tugged him forward toward the next cage. "You've been very neglectful of late, Charles," she said.

"Have I?"

"Yes. I've been missing the conversations we used to have back at home. I feel I hardly know you anymore."

He missed the conversations, too. He missed everything about that time. Sitting with Julia on the dock of the pond, skipping rocks on the water.

"Those were very happy days, weren't they?" he said with a nostalgic crook to his mouth.

"Canoeing in the pond last summer?"

He chuckled. "When you pushed me in? A whig of moss and the stench of frogs that lingered on my clothes for a week."

Julia threw back her head in that way which was so unique to her and laughed. "I warned you not to splash me with the oars."

"An honest mistake," he said, putting his free hand up in a gesture of defense.

"Perhaps the first time," she said. "But surely not five times?"

He grinned and hung his head in mock guilt. Suddenly he frowned. "Things have changed since then."

"Not I," Julia said.

Charles turned his head. Did she really think she hadn't changed?

She looked the same. That small ringlet which always hung behind her right ear. The same shade of pink tinging her cheeks. The dark lashes which framed those cornflower blue eyes he'd looked into a million times.

But no. Nothing else was the same.

"Oh!" Cecilia's cry broke in on their conversation. "Look at these creatures." She stood facing a cage farther down the walkway. She leaned forward toward the cage as if she wished to approach it but didn't dare.

Charles walked toward her, and his arm broke free from Julia's. Remembering their days at home in the country had been bittersweet. It seemed like a different lifetime—before he'd seen a new side of her.

Everyone in the group gathered in front of the cage. Inside were three small, black monkeys with white hair framing their curious faces.

"Colobus monkeys," Miss Holledge said, examining the plaque. "And we are permitted to feed them." She looked in the container attached to the wall.

Isabel went up beside her, peering in. "It looks like a mixture of seeds and berries."

"How fortunate." Charles came up beside her and reached a hand in. "I'm starving. Don't mind if I do."

Isabel's head turned to him. She watched him with a dare in her eyes. "You wouldn't!"

His lip twitched, but he met her gaze with a challenging look of his own. Keeping his eyes on her, he picked out a berry from his palm and tossed it into his mouth.

Her lips trembled as she tried to stifle a smile.

He never let his eyes waver from hers, chewing the dried berry with a gusto very much at odds with his true desire to spit out the bitter thing.

"How odd you are, Charles," said Julia from behind. "I hope you won't fall ill."

"And?" Isabel looked at him expectantly. "Was it everything you had hoped it would be?"

The muscles in his jaw tensed as he forced himself to swallow the berry. "Delectable. It has only whetted my appetite." He grabbed a second handful and offered her some.

"Really?" Isabel's eyes darted hesitantly from his outstretched hand to his eyes.

Charles laughed, dropping his hand. "No. It was terrible." He looked to the monkeys. "How can you eat this rot?" He stuck a hand through the iron bars, but the three monkeys only stared.

Isabel came up beside him, and he inhaled a refreshing waft of violets—a welcome change from what he could only assume was the scent of animal droppings permeating the menagerie.

"May I?" she said, indicating his hand with her eyes. She took a pinch of a few berries from his palm.

It was the second time he could remember her initiating contact between them. More often than not, she seemed to pull away from his touch. He watched her as she put her hand through the bars.

"No need to be afraid," she said. She tossed a few berries toward them. Two retreated, but one looked at the berries for a moment before gingerly walking toward the food, picking up a piece, and tapping it on his teeth.

Soon enough, all three monkeys had eaten the scattered berries and were looking expectantly at Isabel.

"Extraordinary." Charles said to her, tossing a few berries toward the monkeys. "You seem to have a gift with them."

Isabel laughed. "That, or I simply have the food they wish for." She jumped slightly as a monkey came up to the bars in front of her. It looked at her with a round, direct stare. She put her hand through the bars slowly. The monkey looked at her and then at her hand, grabbed the berries, and hopped back toward the others.

Miss Darling gasped, and the others applauded.

Isabel brushed off her gloved hands. "I believe they are as scared of us as we are of them."

Charles looked at the monkeys who were chewing on their berries while staring at the group. "I think you're onto something there," Charles said. He put out a handful of berries, and two monkeys ambled over to take them. He looked over at Isabel, and she nodded her head approvingly.

"I think I should like to try," Julia said, putting a hand into the container. "Pardon me," she said, sidling into the small space between Charles and Isabel with a smile. "This seems to be the best position for feeding them." She extended a handful of berries through the bars, and a monkey approached.

"Easy, Ju," Charles said, seeing the way her body turned away from the bars as if she wasn't sure she welcomed contact with the animal.

The monkey sniffed her hand and began taking the berries. Its fingers touched her hand, and she jumped at the direct contact, closing her hand into a fist and drawing back slightly.

The monkey howled and grabbed her hand. She screamed and tore it away, yelping as the monkey's claws scraped at her fist. She drew her hand toward her, cradling it and let out a small scream when she saw the blood which was seeping slightly through her gloves.

"Ju!" Charles put a hand below hers and leaned in to inspect the wounds. The monkey's claws had only ripped the glove in one place, but blood showed through in three different areas. "This cut doesn't look too deep—your glove stopped a great deal of damage—but the wounds definitely need attention."

"Yes," Isabel said, "we should get you inside where they can be cleaned and dressed. I'll inform the servants."

"Good idea," Charles said, nodding to her. He was grateful Isabel had a practical head on her shoulders. "Are you all right, Ju?"

"I feel delirious," she said, looking up into his eyes with flitting eyelids. She leaned on him heavily.

He glanced at the others.

Cecilia stood with her mouth agape. "I think I shall faint," she suddenly cried. Her body went slack, and Lord Brockway rushed to catch her under the arms.

Charles swore under his breath.

"My thoughts precisely," Miss Holledge said as she assisted Lord Brockway in placing Cecilia's comatose form into his arms.

Isabel hastened back toward them. "They have gone to prepare things inside. Let us make our way there."

Charles nodded, putting a supporting arm around Julia's waist and urging her forward.

She looked up into his eyes, her shoulders slumped over and

brows drawn together. "I don't think I can walk, Charles. I feel so dizzy."

He placed an arm behind her knees and lifted her.

"Thank you," she said, laying her head onto his shoulder and closing her eyes. He expected some kind of internal reaction to her proximity, but he felt nothing but an urgency to get her inside.

The group hastened to the manor where the servants directed them to the library.

Charles laid Julia carefully on the chaise lounge. Isabel stood ready with a bowl of water and a towel.

"Would you care to clean the wounds?" she said, offering the bowl and towel to him. She glanced down at Julia. "I'm afraid it will sting, Miss Darling."

"No, Charles," Julia said in a feeble but urgent voice. "Let someone else do it. I wish for you to hold my hand, please. You know that I can't bear pain."

Charles's eyes flitted up to Isabel.

She stood more stiffly than usual, and her eyes were lowered, looking at the bowl in her hands.

He pressed his lips together in what he hoped was a smile and took Julia's hand in his. Why did he feel so conflicted?

"I am happy to clean the wounds," Isabel said, pulling up a footstool beside Miss Darling. "I am told I have a gentle hand." She wore a sympathetic smile.

Julia's neck was stretched, her face expressionless. She brushed lightly at a hair which had fallen onto her forehead and then winced. She had used the injured hand.

"Well," she said as she inspected it with a frown, "perhaps it makes sense for you to clean the wounds since it was your idea to feed the beasts."

Isabel stiffened momentarily in the act of seating herself, looking at Julia with an open mouth.

Charles was incredulous. "Ju," he said. "That's not fair."

"No," Isabel said, dipping the towel in the water. "She is right. It was unwise of me to feed the animals from my hand. It's unlikely that anyone else would have thought to do such a heedless thing if I had not set a precedent."

"I think," Miss Holledge chimed in as she fanned Cecilia who was sprawled on the settee, "that perhaps things would not have gone awry if the rest of us—" she emphasized the words but her eyes darted to Julia, "—were as calm as you were with them. It seems that they can, indeed, smell fear."

Charles thought that Miss Holledge quite likely had a point. The monkeys had been fine to take their food from his hands and Isabel's hands. Julia's sudden movement was what seemed to have triggered the injury.

Isabel cleaned the wound with delicate but confident movements. Julia was not an easy patient, though, as she frequently called out in pain and drew her hand away, a reaction which only increased her discomfort. She squeezed Charles's hand with every brush of the wet towel.

He tried to calm her with assurances that it would be over soon, but he couldn't deny the small twinges of impatience he felt. The wounds were red and had bled some, but they were far from being serious or deep.

Once the bandage was secured around her hand, Isabel stood with the pink-tinged water and towel. "There," she said. "I don't believe we have much cause for concern. The wounds should recover fairly quickly, and I think the bandage will help reduce the discomfort."

She wore a pained smile. She seemed to truly feel for Julia.

Julia heaved a large sigh, laid her head back, and closed her eyes.

"Isabel," Charles said as he stood.

Isabel turned, looking expectantly at him.

But Julia's eyes shot open as Charles's hand released hers. "Where are you going, Charles? I still need you."

He glanced at Julia and then back at the retreating figure of

Isabel—she hadn't stayed after Julia's call to him. Patting Julia's uninjured hand, he reassured her, "I will only be a moment."

"Isabel," he said as he came up beside her.

She stopped just shy of the door. He took in a breath, his lips pressed together, and his forehead creased. "Julia is"— he grimaced and shook his head, trying to find the right words —"a passionate person, and it can lead her to say rash or ill-judged things. I hope that what she said didn't hurt you." He looked into Isabel's eyes. "It isn't your fault."

Isabel swallowed but smiled at him. "I was not hurt by what she said."

The way she phrased it was strange—almost too exact. And why did he have the impression that her smile was covering something?

He rubbed his hands down the legs of his pantaloons. "You were very kind to dress the wounds. And very forbearing with a difficult patient." A wry smile appeared on his face as he brought up his left hand. There were three red marks from Julia's grasping nails.

"Oh dear," said Isabel with a small laugh. "Perhaps you need this?" She raised the bowl of water.

Charles chuckled and rubbed at the three marks. "Or perhaps I simply showed too much fear."

Isabel repressed a smile, but a dimple peeped out.

He grinned. He always felt a sense of satisfaction when he brought a smile to Isabel's face. Particularly when he knew she was trying to repress her amusement.

"Charles!" Julia's voice rang out.

His head jerked toward the sound, but he brought his gaze back to Isabel. He raised his shoulders in a helpless gesture, inclined his head to Isabel, and turned back toward Julia.

16

Isabel sipped her cup of chocolate. She never took her breakfast in bed. But today was different.

Things had not gone to plan for Cecilia—or for anyone in the group, surely—on their visit to the menagerie, and Isabel was in no mood to subject herself to the aftereffects. She needed time to consider what to do next.

Lord Brockway seemed to be distancing himself from Cecilia without much difficulty. And who could blame him after the way she had been treating him? But if she continued to treat any gentleman who fell in love with her the same way, she would have no prospects at all, much less the spectacular marriage she seemed to expect. Isabel's hope for her sister to come to her senses was fading quickly. And with it, her confidence in her own future.

Charles's behavior had been, as usual, puzzling. At times earnest, at other times teasing, his behavior raised emotions in her that inevitably came crashing down when she remembered that it was all done with the intent to win back Miss Darling—Miss Darling who seemed to lose no opportunity of reminding Isabel that she considered Charles to be hers.

There was an urgent knock on the door.

"Come in," she said, setting her chocolate down on the breakfast tray.

It was Anaïs. Her face was pale, and she was out of breath.

"They've come to take Hetty, *mademoiselle! Venez.*" She motioned for Isabel to come.

Isabel set the tray in front of her and threw the bed covers back. She grabbed her dressing gown and put it on as she rushed through the door, held open by Anaïs.

She could hear a commotion at the front door. Hetty was sobbing, and Mrs. Cosgrove's voice was raised, followed by the voice of someone Isabel had met only once but had no difficulty identifying: Mrs. Robson.

Isabel arrived to see the three women as well as a man dressed in simple but neat clothing. He held a paper in his hands and his chin up with a slight sneer, as if the disturbance occurring in front of him were distasteful to him. Paxton stood to the side of the group.

"Ma'am," Paxton said, "Do you wish for me to see that these people—" he indicated them with a haughty flick of his head "—cease from disturbing you?"

Mrs. Cosgrove shook her head, staring at Mrs. Robson with a stony expression. "Thank you, Paxton. I am well able to handle the situation. You may go."

Paxton bowed and left.

"Mrs. Cosgrove," said the man standing next to Mrs. Robson. "You have no legal right to keep Miss Robson here when her mother wishes for her return."

Mrs. Robson's chin came up, and she nodded soundly.

Hetty let out a large sob.

"Wishes her return indeed," Mrs. Cosgrove scoffed, looking down on Mrs. Robson with distaste. "More likely she wishes to profit off of her."

"Be that as it may," the man said in a loud voice, "it is her right to demand Miss Robson's removal from this house."

Hetty sobbed anew. "Oh, please, Mama, don't take me away from them! I can't marry him. I can't!"

Isabel rushed over, wrapping a comforting arm around Hetty. "There, there, Hetty. We will all come about."

"Come," Mrs. Robson said, reaching for Hetty's wrist. "You heard him."

The man opened the front door, seeing Mrs. Robson and Hetty out before nodding and tipping his hat to Mrs. Cosgrove and Isabel.

Isabel peered outside. There was a coach awaiting. Its door hung open, and a coachman stood at its side. A passenger was already seated inside, and he lowered his head to watch the approach of Mrs. Robson and Hetty.

It was Mr. Farrow.

"No!" Isabel cried out, running toward the door until realizing she was only in her dressing gown. "Hetty!"

Hetty looked back at her as she stepped into the coach. A more beautiful but pathetic image Isabel could not have imagined. Hetty's face was tear-streaked, her expression helpless. On meeting eyes with Isabel, her chin trembled before Mrs. Robson nudged her in through the coach door.

Isabel's mother pulled her back from the doorway. "There is nothing we can do, Isabel. You are not even dressed, for heaven's sake."

They watched as the coach pulled away. Isabel dashed at a tear on her cheek. "We cannot leave her to that woman and Mr. Farrow—you saw how terrified she was. It will break her, Mama."

The muscles in her mother's neck were taut, and she sighed through a clenched jaw as she closed the door. "I don't see what we can possibly do. You heard the solicitor."

"Hired by Mr. Farrow to intimidate us, no doubt." Isabel's breath came out shaky. What would he do with Hetty? Was she overreacting? Was he perhaps well-meaning this time?

Isabel's mother laid a hand on her arm—an uncharacteristically affectionate gesture. "We did as much as we could, my dear." She patted her arm twice and then walked away.

Isabel stood rooted to the spot. There had to be something more they could do. But what?

She chewed her lip then rushed toward the morning room, setting a paper on the desk and dipping the quill in ink. Her hands were unsteady as she scribbled a short note then folded the paper and sealed it, rushing back out of the room. She handed the note to the footman, directing him to take it immediately to the address listed. He nodded and was on his way.

Isabel hastened up the stairs and to her room, ringing the bell for Anaïs. She didn't wait for the maid, though, to shed her dressing gown and begin putting on clothing suitable for walking.

Anaïs knocked lightly and opened the door. "*Oui, mademoiselle?*"

"I need you to accompany me to the church." Isabel didn't look up as she put her arms through her sleeves.

"*Eh bien,*" said Anaïs as she helped Isabel's dress over her head, "Cecilia has need of me."

"Cecilia will have to wait. We won't be gone long."

Within minutes, Isabel was ready to go.

The walk to the chapel was accomplished in only a few minutes. They turned into the courtyard, and Isabel looked around. The churchyard seemed deserted. She hadn't expected Charles to be there yet, and she paced back and forth as they waited, her shoes smacking the pavement rhythmically.

Sending a note to Charles had perhaps been unwise. What could he do, after all? His hands were tied by the law just as the Cosgrove's were.

But who else could she turn to? She couldn't allow Hetty to face whatever future her mother and Mr. Farrow had in mind without making an effort to do whatever stood in her power.

She glanced at Anaïs, who stood watching her with a tilted head and narrowed eyes.

"You await someone?" she said. Her eyes widened, lighting up with interest. *"Un gentilhomme, peut-être? It is a—"* she paused as she searched for the word *"—rendez-vous clandestin?"*

Isabel stopped, looking at the maid with severity. "Absolutely not. You forget your place, Anaïs. Your presence here ensures that it is not a clandestine meeting but a perfectly respectable one."

Anaïs lowered her head in a show of atonement for her outburst. Cecilia had been allowing her far too much license, excusing all manner of lapses due to her French upbringing.

The sound of quick footsteps grew louder, and Isabel whipped around to see Charles entering the courtyard of the church. His eyes met hers, and he took off his hat as a few wide steps brought him in front of her.

"What is it?" his eyes searched hers with urgency. "What has happened?"

"They've taken Hetty," she said, feeling her voice catch as her fingers fidgeted.

His brows drew together. "Who?" He shook his head as if to apologize and said, "Come. Sit down." He led her toward the bench Hetty had sat on when they had first discovered her, helping her onto the seat and then sitting beside her. "Tell me."

Isabel fiddled with the strings of her shawl as she looked at him. "Hetty's mother and a solicitor came to the house, insisting that we surrender Hetty to her mother."

Charles blew a puff of air through his lips and shook his head. "I thought it might only be a matter of time. She stands to gain too much from Hetty to let her slip through her fingers. I admit, though, that I'm surprised that she was able to persuade a solicitor to assist her, given her coarse manners."

"That is the worst of it, Charles," Isabel said, taking her top lip between her teeth as she thought on Hetty's predicament. "I don't believe that it was Mrs. Robson's solicitor at all. Just before the coach left, I saw a man inside. He had been waiting while Mrs. Robson spoke to us."

Charles stared at her with an arrested expression. "Farrow." It was a statement rather than a question.

Isabel nodded, clasping her hands tightly in her lap. "Oh, Charles. If you could have seen Hetty." She swallowed as she pictured Hetty's helpless face, and she wiped a tear. "She looked at me as if I were her last hope."

Charles gripped his lips together and put a reassuring hand over Isabel's.

Isabel could see Anaïs in her peripheral vision. Surely Charles's kind gesture would confirm the maid in her suspicions that this was a clandestine meeting.

But Isabel hadn't the energy to care. What did such things matter with Hetty in such trouble?

"Clearly Mrs. Robson and Mr. Farrow have come to some sort of agreement," Isabel said, feeling impatient and restless, "but I can't think what it would be." She looked up at him. "Do you think he plans to marry Hetty after all?"

Charles stared at her grimly. "I have little hope of that. I have heard enough about Robert Farrow to know that he means to marry as well as he is able."

Isabel stood up in agitation, and Charles's hand dropped onto his lap. "She's only a child, for heaven's sake!" Isabel said. "And soon to have a child of her own." She wrung her hands, the anger inside her bringing fresh tears to her eyes. "I have such an awful presentiment." She put a hand on her stomach and then glanced at Charles.

He was watching her pace, his jaw moving from side to side.

"I'm sorry," she said with a helpless hand gesture. "I didn't know who else to go to."

He stood, going over to her and taking her hands together in his.

She lowered her head, turning it to the side to hide the way her heart jumped.

"Don't apologize." He lowered his head and leaned it forward as he tried to catch her eye. "Look at me, Isabel."

She brought her head up, looking at him through blurry vision.

"You need never apologize for calling on me. I wouldn't wish for you to go to anyone else." His eyes were soft and tender as he looked at her. His hand came up, and he wiped away an escaping tear with his thumb. His eyes moved down toward her lips, which parted slightly as his eyes fell upon them.

Her heart thumped loudly. What was this? Was it part of the charade? It seemed so very unnecessary, with Miss Darling and her father nowhere in sight.

She turned her face away and bit the inside of her lip.

She couldn't dwell on such thoughts. She needed to focus on Hetty. Hetty needed her. She broke her hands free of his and glanced over at Anaïs, seated on a nearby bench. She looked too intent on staring at the sky to be believable. Of course she had been watching the whole interaction.

Isabel sighed. "What can be done?"

"I don't know," Charles said. "I must think. Surely there is something." He stood still for a moment then put his hat back on. "I will send you word if I discover anything. May I accompany you home?"

Isabel shook her head. The last thing she wanted was for him to spend more time with her playing the chivalry card. The sooner they parted ways, the sooner he could discover Hetty's whereabouts. "Thank you, but there is no need. Anaïs will be with me. I think I shall speak with Mr. Safford—to let him know what has happened."

Charles shook his head. "Until we have Hetty safe, I would rather not involve anyone else. "

Isabel swallowed and nodded, wishing she could tell him of her conversation with the rector. She still harbored a hope that Mr. Farrow was changing his ways—perhaps in response to Mr. Safford's letter. Charles knew nothing of that, so it was natural that he would assume the worst.

Isabel could only hope that Mr. Farrow had inherited even a shred of his father's late-blooming piety.

Charles moved as if to come toward her but stopped, and his hand dropped to his side.

He nodded to her. "I will be in touch."

Turning on his heel, he made his way out of the churchyard, leaving Isabel staring hollowly after him.

❧ 17 ❧

Charles's temper was in no happy state after a morning of attempting to find the Robson's residence. When he had finally met with success, a young and unkempt child at the door informed him that Hetty had not been home in days and days, but that she would call for her Mama to come down.

He had sworn under his breath upon hearing about Hetty--a fact which didn't seem to faze the child.

He was left standing at the door until an older child appeared at the doorway and showed him into a small, overdecorated drawing room. It was as if someone had described several London drawing rooms to Mrs. Robson, and she had attempted to incorporate every piece reported to her, going for quantity over quality. An overly sweet *eau de parfum* masked the smell of mildew.

Soon enough, Mrs. Robson stood before him, bringing with her more of the perfumed scent which made Charles feel lightheaded and slightly sick.

The short and stout woman who stood before him was nothing like the picture he'd had in his mind. It was apparent, as well, that Hetty had not had her beauty from her mother. The clothing she wore was vulgarly-colorful, and it bunched awkwardly between her large bosom and round stomach.

Mrs. Robson looked at him with narrowed eyes and heavily-pursed lips, taking in his clothing from his hat down to his polished Hessians. She seemed to like what she saw, though, and her expression morphed into one he could only describe as toadying.

"Good morning, sir," she said. "Quite honored we are to welcome you to our humble abode." It was obvious that she was quite proud of her drawing room. "How may I serve you today?"

He let one of his thick eyebrows climb up and took out his quizzing glass. He took his time studying her through it, appreciating the way her eyes began to shift in discomfort, before dropping it and saying, "I am here to inquire after one of your children."

A glimmer of hope appeared in her eyes. "I have many children, sir —three beauties for daughters." She gave him an enigmatic look as though she knew what he was looking for. Her expression shifted suddenly, though, as if she had remembered something, and she added, "Unfortunately, one is away, but the other two are just as pleasing."

His lip turned up into a sneer. What had she done with Hetty, then? "I have the pleasure of being acquainted already with one—now two—of your daughters. May I suggest that you consider bathing your children before trumpeting the superiority of their physical appearances, ma'am? That is your affair, though. I am here for Hetty."

She wrung her hands. "I hesitate to inform you that my Hetty is away."

"Where?"

Mrs. Robson seemed to sense that Charles posed a threat to her. Her hands went still, and she straightened her shoulders and neck, trying to look at him down her nose despite being a full foot shorter. "I'm sure that's no business of yours, sir."

His half-smile appeared. "And yet I have made it my business. You will tell me where Hetty is, or I shall have to employ the Bow Street Runners to discover her whereabouts for me."

The whites of her eyes grew, her fists clenched and unclenched, and her breath came shallow and quick.

Charles raised his brows, shrugged his shoulders, and said, "Have it your way. You may expect a call by the end of the week." He turned on his heel and made for the door.

"Stop!"

He smiled at the door then recomposed his face into one of stony disinterest as he turned around again. "What is it?"

"Marshalsea." The word was mumbled.

"What?" Charles's voice was dangerously soft, his jaw hard.

"Hetty. She's at Marshalsea." Mrs. Robson didn't meet his eyes. She looked fixedly at her own twiddling fingers. "In Southwark."

"I know where Marshalsea is." His voice was dangerously quiet. "Why is your daughter in debtor's prison?"

Mrs. Robson quaked but said nothing.

Charles swung around and jogged out of the room and through the front door. He had walked to the Robsons, but he couldn't walk to Southwark. He hailed the first hack available and directed the driver to take him to Marshalsea.

His jaw tightened. It had taken every ounce of self-control not to shake the woman in her own house. He realized that his acute anger covered something deeper: fear. Marshalsea was no place for a young woman like Hetty. His only consolation was that she could not have been there even a full twenty-four hours yet.

The hackney let him down in front of the prison, and Charles's nose wrinkled at an overpowering smell of sewage. After explaining to the turnkey at the door that he was there to see a prisoner, he entered into the courtyard and was directed that he would find the women housed above the tap room.

His brow was black and murderous by the time he reached the rooms where he might find Hetty. The sound of raucous laughter in the tavern below only added to his rage. To think of an innocent like her exposed to the sights, smells, and sounds of Marshalsea...it was unthinkable. He shuddered to think what Isabel would feel if she were witnessing it.

He knocked on two doors before a woman was able to direct him to the room Hetty was boarding in. He stood before the door she indicated and let out a deep breath, trying to relax his facial muscles. Hetty would likely be terrified already from her experience—she didn't need to see Charles in anger.

A tall woman with disheveled, mousy brown hair, filthy clothes, and hollow eyes opened the door to his knock.

"I'm looking for Hetty Robson, please," he said softly.

The woman said nothing, only opening the door wider and pointing to the corner of the small room.

Hetty sat on top of a small bed, huddled in the corner with her arms wrapped around her legs and her head resting on her knees. Two more women sat on the only other bed in the room, watching Charles with disinterest.

The dirt on the timbered floor muffled his steps as he walked over to Hetty.

"Hetty." He said her name gently.

Slowly her head came up. Her face was dirty and tear-trailed, though the tear tracks had dried. It took a moment before she seemed to register who was addressing her.

"Mr. Galbraith?" Her voice cracked, and she cleared her throat.

Charles thought he would never forget the pitiful image before him. It was no wonder Isabel had been so affected at Hetty's sudden departure from the Cosgrove house if she witnessed the same hopeless look staring at him from the girl's eyes.

"What are you doing here?" she said.

"I've come to take you away from this place." He extended his hand to her, but she didn't move. "Hetty? Did you hear me? I'm taking you away from here." He beckoned again.

"You can't take me," she said, not even looking at him. A single tear dropped down her cheek, darkening the dirt as it trailed down. "I can't pay my debt."

Charles dropped his hand. "What debt?"

"The one they imprisoned me for."

Charles sat down on the edge of the bed. "What happened? How did you come to be here?"

More tears began to flow, but Hetty's voice remained level, and she stared at the wall. "Mama and Mr. Farrow brought me. He promised he would use his influence in society on Mama's behalf if she would claim I had stolen from them. And then he gave her thirty pounds with a promise of more for later if she kept quiet."

Charles's hands clenched. "And what of a trial?"

Hetty's head shook slowly from side to side. "Mr. Farrow paid the man to ignore the lack of a trial. He said my name needn't even be recorded."

Charles inhaled deeply, but his heart pounded, and he could feel the veins in his neck standing out as the blood pulsed through. "Come." He stood, taking her by the hand and pulling her toward the edge of the bed gently but firmly. "We are leaving."

Hetty didn't resist, but nor did she seem to believe him, based on her lack of energy. Her eyes still had the same defeated look.

The three other women in the room watched as they left, shutting the door behind. They passed through the courtyard, the smell of sewage growing as they neared the door of the prison. The turnkey looked up as they approached.

"This young woman," said Charles, "was wrongfully imprisoned, and she will be leaving with me."

The young man drew back, clearly unaccustomed to such forthright language from those passing through the gate. A mulish expression appeared on his face. "She'll not be leaving on my watch, sir. The only prisoners as leave here for good is them as has paid their dues."

Hetty tugged on Charles's arm. "Never mind, Mr. Galbraith. I shall just go back." She tried to turn away toward the courtyard, but Charles didn't move, keeping a firm hold on her arm.

His eyes stayed trained on the young turnkey. "Then I suggest that your superiors arrange for a proper trial where those dues can be determined—if any such dues exist, which they do not."

The corners of the young man's lips turned down, and he scratched at his cheek. Charles was fairly sure he had intimidated the young man. It was time to strike while the iron was hot. "Because Miss Robson was wrongfully imprisoned through bribery and corruption, she has not received, nor is she likely to receive, a trial."

The turnkey folded his arms across his chest. "Them as brought her in had said she owes a debt of five pounds."

"And yet," said Charles, "if you were to look at the fastidious records no doubt kept by the men who run the prison, you would find no such record on the ledger."

The young man looked shaken by the logic presented, but he tightened his folded arms. "I don't know the particulars, sir. I only know that I can't let her leave without paying the five pounds."

Charles reached into his pocket, pulling out a five-pound note. He held it in the air with raised brows. The young turnkey looked at it with hungry eyes.

"And to whom would she pay this supposed five-pound debt if there is no formal record that she owes it?"

The turnkey's eyes shifted back and forth between the note and Charles's face. "I suppose," he said slowly, "that I could arrange it all for the young miss if she was agreeable?"

Charles nodded and moved to hand the note to the young man only to suddenly pull it back from his reach.

The turnkey's eyes widened, a hurt look in them.

"And what assurance does Miss Robson have that you will truly 'arrange it all,' as you say?"

The man put a hand to his chest, staring back at Charles with the energy and sincerity of a child. "On my honor, sir. I knows just what to do to tidy it all up."

"If I find," Charles said, walking up to the turnkey and looking down on him, "that you have not followed through, you will receive a second visit from me. And rest assured that it will not be so pleasant."

The young man shook his head frantically. "There'll be no need, sir. I swears it."

Charles's mouth broke into a large grin. He handed the five-pound note to the young man and clapped him on the shoulder amicably. "Thank you. You've done a good turn today, my friend. I won't forget it."

The turnkey looked at the note for a moment, swallowing and licking his lips, then glanced around before placing it in his pocket. He nodded at Charles and Hetty then unlocked the gate for them to pass through.

They stepped out onto the street just outside the prison's border wall, and Hetty let out a sob as the door clanked shut and the key turning in the lock sounded.

"Thank you," she said, her hand over her mouth.

Charles grimaced and put a reassuring hand over the arm linked with his. "I am so sorry, Hetty. You should never have experienced such a thing."

She continued to cry, and he handed her a handkerchief. "But they will bring me back!"

Charles shook his head adamantly. "They won't have the chance. I hope to arrange things for you so that you will be rid of Mr. Farrow. As for your mother, you would only need contact her if you desired it."

"Really?" Every bit of the earlier hopelessness in her eyes had been replaced with an equal measure of hope.

"Yes," he smiled at her implicit trust in him. "But it will take some arranging. I will take you to Isabel until everything is in order."

Hetty began to cry again, this time with a smile on her face.

She had been through quite an ordeal, and it was natural and understandable for her to express it all through tears. But Charles felt exhausted. He clearly wasn't cut out for high-strung females like Hetty.

18

Paxton looked at Isabel with an impassive countenance. "Mr. Galbraith is here to see you, Miss. I've shown him into the morning room."

Isabel blinked rapidly. She had not been expecting any visitors, and definitely not Charles. When he had said he would be in touch, she had assumed that he would send a note if he had any news of Hetty.

She dismissed Paxton and rubbed her lips together with a large intake of breath. Her interaction with Charles the day prior had been...confusing. She had been blue over Hetty's sudden departure, and she had not known how to react to the intimacy of the interaction they had shared. It had felt so real and yet so contrary to what they were working toward.

When she opened the door to the morning room, she stopped in her tracks. Hetty stood next to Charles.

She rushed over and wrapped her arms around Hetty, looking up at Charles with gratitude and wonder. She knew an impulse to wrap her arms around him next, but instead she only whispered, "How?"

The half-smile he had been wearing was replaced by more of a grimace. She nodded her understanding. He would tell her more about it when he could.

"I have a few matters to arrange on Hetty's behalf, but she cannot, as you know, stay with me. I hope this isn't a problem, though. If it is, perhaps Miss Holledge could take her in for a night or two?"

Isabel wrapped an arm around Hetty's shoulders and squeezed her. "It is no problem at all."

"Are you sure, Izzy?" Hetty said, looking up at her with anxious eyes.

Isabel's dimple peeped through. "I'll have you know that even Anaïs has been blue since you left. She has taken to muttering in French even more than usual, and, what's more, I saw her attempt that new coiffure you tried on Cecilia the other night—the one she criticized so heavily."

Hetty laughed, and Isabel went to ring the bell. "I would like to be present when she sees that you've returned. I'm sure you'd like to clean up a bit and perhaps have something to eat?"

Hetty's eyes widened, and she nodded quickly. "Yes, please."

The door opened to reveal Paxton, and Isabel instructed him to fetch Anaïs. She arrived shortly, opening the door and standing with her hands clasped in front of her as she looked at Isabel for instruction.

Isabel only smiled, waiting for her to see Hetty.

Anaïs' gaze shifted to Charles and then to Hetty, and her eyes ballooned. She hastened toward her with all the grace of a French-woman, hugging her and saying, *"Mais quelle surprise!"* and contin-uing in French too rapid for Isabel to understand.

Isabel looked at Charles, who blinked slowly as he listened to the French maid babble away.

Hetty stood stunned for a moment, clearly unprepared for the suddenly-warm treatment she was receiving. "English, Anaïs. English!"

Anaïs's chin came up. *"Jamais. Le français, c'est la langue des anges."* She paused and then said in slow and heavily-accent English, "Engleesh eez a language of —" she sputtered "—cows."

Isabel laughed as she glanced at Charles's stunned expression. "Anaïs, will you please make sure that Hetty has a chance to clean up and eat some food?"

Anaïs nodded, wrapped an arm around Hetty, and began to scold her in French for the filthy state of her clothing. The door closed, and Isabel found herself alone with Charles.

"Remind me never to employ a Frenchwoman," said Charles, still staring wide-eyed at the door.

Isabel laughed out loud. "If you say that now, I wonder what you would have said to see her before Hetty's departure. The two were always at one another's throats, disagreeing on every detail of Cecilia's and my toilettes. But Hetty has found her way into the hardest of hearts in this house." She gestured for him to take a seat. "But come, tell me how it comes to be that she is here."

She knew that it was not at all *comme il faut,* as Anaïs would say, for her to entertain Charles alone. But what about their relationship had been *comme il faut?* Besides, she needed to speak to him in confidence.

Charles shrugged and let out a breath as he sat. "It is not a happy story. It is even more diabolical than you had feared." He relayed to her his interaction with Mrs. Robson and then his experience at Marshalsea. Her horror grew as she listened to him recount it all.

When he finished, she sat in stunned silence for a moment, staring at nothing in particular. "I don't even know what to say." She looked at Charles, who was watching her with concern.

"That's not entirely true. I do know one thing I wish to say," she said. She paused and took in a breath, looking into his eyes intently. "Thank you." The words seemed so feeble compared to what she felt.

"It was nothing," he said, waving a dismissive hand as he shook his head.

"It was not nothing to me, Charles." She shook her head. "You went to much trouble for Hetty."

He looked at her with an almost blank expression. "I did it for you just as much as I did it for Hetty," he said.

Isabel's lips parted. She clamped her jaw shut. He didn't mean anything by it. At least not what she had hoped he meant. They had become friends, had they not? Friends helped one another when they were in need, and that is what he had done. "You are a true friend," she said, smiling at him through the bittersweet emotion she felt.

For a moment, it seemed as if anger or hurt flashed in his eyes, but it was gone as soon as it came—if it had truly been there at all. Whatever the expression was on his face after, it was unreadable to her. "I hope we shall always be friends," he said.

Isabel thought of the future. If they could always be friends as they were now, she might have agreed with him.

But it would not always be as it was now. He would marry Miss Darling, and to continue their friendship then would be a choice to willfully inflict physical pain on herself each day. What need would Charles have of her then, anyway?

She smiled wryly. "Wouldn't that be wonderful?" He looked ready to inquire her meaning, so she rushed to add, "I won't forget what you did, and neither will Hetty."

She shook her head as she thought on what Hetty had been through over the past day and a half. "What kind of people would throw their own child to the wolves for such reasons and for such a paltry sum of money?"

Charles grimaced. "Thirty pounds? Much like thirty pieces of silver, isn't it? So, someone with the heart of Judas Iscariot, I suppose."

Isabel stood and shook her head, blinking slowly. "Indeed. But Mrs. Robson had set her sights on marrying Hetty to Mr. Farrow."

Charles shrugged. "Perhaps she saw Hetty as a sacrifice for the greater good of her family. Besides, I imagine Mr. Farrow can be quite convincing when he chooses to be."

"Menacing, more like," Isabel said. "He is more dangerous than you know." She glanced at Charles.

Charles's frowned. "What do you mean?"

She wrung her hands as she paced. Could she tell him what she had learned from Mr. Safford?

No, she couldn't betray the rector's confidences. The more people who knew, the more likely Mr. Farrow was to obtain the information he needed to find the will. "I can't say more than that, but please believe me when I say that he is capable of doing harm to anyone who stands in his way."

Charles drew back in his chair. "Can't say more?"

Isabel sat down and folded her hands in her lap, looking down at them and feeling conflicted. He had done so much for Hetty—didn't he deserve to know? But she couldn't in good conscience tell him without first asking permission from Mr. Safford. "It is not my secret to tell," she said, gripping her lips together.

His eyes were tight as he looked at her with incredulity. "What are secrets when Farrow poses a danger to people?"

Isabel's head snapped up, her body stiff. "People," she said softly. "You mean Miss Darling?"

His returning stare challenged her. "Is it wrong to be concerned for her safety? Surely she doesn't deserve to suffer due to unnecessary ignorance."

Isabel swallowed, speaking slowly. "You believe she is entirely ignorant of Mr. Farrow's character?"

Charles stood, his eyes hard. "Yes. I know Julia."

Isabel turned her head away. Hearing him defend Miss Darling made her stomach tie itself in knots.

Perhaps he was right, though. Perhaps Miss Darling was unaware of Robert Farrow's true character. And if that was so, she deserved to be made aware. Besides, this could be what they had worked for all along: the proof that would lead Miss Darling to let go of Mr. Farrow and reconcile with Charles.

"No one who is innocent should suffer needlessly," she said, staring at the wall. "But if telling someone's secret puts them in greater danger, how have we solved anything?"

Charles said nothing, his jaw moving left to right as he stared at

Isabel. His thick, dark brows made him look particularly angry. She couldn't stand to look at him, knowing he was upset with her.

"In any event, Hetty must be kept safe from Mr. Farrow," she said. "And if her parents insist on having dealings with him, they are every bit the danger that he is."

Charles walked toward the window, looking out it as he responded. "I will be sending a note to the Robsons' instructing them to stay away from Hetty. I believe I made Mrs. Robson to feel that I was in earnest. As for Farrow—" his jaw clenched shut for a moment "—I must find a way to ensure he understands that his dealings with Hetty are over."

Isabel shook her head. "You have done enough. The information I have will keep Mr. Farrow away from Hetty. Let me arrange that side of things."

Charles's head came around. The anger was gone, but the frown remained. "If Farrow is as dangerous as you say, threatening him will only put you in harm's way."

Isabel smiled wryly. At least he seemed to care for her safety, too. "I will make sure he does not know my identity."

Charles took in a deep breath, not looking entirely convinced. But he seemed not to have an alternative plan and simply nodded.

Once he had taken his leave, Isabel's arms fell to her side limply. She sat down on the settee, her eyes glazing over. The way she had been affected by Charles speaking of Miss Darling told her that she had let herself hope far too much after their interaction in the churchyard.

She could have sworn there was something between them there. But no. Nothing had changed. His sights were still on Miss Darling.

Charles rubbed his forehead as he sat in the library, reading over the letter he had written to Mr. Solomon Abbott. It was a waste of time, really. Of course the man would have no interest in assisting Hetty, knowing the particulars of her situation. But he was running out of ideas.

He stood up and walked over to the window. He needed to get out of his own head. When had things become so tangled and confusing?

His visit to Belport Street with Hetty had left him in a strange state of frustration and worry. But unraveling toward whom those feelings were directed had been perplexing. Was he worried for Julia or Isabel? Or both?

Why had Isabel's comment about him being a true friend hurt him? It made no sense to take offense at a compliment. Nor had she meant ill when she had suggested that perhaps Julia didn't need to be informed about the danger Farrow was.

And yet Charles had been bothered by the insinuation. The Julia he knew wouldn't have anything to do with a man like Farrow if she knew. But how well did Charles know Julia anymore? The amount of time she passed in Farrow's company seemed ample to show her what a rake he was.

He rang the bell and then picked up the stack of papers in front of him, tapping them on the desk to organize them neatly, and setting them in the top drawer.

Charles instructed the footman to have his horse made ready—perhaps a ride in the park would do him some good. Fresh air, a change of pace, and conversation to redirect his thoughts.

Once he had changed clothes and was mounted on his horse, he headed in the direction of the park. He would likely see any number of people there. Julia made a habit of strolling in the park at this time of day.

He took in a large breath at the thought of seeing her. Time in her company always left him feeling confused now. He had hoped that more time with her would bring about a change in her, that the woman he had loved for so long would return in full force. So far, though, he had only caught glimpses of that woman.

Sure enough, the park was full of ladies and gentlemen walking and riding. He ran into a number of acquaintances, though, before he spotted Julia and her mother, strolling arm in arm down the lane ahead of him with their backs to him. He gave his horse a gentle nudge and trotted up toward the Darling women. Dismounting when he caught up with them, he greeted them both.

The skin around Julia's eyes wrinkled as she recognized him, and his heart skipped a beat to see her smile. She was so much more beautiful with that genuine smile than with the arch one she often wore in society these days. It was the smile from their days at home; the one he had fallen in love with.

He led his horse by the reins, walking alongside Julia. Mrs. Darling stayed silent, letting the two talk and laugh, as they reminisced. Charles hadn't felt in such charity with Julia since the beginning of the Season. She seemed to be in an agreeable mood, and he couldn't help but admire her beauty as she threw her head back in laughter again and again.

Charles's brows jumped as he noticed Mrs. Darling falling back behind them. It was a gesture which Charles appreciated, but it surprised him. Mrs. Darling had been the most vocal opposition to the prospect of them becoming engaged before Julia's Season.

Julia seemed to notice his observation, and she smiled. "Mama looks more favorably upon your suit now than she did at the beginning of the Season."

Charles drew his head back a bit and offered his arm to Julia. "And why is that?"

Julia's smile became more forced. "Oh, she does not approve of my association with Farrow. She thinks I am ruining my chances with other eligible gentlemen by spending so much time in his company. She believes that my reputation has suffered and that you are the best we can hope for now."

"Very flattering," Charles said grimly.

He thought of what Isabel had said. Perhaps she had a point— Julia's mother at least seemed to think Farrow was not the sort of character her daughter should consider eligible for marriage. Surely whatever reason she had for thinking that would also be known to Julia.

"And what do *you* think?" he said, turning his head to watch her.

"I think," she glanced back at her mother with a smile and leaned closer to Charles, "that my mother has any number of antiquated notions."

Charles looked down to the ground, pursing his lips. He wasn't sure how earnest Julia was. She seemed not to take her mother's reasons seriously. But how much did she know? And how much did her mother know or guess?

There had always been something off-putting about Farrow— perhaps his arrogance. So, when Charles had learned of Hetty's predicament—and that it was at the hands of Farrow—his dislike of the man had been cemented.

If Farrow had done the honorable thing and taken responsibility for Hetty, perhaps he could have overlooked his actions. But he had not taken responsibility. He had taken advantage of Hetty's youth and naïveté and then left her with nothing. It was despicable. And his role in sending her to Marshalsea? It was outside of any bounds.

This was the man Julia was allowing to court her. She couldn't possibly know how black his character was.

"I admit," Charles said, "that I, too, dislike seeing you in his company."

"Jealous, Charles?" Julia said with a teasing look.

"Perhaps," he said. "But more than that, I don't trust him. He is not who you think he is, Ju."

Julia laughed. "You think you know him more than I?"

He looked over at her as if he could gauge how much she knew by simply looking at her. Surely, she couldn't treat the things that Farrow had done with such levity if she were aware? "Perhaps," he said slowly, "he has only let you see the side of himself that he wishes you to see."

"Good heavens, Charles," she turned her body toward him with an incredulous look, "What has Farrow done to set you so at odds with him? Aside from courting me."

Charles's jaw shifted from side to side. How was he to explain everything to her? "It is nothing fit for a lady's ears."

"Ah," she said, turning away from him with a smile. "You mean the women of easy virtue Farrow keeps company with?"

Charles drew back, and she laughed when she saw his face. "Surely you can't be so prudish, Charles, to begrudge Farrow his adventures."

"Adventures?" His expression was pained, his brows drawn together. "I don't think that the pain he has left in his wake can accurately be described as an adventure, Julia."

Julia looked at him with a patronizing smile. "Charles, if I were as fastidious as you seem to think I should be, I should have no prospects at all for marriage."

Charles shook his head. "You hold far too low an opinion of the male sex. Even if Farrow is in the petticoat line, no gentleman worth the title would prey on innocents nor leave them uncared for."

Julia's chin went up, and her lips pursed. "These women you speak of should perhaps take more care to guard their virtue."

Charles could think of no response. It seemed Isabel hadn't deserved his offended reaction when she had implied that Julia was aware of Farrow's character.

This wasn't the Julia he knew. But he had to believe that she would feel differently if she knew the details of the situation. If she had seen Hetty in distress as he and Isabel had, she would have done the same thing Isabel did. Wouldn't she?

Julia nudged him playfully. "Oh, Charles. Do stop being so very serious. Besides, if you are trying to convince me that you are a more eligible husband than Robert, you will have to do better than that. He is very wealthy, you know." She gave him a significant look. Her eyes still teased him, but he was in no mood for it.

He drew away from her. "Since when did such concerns matter to you so much? Whatever his wealth, I shouldn't have to convince you, Ju." He looked her in the eye. "I would care for you in a way Farrow isn't capable of, even if he has more money. I think you know that. And if wealth is more important to you than that—" he shrugged his shoulders and stared ahead "—then I wish you well."

There was a pause before Julia said, "And what of your muse?"

Charles's brows snapped together. "My muse?"

"Miss Cosgrove, of course," she said with an eyebrow raised.

He opened his mouth and then shut it. Yes, what of Isabel? He could tell Julia that his relationship with Isabel was just a result of her *own* rejection of him—a means to an end, no more. But was that true? Perhaps it had been at one time.

Besides, Julia was supposed to question Charles's affection for her. That had been what they had wanted all along, wasn't it? For Julia to believe Charles was falling in love with Isabel Cosgrove.

"It is true that I hold Isabel in great esteem," he said. And it *was* true. "She is unlike anyone I know—selfless, caring, loyal."

"Well," said Julia in a clipped voice, "she sounds a terrible bore, just as I had suspected."

Charles's half-smile appeared as he stared at the ground they were treading. "Quite the contrary. She has an unexpectedly keen sense of humor." It was one of the things he best loved about Isabel—she was amusing without even realizing it.

He looked over at Julia—her eyes stared forward, hard and bright, and her nostrils flared slightly.

Her expression changed suddenly, and she moved closer to him, reaching up to brush something from his face. He blinked rapidly at the abrupt change in demeanor and the intimate gesture. She was as confusing as ever.

"What was that?" he said, the corner of his mouth turning up in a curious and surprised smile.

Her gaze shifted to the side and then back, and she looked into his eyes with the coy smile he had grown to despise. "You had something on your face." She was closer to him than ever, keeping the entirety of their upper arms locked against each other as she turned back to face the path. "Ah," she said with a large smile, turning at the approaching group of people.

20

When Isabel had seen Charles and Miss Darling up ahead —followed by a woman she could only assume was Miss Darling's mother—she had hoped to pass by unnoticed. The two were turned toward each other, after all, and sharing a moment which looked to be intimate. Seeing it made Isabel feel sick, and she had turned her head away, addressing a remark to Mary and Hetty to avoid observing anything more. She felt ridiculous as she thought on the moment she and Charles had shared in the churchyard.

Miss Darling had definitely noticed her though—the furtive glance she shot in their direction as she reached up and touched Charles's face was evidence of that.

Charles, on the other hand, was oblivious to their approach until Miss Darling turned and called their names. They had no choice but to return her smile and stop, while Mary said through her clenched, smiling teeth, "Don't let Miss Darling get to you, Izzy. She means to provoke you."

It was only what Isabel should have expected. It meant that the plan was working: Miss Darling felt threatened by Isabel. A part of

Isabel could even feel for Miss Darling—the fear that she might be losing the man she loved to another.

The groups exchanged greetings, and Isabel forced herself to meet the eyes of both Miss Darling and Charles. The last thing she needed was for Charles to realize the truth: that she didn't have to pretend at all anymore; that her smiles for him were genuine; that she had been miserable after their last meeting, knowing that he was upset with her; that she was in love with him.

If there was one thing that could increase the obligation he felt toward her, it would be the knowledge that she was fast beginning to wonder how she would ever find joy outside of the relationship they had formed.

And to allow Miss Darling to sense the jealousy or inferiority Isabel struggled against in her presence—it would be to undo much of Isabel's work.

Miss Darling never broke arms with Charles as she greeted the group. Her eyes landed on Hetty, and Isabel couldn't help but bite her lip as she saw the competitive gleam which came into Miss Darling's eyes in that moment. Hetty, on the other hand, was characteristically open and guileless.

She extended a hand to Charles, saying, "I was about to embrace you, but I have been sternly informed by Izzy that it is not at all the thing, and that I must not go about embracing gentlemen."

Charles's lip twitched and he caught Isabel's eyes. "She is quite right," he said as he shook hands with Hetty.

Isabel watched Miss Darling send an elbow into Charles's side, indicating with a significant look that she wished to be introduced to Hetty.

"Ah," Charles said, "Miss Darling, let me present to you Miss Hetty Robson."

Hetty smiled and curtseyed, while Miss Darling inclined her head slightly. "Are you a relation of Miss Cosgrove's then?" Miss Darling asked.

"Yes," Isabel chimed in. "She is my father's cousin's daughter. Visiting from up north."

"And what of you?" Hetty said, unaffected by the daunting reaction. "Are you a relation of Mr. Galbraith's?"

Isabel stiffened slightly. It would only be a matter of time before Miss Darling could respond that she was Charles's wife.

"No," said Miss Darling, looking up at Charles with an arch look. "But we have known one another since childhood."

"Oh dear," said Hetty with a self-censuring grimace. "I am forever making foolish mistakes like that. I thought that Izzy and Mr. Galbraith were married when I first met *them*."

"Mrs. Darling," interjected Mary, drawing a grateful look from Isabel, "I understand that your oldest son has just bought a commission?"

The subject changed, and Isabel found that she, Hetty, and Miss Darling were left to converse amongst themselves. Isabel wondered what she could say to this woman who seemed to have taken her in dislike and who obviously looked down upon Hetty.

Miss Darling spoke before she had time to consider, turning toward Hetty and saying with an overwrought smile, "You mentioned your relationship with the Cosgrove family, Miss Robson. How do you come to know Charles?"

"Oh," Hetty replied with the extra measure of energy which always permeated her voice when she spoke of Isabel or Charles, "I met him at the same time as I met Izzy. He is the most obliging and kind gentleman I know. I owe him my very life!"

Isabel put a hand on Hetty's shoulder, hoping to quell her enthusiasm and the dangerous direction the conversation seemed to be taking. "Yes, Charles has been very good to you, hasn't he?"

Miss Darling's smile became even more brittle. "To be sure, Charles has always been one to show kindness to the young ladies neglected by everyone else." Her bright eyes flitted to Isabel as she spoke.

Isabel felt her cheeks heat up, but she smiled back at Miss Darling.

"He seems to be very kind to you," Hetty said.

Isabel's eyes widened. She glanced at Hetty, but there was no trace of impudence in the expression she directed at Miss Darling. Had she intended to put Miss Darling in her place?

Isabel cleared her throat. "You mentioned that you grew up with Charles?"

"Yes," Miss Darling said, her gaze lingering on Hetty for a moment before she pulled it away to meet Isabel's eyes. The brilliant blue eyes held a challenge. "We have always been on very close terms, naturally, and we always shall be, I hope."

How did she manage to make a smile seem so full of hostility?

"Hmm," Hetty said.

"What is it?" Miss Darling replied.

"I am just surprised," Hetty said, the picture of innocent confusion. "Surprised that, close as you are, I have never once heard Charles speak of you. Not in all the times he has come to visit Izzy."

Isabel's jaw went slack, and she grabbed Hetty's arm before Miss Darling could strike back. "Oh!" she cried, looking down the lane, "I see Lord Brockway, and I have been meaning to ask after his mother." She inclined her head at Miss Darling with the most genuine smile she could muster. "Please excuse us, Miss Darling. It was a pleasure." She tore Hetty away from Miss Darling's reach and tapped Mary on the shoulder to inform her that it was time to go. Isabel smiled at Mrs. Darling and Charles as she put a firm hand around Mary's arm, guiding her away as Mary made her excuses.

"Wait," Charles said. He took two strides over to Isabel, bringing him back in front of Miss Darling.

Isabel looked at him, waiting for whatever he had to say while she tried to ignore Miss Darling as she laced an arm through Charles's and stared at Isabel.

"I had been meaning to speak with you," he said. Isabel said nothing, and his eyes darted to those surrounding them. "No matter, though. I will wait upon you instead."

Isabel avoided Miss Darling's eyes determinedly, nodding at Charles with something between a smile and a grimace, and leading Mary and Hetty away.

"Good heavens, Izzy," Mary said as she tried to keep up with the persistent forward tug of Isabel. "What was the meaning of all that?"

"Perhaps you should ask Hetty," Isabel said with a mouth trembling as she tried to stave off a smile. She nudged Hetty with an elbow and looked at her.

Hetty held her chin high. "It was high time someone gave that woman a set-down. She is quite odious, trying to make you look silly, Izzy."

Isabel gripped her lips together and tilted her head to the side. "I'm sure she is not an odious person. It is only because she feels Charles's regard for her threatened by my presence."

"Oh, Izzy," Mary chimed in, "you are too charitable, if there is such a thing. Mama has always said that it is not the circumstances which are to blame for a person's rudeness; the circumstances simply bring existing rudeness to light."

They quickly came upon Lord Brockway, approaching them at the front of a small group of people. On his arm was a petite young woman who seemed to frequently look up at him with warm eyes. Isabel thought he looked happier than she had seen him in ages. He was relaxed, and there seemed to be a lightness to his step as he came upon them.

He came to a stop in front of the three women, greeting them in his customary polite way. The rest of the group who had been following behind Lord Brockway walked around him and continued on their way.

Lord Brockway looked down at the young woman on his arm and said, "Miss Bernard, allow me to introduce you to Miss Holledge, Miss Cosgrove, and Miss Robson. Miss Bernard is only recently arrived from the Continent where her father was stationed for some years."

Isabel's eyes shifted to Lord Brockway's, a significant look on her face. Was this the young woman he had mentioned at the menagerie?

He met her look with an almost imperceptible incline of his head, confirming her suspicions. She smiled at him and greeted Miss Bernard with a friendly smile.

They didn't tarry with the two for long, not wishing to keep them from the company who had gone on ahead of them, but when Isabel said farewell to Lord Brockway, it was with an expressive look, indicating her approval of Miss Bernard.

"Well," Mary said as they walked away, "if those two haven't tied the knot by Michaelmas, then I know nothing of love."

"Yes," Isabel said, "I believe you're right."

"Happily for them." Mary glanced at Isabel. "Not so happily for you, though, Izzy."

Isabel took in a deep breath, staring at the hem of her dress as it shifted with her moving feet. "Indeed, it does make things more awkward for me. But I am very happy for Lord Brockway, and perhaps it will help Cecilia learn a valuable lesson." She tried to make her voice sound light as she added, "Charles and Miss Darling look to be well on their way to burying the hatchet and reconciling." She saw Mary look at her through the corner of her eye and kept her eyes on the path ahead.

"Izzy," said Mary with suspicion in her voice.

Isabel looked at her, eyebrows up, affecting ignorance. "What?"

Mary sighed. "And I suppose you are every bit as happy for them as you are for Lord Brockway and Miss Bernard?"

She leaned away, looking at Mary with disbelief. "Why should I not be? It is what we have been wishing for all along."

"It is decidedly not what I have been wishing for all along," replied Mary, turning her head away from Isabel.

"Nor I," said Hetty.

Isabel's throat felt tight, and she felt the back of her eyes burning. She forced a laugh. "Good gracious! Whatever can you mean?"

"You know, Izzy," Hetty said prosaically, "You think that you are acting kindly by encouraging Mr. Galbraith to marry Miss Darling. But it is not at all kind to encourage someone as good as he is to marry someone as bad as she is."

Isabel's head whipped around to stare at Hetty who seemed to be suddenly full of wit and wisdom. She glanced at Mary, wondering if she, too, was surprised by this new side of the wide-eyed young woman they had taken under their wings. Mary was not smiling, though. She was looking at Isabel with a straight face and raised brows, as if challenging her to respond to such a home thrust.

"Perhaps, Hetty," Isabel responded. "But Charles is a grown man. He is very capable of determining what is best for himself. Besides, even if Miss Darling is not the most fitting wife for him, it does not necessarily follow that I am."

"It does for anyone who has spent any time around the two of you," said Mary flatly.

Isabel's mouth opened to respond, but she closed it again. Her heart was beating fast, and she felt desperate to change the subject while also wanting fiercely to ask Mary what she meant.

A sharp intake of breath erupted from Hetty. "Oh dear," she said as she scooted in toward Isabel, lowering her head with eyes darting up toward the path ahead and then back down to her feet. "This was a terrible idea. I should not have come!"

Isabel and Mary exchanged confused glances and then looked ahead. Isabel's heart skipped a beat. Mr. Farrow was riding toward them on a gleaming chestnut.

"Don't fear, Hetty," said Isabel in a low voice. "We will not acknowledge him, and he may pass by. Don't give him the satisfaction of seeing your fear. We will keep you safe. Charles promised, remember?"

Hetty seemed to calm slightly at the words, but Isabel could feel her arm trembling.

Of course, it was ridiculous to think that Mr. Farrow would do anything in the middle of the park in the afternoon, but the man was unpredictable and determined enough to set Isabel on edge. Why had she insisted that Hetty accompany them to the park without the escort of a gentleman? She had wanted so much to treat Hetty to an outing she would enjoy after spending so much time in the house.

Isabel had little hope that Mr. Farrow would pass by them, and she watched uneasily as his gaze came to rest on Hetty. His eyes widened, his nostrils flared, and his jaw clenched.

He reined in his horse, and his eyes lingered on Hetty as he nodded his head at the ladies in greeting. He seemed to be attempting a smile, but the top of his lip was raised in an unmistakable sneer.

"Ah, Mr. Farrow," Mary said in a sweet voice, breaking the strained silence. "What a pleasure to find you here on this lovely afternoon."

His eyes flitted to her, and he nodded with another attempt at a smile. "Yes, quite." His eyes moved back to Hetty. "Miss Robson, I confess that I did not expect to meet you here."

Isabel breathed a sigh of relief as she noted how collected Hetty looked. If she hadn't been able to feel Hetty's stiffness, she would have had no idea that she was anxious to be confronting Mr. Farrow.

Hetty smiled as she raised her brows politely and said, "Oh? Why not?"

Isabel took her lips between her teeth, fighting one desire to laugh and one to shake Hetty for her daring.

Mr. Farrow glanced at Isabel but otherwise kept his eyes trained on Hetty, "It seems you have found your way back to the Cosgrove family. How comforting it is to know where to find you in case I have need of you." His eyes threatened Hetty as his horse fidgeted underneath him.

Hetty shivered, and her smile faltered.

Isabel tightened her arm around Hetty's. Mr. Farrow clearly felt no compunction threatening Hetty in broad daylight with both Isabel and Mary as witnesses. She had no doubt that he would dare to have

Hetty followed or taken whenever the opportunity presented itself, so long as he thought it would safeguard him from the damage Hetty could do to his reputation.

Isabel could not allow him to think such a thing when she had ammunition to prevent it.

"We are likewise comforted in our knowledge of where to find you, Mr. Farrow," she said with a challenge in her eyes.

He seemed annoyed at the comment and made no response.

"Please make no mistake, sir" Isabel continued, "if I find that you refuse to leave Miss Robson alone, you can rest assured that hitherto-secret information will come to light, ensuring both your financial and social ruin."

Mr. Farrow's lips pulled back to bare his teeth, and his hands clenched around the reins. "Impossible," he spat out.

"Indisputable," Isabel countered, her cheeks warm to the touch. "You stand on thin ice, Mr. Farrow. I recommend that you do nothing to further compromise your position. Leave Hetty be, and she will return the favor, though it is far more than you deserve."

She began walking forward, pulling Hetty and Mary along with her. Both had to hasten to match her speed.

"Bravo!" cried Mary with admiration, looking back behind them after an admiring glance at Isabel. "I believe you've successfully confounded Farrow, Izzy. He and his horse are still at a standstill in the middle of the path."

"You were marvelous!" cried Hetty. She seemed completely energized.

Isabel took a deep breath but didn't slacken her pace.

She chewed her lip distractedly. She had grave doubts as to whether she had been wise to say what she had. Charles, for one, would be aghast at what she had done. Hadn't she promised him that Mr. Farrow would be unaware of her identity as the person who knew the information he wished to keep secret?

She only hoped that Hetty was indeed safer for the interaction.

21

C harles had just sat down for breakfast when he heard the bell to his lodgings ring. Who in the world would be paying a call at this hour? He trusted that Morton would turn away whoever it was.

He had only taken one bite of his toast when a knock sounded on the door.

"A man here to see you, sir," said the footman.

Charles noticed the absence of any calling card in the footman's hand.

"I told him you were not at home to visitors, but he requested that I let you know his name is Abbott."

Charles looked at his footman dazedly for a moment before clearing his throat and putting his napkin down. "Show him into the library, please."

He had written to Abbott, of course, and requested a response as soon as possible. He had not expected an answer, much less an actual call.

This meeting was bound to be quite an interesting one.

He took another bite of toast and a sip of ale before rising to walk to the library.

The man inside was tall enough to have to look down at the hands of the mahogany clock in the room, his hair a rich brown, and his expression grave. He betrayed none of the nerves Charles had expected to see, given their difference in station. His clothes were neat and simple, though obviously not well-tailored.

What kind of man was this Mr. Abbott, and what was the purpose of his visit?

"Hello, Mr. Abbott," Charles said, offering the man a seat in a gilt armchair.

"Very pleased to meet you, Mr. Galbraith," Mr. Abbott said without expression. He stayed standing. "Thank you for the offer, but I would prefer to stand. I know you were not expecting my visit, so I will keep it short."

Charles inclined his head. "I admit my surprise at receiving news of your presence, but I am glad of it, all the same. What can I do for you?"

"If you please, sir, I wish to know, in quite plain terms, what the situation is of Hett—" he cleared his throat "—Miss Robson. I believe I understood enough from your letter to infer how things stand, but I would like to be certain."

Charles looked at Mr. Abbott with a measuring gaze. The man seemed unflappable, nothing like that ignorant youth Charles had envisioned when Hetty had first spoken of her prior attachment to him. Charles had spent time around a fair number of untrustworthy gentlemen over the years. Mr. Abbott was very clearly *not* one of them. He was a bit stiff, surely, but Charles liked what he saw so far.

He spent a few minutes recounting his first and subsequent encounters with Hetty, what he had come to learn of her situation, and where things now stood.

Mr. Abbott stood motionless but attentive, no expression crossing his face but for a brief grimace upon hearing of Mrs. Robson's role and a pulsing of the vein in his neck when Marshalsea was mentioned.

"I wish I could say that I was surprised," he said when Charles had finished speaking. "When her mother informed me that they were moving to town and that I was not on any account to contact Hetty, I greatly feared what would become of her. She is naïve in the extreme and has always wished to please her parents. Allow me to express my gratitude to you and your friends for ensuring her safety when no one else would."

Charles executed a shallow bow.

"I have both the power and the desire to help Hetty, Mr. Galbraith. My financial situation is stable, though quite modest. But I love her very much, and I will take the best care of her I possibly can."

Charles cleared his throat and clasped his hands. Had the man understood him clearly? "Mr. Abbott, allow me to be plain with you. You do realize that Hetty is with child?"

Mr. Abbott nodded curtly. "I will certainly not be the first person to raise another man's child, sir."

Charles acknowledged the truth of the statement.

"Hetty doesn't deserve ruin," Mr. Abbott continued, "simply because she was too innocent to understand the malicious intentions of those around her."

Charles stared at the man in wonder. Behind Mr. Abbott's stoic façade, there was clearly a deep, abiding, and unselfish love that Charles found himself admiring.

"And what of obtaining permission from her parents?" he said. He doubted Mrs. Robson would consent to a marriage between her daughter and a plain, working man like Mr. Abbott.

"I believe I can persuade her father to agree to it. He is much more reasonable than his wife, and his is the permission I need. I shall obtain a license and ask that the banns be read at once. Then I shall return for Hetty and convey her to my mother's home."

Charles nodded slowly. "I should like to do something more to help you and Hetty. Allow me to pay for the license, Mr. Abbott."

Mr. Abbott seemed to hesitate. Likely it was a matter of pride for him.

"You will have plenty to do in caring for Hetty over the years," Charles continued. "Allow me this one gesture."

Mr. Abbott frowned but nodded. "It is very generous of you, sir."

Within minutes, Mr. Abbott had departed, leaving Charles to marvel at the man's cool and collected confronting of an unfortunate situation—and one he had no duty to involve himself in.

The contrast between Mr. Abbott and Mr. Farrow could hardly have been more stark.

Charles's mother would have greatly admired such a man. And Charles found himself in full agreement. He had no doubt Hetty would be well taken care of by Mr. Abbott, which was more than he could say of her parents' care.

❦

CHARLES STOOD in front of the mirror, his tongue between his teeth as he put the finishing touch on his cravat. Two crumpled cravats lay on the floor near his feet, and tiny beads of sweat were forming near his hairline.

He let his arms drop to his sides and examined his work through narrowed eyes. It would have to do. It was rare for him to retie a cravat, but his fingers had been unreliable and impatient all morning. He shrugged on his blue coat and took in a deep breath. The carriage and his horse would likely be waiting outside.

The ride to Belport Street was undertaken at a brisk pace, but Charles was glad for a few minutes of reflection. Things had been going well with Julia the past few days. While she was still to be seen in Farrow's company more often than Charles liked, she seemed to be equally as interested in Charles's company once again.

The frustration Charles often felt in her presence he ascribed to lingering feelings of bitterness or resentment at the way things had been handled since the Season had begun. Julia continued to say things that Charles often found tasteless, disappointing, or even cruel, but it was reasonable to expect that the effects of London and Farrow would take time to wear off.

She had let drop several hints that she would welcome a more assertive courtship on Charles's part. On one or two occasions, she had even spoken of a future together as if it were a foregone conclusion. Charles had been surprised to find that such comments had made him feel anxious rather than elated or confident.

He found himself wondering how Isabel was faring. Was her father pestering her about a date for a wedding? And what of Miss Cecilia and Lord Brockway? He had not seen them in company recently. In fact, the other night Lord Brockway had danced numerous times with an unfamiliar young woman. If it was evidence of an attachment forming, it would throw a wrench into Isabel's plans. Did she have an alternative in place in the event that Miss Cecilia didn't marry Lord Brockway?

He hoped that she was pleased with the arrangements for Hetty. He imagined that both Isabel and Hetty must have been as surprised as he was upon receiving his letter detailing the plans for the latter. Charles felt that there could hardly have been a happier result to the whole situation. He could only be grateful that he had written to Mr. Abbott against his better judgment.

He was shown into the morning room when he reached Belport Street and had only to wait a few minutes before the door opened to admit Isabel and Hetty.

Isabel's expression held a friendly smile as she walked in, but Charles thought he saw a hint of dark circles under her eyes.

Hetty looked glowing in a dress of pale pink muslin. She twirled as she approached Charles. "What do you think?" she said, indicating the dress. "Miss Cecilia gave it to me—says she didn't wear it above three times, so it is practically new!"

Charles's mouth twitched, but he tried to look as interested as

Hetty expected him to be. He knew that Isabel would appreciate the naive candor of Hetty and glanced at her. Her eyes twinkled as they met his, just as he had expected and hoped they would.

"You look very smart," he said to Hetty with a nod of approval. "Have you all your things? The carriage is waiting outside. My sister will greet you when you arrive at Wembley where you will remain with her until Mr. Abbott is able to convey you to his mother's home."

Hetty's expression became timid, a blush stealing into her cheeks, and she rubbed the fabric of her dress between two fingers. "I can hardly believe that I shall see him again! I never thought to."

"You are very fortunate in him, to be sure," Charles said. His eyes traveled to her bare head. "But where is your bonnet?"

"Oh," Hetty said, looking around her for the bonnet. "How silly of me! I shall go fetch it." And with that, she scurried out of the room.

"Is your sister truly prepared," asked Isabel with an indulgent smile lingering after Hetty, "for the impetuous and unaffected Miss Hester Helena Robson?"

Charles chuckled. "I have done my best to prepare Jane for Hetty's personality, but some things must be experienced to be understood."

Isabel clasped her hands together, lightly twiddling her thumbs and looking at Charles with a frown. "How ever did you convince Mr. Abbott to accept Hetty? To marry her?" She shook her head, bewildered. "I am sure it has been no small ordeal for you to arrange it all."

Charles set his hat down on a side table, shaking his head. "I admit that I was at point non-plus for a few days, but circumstances suddenly combined in a very serendipitous way. Mr. Abbott appeared at my door one morning—I had written to him of course, but I had no expectation of a response. He was shockingly composed and unruffled upon hearing Hetty's story and himself declared his intention of marrying her. It seems that they had every intention of marrying prior to the Robsons arrival in town, had Mrs. Robson not intervened.

"He told me that he only needed a bit of time to make arrangements. And as if I had not already sustained enough surprises for one day, that very same evening, my sister Jane visited and offered her assistance until Mr. Abbott is able to convey Hetty to his home. She is involved in a society for the betterment of unfortunate women, you know." He took in a large breath and shrugged his shoulders.

"Divine providence," Isabel said with wondering eyes.

"I am inclined to agree with you," Charles said.

Isabel looked at him with her candid, direct gaze. Her eyes held that same sincerity he had come to appreciate. "Thank you again for —" she took in a breath, seeming to search for a word "—saving the day. Having Hetty's affairs arranged has relieved a great burden from my mind."

He wasn't surprised to discover that Isabel worried for Hetty. She seemed the type of person who likely worried for others a great deal, though she managed to maintain an appearance of placid confidence. The circles under her eyes, though, betrayed that façade for once.

"I'm sorry not to have been able to arrange things sooner." He pursed his lips. "But come, has something in particular increased your worry on her behalf?"

Isabel didn't respond for a moment. "Only that I fear what Mr. Farrow might do."

Charles's brows snapped together. The mention of Farrow's name never improved his mood, but it rankled even more than usual since Isabel's refusal to trust him with whatever secret she knew of him. He resisted the desire to revisit the debate, though, instead saying, "I still can't say that I feel comfortable with your plan to warn him against any interaction with Hetty. If he is as dangerous as you say he is, he will not like to be threatened."

Isabel averted her gaze, her cheeks reddening. What had he said to elicit such a reaction?

"I will feel more at ease," she said, "when she is at your sister's. Have you told anyone else?"

"No," he said, shaking his head then rearing back slightly. "Good heavens, do you think Farrow would really follow her all the way to Wembley?"

Isabel paced, her hands still clasped in front of her. "I don't know. I believe he would harm her if he could. She threatened him, you know, so he fears that she will parade the baby around along with his name. Much is at stake for him, and I haven't felt at peace knowing that he can find Hetty here as easily as he did a few days ago."

Charles frowned. "How should he know to find her here? He believes her still to be at Marshalsea, I imagine."

Isabel's eyes flitted to him and then away again, but she didn't respond.

"Doesn't he?" Charles asked. Receiving no answer still, he kept his unblinking eyes on Isabel. "Does he have reason to believe otherwise?"

Isabel stopped pacing, wiping her hands down her dress as she looked at him with fear in her eyes.

The door flew open.

"I'm terribly sorry," Hetty said in a breathless voice, a chip straw bonnet and its ribbons dangling from her hands. "I had set my bonnet upon the bed when I came down the stairs but found it to be missing when I returned. I was obliged to go find Anaïs only to discover that she mistakenly packed it into my valise, thinking that I had forgotten to do so."

Charles glanced at Hetty for a moment as she spoke, but his eyes returned to Isabel. She had again turned her gaze away, though, and was looking at neither him nor Hetty. He squeezed his hands into fists, feeling strangely infuriated that Isabel's normally-frank demeanor had somehow been replaced by mistrust and secrecy. If she sensed real danger, how could she not tell him?

"Hetty," he said, trying to muster a smile, "if you would please make sure that all of your belongings are in the entryway, I will join you in a moment."

Hetty's eyes shifted back and forth between him and Isabel, the energy which she had brought with her on entering completely faded. She seemed to understand and then nodded and walked over to Isabel.

"How I shall miss you, Izzy!" Her hands and bonnet hung awkwardly at her sides until she suddenly threw her arms around Isabel and buried her head in her chest.

Isabel wore a sad smile as she returned the embrace. "We shall write, of course."

"I would like that," Hetty said as she pulled away. She put a cupped hand on her rounding belly. "If it is a girl, I shall name her Isabel."

Isabel's lips pursed, and she brushed away a tear.

Hetty turned to Charles. "And if it is a boy, I shall name him Charles."

Charles had been watching the interaction with appreciation, but such a comment caused his jaw to slacken and his eyes to blink in rapid succession.

Hetty only smiled at his reaction, turned to Isabel with a sigh, and then left the room.

Watching the interaction between Hetty and Isabel had softened Charles's frustration. Whatever reason Isabel had for keeping her own counsel, he didn't desire to guilt her into telling him. He only wished that those confidences would be given freely.

Her face looked drawn and tired, and he couldn't help but move toward her.

"Isabel," he said gently. "I can tell that you are troubled. Can you not relieve whatever burden you carry by sharing it?"

Isabel looked at him, and her eyes were filled with...what was it? Pain? But she made a valiant attempt at a smile. "You have already relieved a burden, Charles." Her eyes flitted to the door Hetty had gone through.

"Then surely I can manage a little more?" He reached out toward one of her hands which hung at her side, but as his fingers met hers, she pulled them away, clasping her hands together.

His stomach lurched, and he dropped his hand. What had he

been thinking? She didn't wish to confide in him—why would he assume she would wish for comfort from him? Their entire relationship had grown out of one goal: her desire to avoid a future with him. He was forcing himself on her.

He took a step back, swallowing, and then manufactured a smile. "Forgive me. I should go help Hetty into the carriage."

He turned on his heel and left.

🪰 22 🪰

Isabel's eyes stared blankly at the door Charles had gone through. Behind her impassive face, though, her emotions warred.

Every interaction with Charles became more haunting to her—a reminder of what she wanted but could not have. It made her sorely regret his presence in her house that fateful night and her own naïve offer to help him win back Miss Darling.

Guilt pinched at her for not being honest with him about her interaction with Mr. Farrow. She hadn't been able to bring herself to tell him what had passed between them at the Park. To do so would have been to draw his ire, to wipe the smile from his face in exchange for the thick, furrowed brows which made him look so intimidating.

With Hetty gone from Belport Street, though, the only remaining threat from Mr. Farrow was to Isabel, and Charles need not concern himself with that. He was not bound to protect her, after all. And she did not want him to feel duty-bound more than he already did.

A general and persistent anxiety loomed underneath all her other emotions, ready to temper any happy moments with a reminder of her increasingly-desperate situation. The part of her plan integral to her own happiness was floundering; things seemed to be at an end between Cecilia and Lord Brockway.

Cecilia's moods reflected the emotional upheaval that it was causing her. She was by turns sullen and lively, though the latter moments had a brittle quality to them.

It seemed that Cecilia was trying to hide the emotions she labored through by appearing more energetic and animated than ever. Those moments were most often to be observed when she was in company, but Isabel watched with some sympathy as Cecilia's demeanor changed drastically when she thought no one was watching, falling into fits of abstraction.

Whatever suitors Cecilia had imagined to be both superior to Lord Brockway and ready to make an offer for her, they had proven to be more interested in flirtation than in any more serious courtship.

But Cecilia would never admit such a thing.

Without the prospect of a brilliant marriage for Cecilia, Isabel had to face a difficult reality: her future was in her father's hands. She had little hope that he would show any more mercy to her now than he had previously.

If anything, he would be furious at her dishonesty besides being even more set on the marriage than ever, having accustomed himself to the idea. To take that away from him would be to rob him of something he had come to think as rightfully his. He would not sit quietly; he would exert all the pressure he could manage onto Isabel and Charles to force them to marry.

Isabel shuddered as she thought of such a confrontation between Charles and her father. She knew that Charles would honor his word in such a scenario, and that it would mean throwing away the future with Miss Darling which seemed now to be at his fingertips—it would make him a martyr.

Isabel thought she could face anything if it meant avoiding that.

She could throw herself on the mercy of her father, hoping for the minute probability that he would understand. She had to at least try.

She raised up her shoulders with a large breath and then exhaled, moving with determination toward the door. From Paxton she learned that her father had asked for the carriage to be pulled around so that he could visit Brooks's, but that he could currently be found in the book room. Isabel hesitated a moment. It might be wiser to wait to speak with her father until he had returned from Brooks's. She had no idea, though, when that might be. Some days, he stayed there until dawn. She couldn't wait that long.

She knocked lightly on the book room door, feeling her heart beat rapidly in her chest, and stepped into the room.

Her father looked up from his desk chair as he placed a stack of papers into one of the drawers.

"Ah, Isabel," he said, standing up and smiling at her. "I have been meaning to have a word with you." He placed a stack of papers in a drawer and then looked back toward her. "Even if you and Galbraith wish to put off the wedding—though why a dead woman should have anything to say about such a thing, I don't understand—I believe it will be better for us to make all the arrangements we can now."

Isabel hesitated before taking a slow step forward and placing a hand on a nearby chair back. "What sort of arrangements do you mean?"

Her father put his hands and fingers together, looking down at a paper on the desk and straightening it with one hand before clasping his hands back together. "Oh, only the usual things: when to have the banns read, settlement talks—nothing you need worry your head over. Galbraith and I can arrange the details. But perhaps you and your mother can begin making preparations for the dinner party where the engagement will be announced."

Isabel took her lips between her teeth. This was not a promising start to the conversation. But it was a conversation that must be had. "Father." She stood behind the armchair, feeling more confident with its mass standing between her and him. "I'm afraid that such a discussion with Charles would be a waste of time."

"Don't be silly, Izzy," he said with a chuckle. "These things must be discussed at some point." He waved a hand. "But I should not have even said anything. It is not a matter for women to worry their heads over—leave it to us." He reached for his hat and cane. He was obviously under the impression that the conversation was over.

Isabel's grip tightened on the leather chair back. "Please don't make me marry him, Father."

His head snapped up. "Eh?"

She clasped her hands together in front of her chest, looking at him in the eye. "I know it is a great wish of yours to see us married, but please—" she shook her clasped hands in a pleading gesture "—it is not what Mr. Galbraith or I want. It would be to consign us both to a state of misery and—"

"Stop." Spit flew from the corner of Mr. Cosgrove's mouth, and his face was mottled red and white. "Ungrateful jade." His voice shook. "You had no prospects of marriage until I arranged this extremely providential union for you, and you dare to ask me to undo it all? To agree to your living out the remainder of your life hanging upon my sleeve?"

Isabel's nostrils flared. She should have anticipated that he would react by making her out to be a thankless child. He could never face his own selfishness, always casting blame upon those around him.

Her voice was quiet and calm when she spoke, staring down at her splayed fingers. "A providential union? Providential for whom, Father? Not for Mr. Galbraith. And though it must seem strange to you, I can assure you that it is not providential for me."

"Listen to me," her father said, grabbing her arm with a white-knuckled hand. "You will marry Galbraith as agreed or you will be a stranger to this family—unrecognized and unwelcome."

Isabel stared forward, not meeting her father's hard stare. "Like Aunt Eliza?"

He slapped her across the cheek. Her eyes stung, and her cheek burned.

"You dare speak her name in front of me?" he spat. "Take her as evidence that I speak truth when I tell you that you *must* do as I say."

She swallowed and nodded once.

Her father thrust her arm from him and stormed from the room.

ISABEL CLASPED AND unclasped her hands, sitting on the cool wood pew and feeling the rector's gaze on her. She had come in hopes of gleaning wisdom from him and calming her anxious and confused mind and heart. She needed reassurance that she had chosen the right path, even if it meant dishonor and disownment for herself.

"And Mr. Galbraith does not know that things are at an end between your sister and Lord Brockway? Or that you face being disowned if he does marry Miss Darling?" he asked.

Isabel didn't look up, only shaking her head. She repressed a desire to squirm under the rector's gaze. She had not set out to willfully deceive Charles, but it had become impossible to avoid. What was worse? Withholding information from him or taking away a future of joy?

"Does Mr. Galbraith have any idea of your feelings?" the rector asked gently. He sat in the pew in front of her, his body turned and his arm resting on the back of the bench.

"He must," Isabel cried softly. "I have tried to conceal the truth, but I believe I have done an ill job of it."

"Ah," said Mr. Safford, nodding his head. "Therein lies the problem, child." He took the Bible from his lap and handed it to her, nodding toward it. "Open it. The eighth chapter of the Gospel of John, verse 32."

Isabel looked at him with skepticism in her eyes but obediently opened the book and searched for the New Testament.

"What does it say?" Mr. Safford asked.

Isabel put a finger on the page of Chapter 8, searching the verses until she came to the right one. She read aloud, "'*And ye shall know the truth, and the truth shall make you free.*'" She looked up at Mr. Safford with incredulity on her face. "You think I should tell him?"

Mr. Safford smiled at her expression and nodded.

What he was saying was not at all what she had come to hear. She had come for reassurance from him that she was doing right. Seeking the happiness of others was more important than her own happiness, wasn't it? She stared at the page, her stomach knotting.

The verse was wrong. If Charles knew the truth, it wouldn't set him free. It would bind him. It would take away the happiness he was so close to. His sense of duty would demand that he sacrifice himself for it—sacrifice himself to save Isabel from the future she faced if she didn't marry him.

She closed the Bible with a snap and jumped in her seat, surprised by the violence with which she had shut it. She sent an apologetic glance at Mr. Safford before saying, "The truth is impossible."

"It is not," he said. "What if the truth changed things?"

"It would change everything," she argued. "But it would not be a change for the better. Do you not see? For Charles to know the truth would mean one of two things: rejecting me for the life he truly desires or, much worse, making a martyr of himself to save me. I may be in pain right now, but to tell the truth would only add to my pain *and* to his. That cannot be right, surely?" She let out a large breath. "What I want cannot be. It is as simple as that."

"How can you be so certain of that?"

Isabel laughed harshly. "Quite easily. The first time we spoke alone, I asked Charles if he still wished to marry Miss Darling, despite their falling out. He confirmed that he did indeed wish it; that his feelings for her remained unchanged. Everything we have done since then has been a result of his desire to marry Miss Darling."

"Or," said Mr. Safford with raised brows, "perhaps things are not now as they were then. Why not be sure? It might be as simple as asking the same question you asked him before."

Isabel clenched her teeth. There was nothing simple about asking if he still wished to marry Miss Darling. To be sure, it was easier than confessing everything to Charles, putting herself undeniably open to rejection, risking the weight of obligation that the truth would crush him with.

"The alternative," continued the rector, "is to spend the rest of your life wondering what would have happened if you hadn't concealed the truth; wondering if you made the right decision. You have to live with the results of this situation every bit as much as does Mr. Galbraith. It will affect you in much more drastic ways than it will affect him. I do not think that a desirable path for you, child."

She stared down at the Bible in her hands, turning it so that the gold letters on the cover caught the light and gleamed. Would she wonder for the rest of her life? There had been moments with Charles when she had questioned what he felt for her, whether there was something more than common regard or friendship. But what did it matter when both Charles and she worked toward a common goal: reuniting him and Miss Darling? Would he not have told her if his desire to marry Julia had changed?

But he had never communicated anything like that to Isabel; those moments could not have meant what she wished for them to mean.

"I will just say a final word before I leave you to your own reflections," the rector said. "I applaud you for your desire to bring happiness to those around you, no matter the cost. I have never doubted your warm heart, child, and I think God is pleased by your desires. But is your happiness less to God than is the happiness of Mr. Galbraith? Or of Miss Robson or Miss Darling? I don't believe so. Perhaps your heart is troubled in part because you have not allowed its full expression and honesty. Your conscience urges you to rectify that.

"So, tell the truth to Mr. Galbraith, difficult as it may be. Tell him of your regard, for love is never wasted—it begs to be expressed. God made us thus. I cannot promise that the truth will lead to the outcome your heart now desires. But I believe that it will ease some of the burden you are carrying and will allow you to move forward with confidence. Have faith in God, put your trust in Him that the truth will set you free in the way that He sees fit to free you. He works in mysterious ways."

He set his hand over hers with a gentle squeeze and then stood, leaving her to her thoughts which were every bit as muddled as when she had first arrived at the church.

What the rector said made some sense. Why was it better to sacrifice her own happiness in favor of Charles's happiness? And was it truly right to deprive him of the truth in doing so?

Whatever the case, Mr. Safford had given her permission to tell Charles of Mr. Farrow's desperate situation. He had received no response to the letter he had sent his nephew and had determined he would wait one more day before taking action with the will.

Isabel felt relieved that she could at least share that much with him, though it would very likely remove any doubt at all from the question of Charles's future with Miss Darling. With Mr. Farrow removed as competition, there was only one plausible path for Miss Darling: marriage to Charles.

Isabel stared at the east window. She held powerful information, and for a moment, she considered keeping it to herself; letting the chips fall as they may between Charles and Miss Darling without any further meddling from herself. She shut her eyelids for a moment then shook her head and lowered it to look at her clasped hands. She couldn't do that. Her conscience wouldn't allow it.

But perhaps it was the last thing she did need do. Armed with the information about Mr. Farrow, Charles had everything he required from Isabel. She could confidently leave things in his hands with no further obligation to punish herself by spending more time in his presence, by strengthening a regard which was not returned.

She straightened suddenly. Knowing what needed to be done, she felt an urgent need to act. There was no reason to wait, to postpone the inevitable. With Lord Brockway's newfound love and with things as good as arranged between Charles and Miss Darling, her future was essentially decided. She would no longer be at home. She would have to decide upon a way to support herself.

She smiled wryly as she thought of the position Hetty had nearly sought as lady's maid and how desirable such a situation might seem to Isabel in a week's time.

Most urgently, she would need a place to live—a roof over her head and food in her stomach. Her father's temper was volatile enough that he might well expel her from the house as soon as he discovered that she had no intention of marrying Charles, even if he intended to try to force the issue upon Charles himself. It was best to be ready with a plan.

Mary Holledge came to mind only to be dismissed quickly. Once it was known that Isabel had been disowned, she could hardly take refuge within society. Her marriage prospects wouldn't improve upon such a thing becoming known, as it inevitably would be. Nor did she wish to bring problems to the Holledge family by her presence. She would have to look elsewhere for refuge.

Aside from her brother Tobias, who was undoubtedly off kicking up larks with his friends, all of Isabel's relations were in town for the Season. Except one.

Isabel traced the letters on the Bible with her forefinger. The last time she had seen Aunt Eliza, Isabel had been a young girl. For years, Aunt Eliza had been the favorite aunt and a regular face among the Cosgroves. Isabel's memories of her were fond ones—picking daffodils together in the early spring, conspiring with her and Cecilia to neglect their needlework in favor of adventuring outdoors, teaching tricks to the dog.

But Aunt Eliza's name had been suddenly banned from the home after her decision to marry an artisan from the nearby village.

Cecilia and Isabel would sometimes whisper to one another when their father wasn't around, laughing as they remembered the times they had spent with Aunt Eliza, plotting to discover her whereabouts in order to orchestrate a secret visit.

It had only been years later that Isabel had discovered Aunt Eliza's whereabouts by accident, happening upon a note from Eliza to her father. Aunt Eliza and her husband were struggling to make ends meet with four young children in a small village outside of Colchester, and she was asking—begging, really—for any assistance her brother might lend. Isabel had never discovered whether her father had answered the letter, but she knew him well enough to guess that he had not. When she had gone to show the letter to Cecilia later, it was nowhere to be found.

Aunt Eliza would welcome Isabel with open arms. She had no doubt of it. But to seek refuge with her would be no small thing—it would be a burden upon Eliza's family, and it would put Isabel in a world very different from the one she had become accustomed to. Nor would she know anyone who could provide her with a reference if she wished to apply for work somewhere in the vicinity.

She inhaled deeply, setting her hands atop the Bible and willing her heart to calm itself. She would have to discover when the next Mail Coach would depart for Colchester and decide how much she could manage to bring with her. Her body shivered as she thought on the bleak future she faced. But it was no use to dwell on the difficulties she could not change. Nor was there time to write ahead to Aunt Eliza to forewarn her.

She stood, setting the Bible on the pew and brushing her skirts downward. There was much to arrange before a departure to Aunt Eliza's could be undertaken. The most urgent matter—and one she little relished—was to inform Charles of the information about Mr. Farrow. Such a thing could only be communicated safely in person. It wouldn't do to send a note with such a report—she needed to be sure that Charles—and only Charles—received it and could act on it.

She walked swiftly out of the church, down the stone steps, and through the courtyard and gate, rubbing her hands together as she walked in the opposite direction of home. What she was about to do was highly improper. But what did propriety matter? Such considerations seemed ridiculous in the face of the future she was confronting.

She signaled a passing hackney, instructed the driver where to take her, and stepped in with palms beginning to sweat. She would tell Charles everything she knew about Mr. Farrow. That was certain. Whether she would decide to follow the rector's advice and be fully honest about her own feelings was another matter entirely. Her heart seemed to pound more and more loudly with each street the hackney passed.

When the driver pulled in front of Charles's building, Isabel took a moment to compose herself, straightening her shoulders and neck. Perhaps if she looked in control, she would feel in control.

She took her lips between her teeth as she stepped up to the door, resisting an impulse to look around her and see whether anyone was watching her—a young, unchaperoned woman at the door of a bachelor. She pulled the bell.

The liveried servant who answered the door raised his brows upon seeing who sought admittance, but after inspecting her clothing and comportment, he seemed to be satisfied enough that he said he would check whether Mr. Galbraith was at home to visitors.

Isabel wiggled her toes in her half-boots as she waited, trying not to think about what Charles's servant must think of her showing up on his doorstep, unescorted, or how many of his servants would soon hear of the strange occurrence.

"Isabel!"

She looked up, surprised to see Charles instead of his servant. He beckoned her to enter, his eyes alert with worry. "Come," he said, leading her swiftly through the entry hall and toward one of the few doors leading off the landing at the bottom of the staircase. He closed the door behind them, offering her a seat on one of three chairs in the room.

"Is something wrong?" he said as soon as she had taken a seat.

She shook her head quickly, hoping to allay his fears. "That is, nothing is urgently wrong. But I needed to speak with you on a matter of business—" she swallowed, debating whether to add anything "—and on a personal matter."

He pulled one of the empty chairs toward her, sitting so that his knees were only inches from hers.

She readjusted in her seat, angling her own knees to the side and tucking one foot under the other. She looked up, meeting Charles's earnest gaze.

His hair was slightly disheveled as if he'd put a hand through it one too many times, and he appeared to have loosened his cravat, probably not expecting any visitors. The subtle unkemptness of his appearance sent a wave of sadness over her. There was so much of Charles that she wished to know better, and yet she sat in front of him, keenly aware that she might never see him again.

He sat waiting for her to elaborate, an intent look in his brown eyes.

"You remember, I'm sure," she said, "when I told you that Mr. Farrow is extremely dangerous."

He grimaced in response with a curt nod.

"I was unable to elaborate at the time simply because I had been told everything in confidence. I know it was upsetting to you to find me so uncommunicative after making such a claim."

Charles put up a hand. "I should not have pressed you as I did."

She smiled appreciatively. "I understand why you did, and I'm sorry I couldn't tell you then what I will tell you now. Mr. Safford has given me leave to communicate the entirety of the situation to you. I hope it will allow you to take the necessary action to protect those you love." She cleared her throat after saying the last word, her eyes flitting away from his for a moment.

Charles's mouth turned down in a frown. "What has the rector to do with Mr. Farrow?"

"Everything, it turns out." She took a deep breath and tried to concisely but clearly recount what the rector had shared with her about Mr. Farrow's relationship to him, the violent turn Mr. Farrow's visit had taken, and the existence of the secret will, left by the rector's estranged brother. She watched as Charles reared back in his seat twice and his eyebrows took turns raising up and knitting together.

He let her speak uninterrupted, and when she had finished, he sat with his elbows resting on his knees and his clasped hands covering his mouth.

"You see," Isabel said slowly, "why I have been so concerned for Hetty's safety." She paused and kept her eyes on him, wondering if his mind had already jumped to Miss Darling. "And why I think it important for you to have this information, even now that Hetty is taken care of."

His head came up. "For Julia's safety, you mean?"

Isabel nodded. "For her safety, first and foremost." She readjusted in her seat and cleared her throat. "But I think that it may also be the final card you have needed."

His head tilted to the side slightly. "What do you mean?"

Her hands fidgeted. She felt reluctant to explain her meaning. Surely he had already seen the hand fate had dealt him? When she spoke, it was in a softer voice than she was accustomed to using. "Once Miss Darling understands the character of Mr. Farrow, she will naturally lose interest in his attentions, leading her to...." She trailed off as she saw his eyebrows snap together.

He stood up hastily. "I have no desire to win Julia's hand in such a way. To be chosen by default." He shook his head quickly.

Isabel stared at the carpeted floor. "You want her heart."

Out of the corner of her eye, she saw Charles turn his head to look at her. His hand paused in the act of stroking his chin distractedly. "Yes," he said simply. "To marry her without it would be worse than to lose her."

Isabel smiled wryly. "I understand."

She looked up, and their eyes locked for a moment. With both hope and dread, she wondered whether he sensed the meaning behind her words. His eyes never wavered from hers.

"I have never asked you," he said, "whether your own affections are engaged."

Isabel swallowed. "What do you mean?"

His arms fell to his sides, and his shoulders came up slightly. "From the beginning of our acquaintance, you have been very driven to release us from the duty to marry one another. I thought perhaps the reason was that there is someone else whom you wish to marry."

Isabel's eyes began to sting, and she blinked rapidly, taking a steadying breath. If there was any time to tell Charles her true feelings, this was the moment.

"Or perhaps you have taken me in greater aversion than I realized." His tone was one of sad humor, and it twisted her heart, so much did she desire to refute the suggestion.

She chose her words carefully. "My wish has always been that you could marry where your heart led you."

"And for you to be able to do the same?" he suggested.

She smiled unevenly, but her brow was drawn. She didn't trust herself to respond. "In any case, you may do what you will with the information I have armed you with. I believe, though, that my role in all of this has played out. I can confidently leave you to arrange everything and wish you all the best in your future with Miss Darling." She smiled at him, but he only chewed his lip, staring down near her feet.

"And what of you?" He looked up at her.

"What of me?" she said with an attempt at a lighthearted shrug of her shoulders.

"Is everything arranged for a union between your sister and Lord Brockway, then?"

She gripped her lips together, and the words from the Bible flitted through her head. *The truth will make you free.* What if she could only manage a portion of the truth? "I believe Lord Brockway's offer to be forthcoming." She swallowed, disliking the way her stomach clenched. The words themselves were true, but she had used them to make Charles believe an untruth.

He nodded and then said, "Very well. But I cannot, in good conscience, allow you to communicate the news of our situation to your father. It was an agreement between him and me. I must be the one to inform him of the breach."

"No!" Isabel said, straightening in her chair with a tense hand on each of the chair's arms. If Charles spoke to her father before she had left, her father would undoubtedly attempt to force the marriage by demanding Charles abide by the terms of their agreement. All of her sacrifice would be in vain, and they would be back where they started.

No, she needed Charles to wait. By then, she would be gone, and her father would be in possession of a note explaining everything. Charles would bear no blame.

Charles reared back on seeing her reaction. "I must insist on this point, Isabel. It is a matter of honor."

Isabel clasped her hands together in pleading, "I understand. But I beg you to wait a few days before doing anything. He must not hear from you before things are arranged for Cecilia. Surely you understand."

He nodded his assent though he looked grave. "And you are sure that he will be satisfied by Miss Cecilia's marriage to Lord Brockway? That you will not be adversely affected by all of this?" He looked at her expectantly and seeing her pause, he said softly, "I know that you have no desire to marry me, Isabel. But I couldn't bear to discover that you had been made unhappy as a result of this entire mess I've created."

She could feel his eyes on her, but she couldn't bear to meet them.

"You are sure that this is what you want?" he asked.

Something about the note in his voice brought her eyes up to his. What was that gleam in his eyes? Was it sadness?

She nodded in response—it was all she could manage, and it somehow felt less dishonest than saying the words aloud.

Her response was the truth, in a way—this *was* what she wanted. And yet also so far from what she wanted. She *would* be adversely affected by it all, but perhaps the knowledge that her own suffering had made his happiness possible would buoy her up in the days to come.

He seemed so grave as she looked at him. But why? She needed to know that there was meaning to her sacrifice.

She hoped the smile she put on was convincing. "How do you feel? Being so close to attaining the happiness you have wished for all this time?"

He ran a hand through his tousled hair. "Strange, to be honest. Not at all as I apprehended I would feel."

It was not the answer she had expected. And it was one that, left to itself, might give her hope that she had no right to feel. "Perhaps," she suggested, "you won't be able to truly exult until you are engaged to Miss Darling?"

"Yes," he said, seeming to consider her words. "Perhaps you are right." He stood straighter, more confidently and smiled his half-smile. "It will all feel right when everything is finally arranged, when I've heard Julia reassure me of her love."

Isabel shot up from her seat to leave, not sure she could bear to hear more. She had heard enough. Charles was still consumed with the desire to have Miss Darling's affection again—he was obviously struggling with the anxiety and anticipation of achieving a long-held goal. And how could he not have Miss Darling's affection after all? She would have to be a simpleton not to love Charles.

Her feet felt rooted to the spot. How could she leave, knowing she wouldn't see his face; knowing that she couldn't explain to him, say a proper goodbye?

"Was there not a personal matter you wished to speak of?" Charles asked, coming out of a reflective state.

Isabel's heart pounded as she looked at him. *Love is never wasted,* the rector had said. Surely he was right. But did love have to be expressed in words to be shown? Wasn't the show of her love the fact that she was allowing Charles to have the life he wished for rather than the life that his honor would require of him if he knew the whole truth?

"I..." she stammered. To her horror, she felt her chin begin to tremble and her eyes sting.

Charles's brow furrowed, and he came toward her, holding both hands out to receive hers. "What is it? What's wrong?"

Her hands hung at her sides, and he picked them up gently,

causing her heart to beat erratically for a moment. He searched her eyes, and she smiled weakly at him.

"It is nothing," she said, trying to store up the feeling of her hands enclosed in his.

Anger seemed to flash through his eyes momentarily, and he let go of her hands. "If you say so," he said, turning away.

She moved toward the door, and he followed, turning the handle and opening it for her. His jaw was set tightly when she looked at him a last time.

"I wish you every happiness, Charles. Goodbye."

❦ 23 ❦

Charles's jaw slackened as the door closed behind Isabel. He stood for a moment, staring with unfocused eyes at the wooden door before turning and sitting on the couch.

She had asked him how he felt being so close to attaining what he had hoped for for so long. And he had spoken truth when he had said that he felt strange. She had indeed given him the final tool to bring Julia back to him. Without Farrow muddying the waters, Julia was much more likely to give her undivided attention to Charles. She had, after all, made it quite plain that she still wished for Charles to court her, to win her hand back. Aside from Farrow, she had seemed to show only passing interest in the gentlemen who vied for her hand at balls, parties, and routs.

So why did he feel troubled? Was it, as Isabel had suggested, because he couldn't feel sure of the victory until it was truly had? Was it because, despite Julia's attention and flirtation, he couldn't be sure that her heart was engaged as it had been prior to coming to London?

That might account for some of his feelings, but it didn't explain everything. When Isabel had claimed that her part had been fully played in their act, he had felt an impulse to suggest one more endeavor together, a reluctance to put an end to the arrangement they had. Were those feelings simply a desire to ensure that Julia understood that he was not simply waiting for her, hoping for her to choose him? But wasn't that exactly what he was doing?

He shook his head, running a hand through his hair. In any case, he needed to make Julia understand that Farrow was a reprobate. She could not be left ignorant. If Farrow truly faced the financial difficulties Isabel mentioned, he would be foolish to let Julia slip through his hands with a dowry such as she would bring to marriage.

He took his pocket watch out, realizing that he had less time than he thought before he was set to meet Julia and her friend in the Park for a stroll. He rang the bell, requesting his horse be made ready, and then trotted up the stairs to his room to make himself more presentable.

He took the most direct route to the Park, going as quickly as was feasible in the traffic of the London streets. He was anxious to find Julia, hoping that being in her presence would reassure him that the chips were falling into place the way they should be. He found Julia, her maid, and her friend Miss Burton standing under the shade of a large tree—Julia's favorite in the Park.

He dismounted, greeting the group, and leading his horse to a nearby bush where he looped the reins around one of the larger branches. The horse seemed contented to nibble on the available grass.

He stepped toward the three women, and Julia immediately slid her slender arm into his with a wide smile and an upward glance. It was the same way she had looked at him for years—the look that had made his heart stop and then thud. But after observing her direct the same look toward Farrow a number of times, it had lost much of its effect upon him.

"I'm so very glad to see you, Charles," she said, pulling him along to walk in a large circle around the base of the tree. "It feels an age since I saw you."

He looked down at her with a half-smile. "I saw you only two days since."

"An age," she reiterated with a teasing smile. "I depend upon you not to let it happen again."

"What? Let a day pass without seeing one another?" he said incredulously.

She nodded.

"That is a tall order, Ju. I don't know that it is achievable. We didn't even see one another daily before coming to London."

"Oh, but Charles, anything is possible if you but have the will." She looked up at him expectantly. "Do you have the will?"

His lips parted, and he stared back down at her, a thousand memories flooding his mind as he looked into her lash-framed blue eyes.

"I think," she said matter-of-factly, "it might be accomplished quite easily, you know. A simple visit to my father would do wonders in setting us upon that path." She pursed her lips to suppress a smile, but her brows wagged up and down once.

Charles's own brows lifted. Julia had always been driven, never shy to state what she wanted. His heart quickened slightly as he considered what it meant to have her suggest such an action. Was this it, then? What he had been hoping for?

He thought of what a visit to Mr. Darling would entail. The Season wasn't over, after all, and that had been a main stipulation of the Darlings when he had been forbidden from paying his addresses to Julia. Mr. Darling had also been clear that he thought Julia could do better. With Farrow's old family name and the estates they owned, he was just the type of person Mr. Darling would likely welcome as a suitor for his daughter.

"Ju," Charles said, stopping and turning to face her, "I need to tell you something. Something important."

Julia tilted her head as she looked at him, her arch smile appearing again. "I already know," she said.

Charles blinked. "Know what?"

"That you love me," she said, lifting her shoulders. "Everybody knows."

He was momentarily diverted from his purpose. His jaw shifted from side to side. "What do you mean by that?"

"Oh, come, Charles! It is quite obvious that you wished to teach me a lesson. I can't say that I admire your decision to choose Miss Cosgrove as the instrument of your plan—there are plenty of other lovely and eligible ladies who would have served the purpose better— but—" she put up her palms in a gesture of surrender, accompanied by a little laugh "—you win."

Charles's brows were drawn, his face in stark contrast with the humor written on Julia's. Anger made his veins pulsate, but he didn't know whether it was because she was so near to being correct or because she was also so terribly wrong.

It was true that he and Isabel had hoped to remind Julia of her regard for him. It was not something he felt particularly proud of. But he and Isabel had also been keeping up appearances for her father's benefit. Isabel had simply recognized the additional opportunity it might provide for Charles—killing two birds with one stone, in a way.

Julia's conceited treatment of Isabel, her assumption that she had been nothing but a puppet to Charles—it sickened him and made him feel sudden unease. Did Isabel feel that she had been a pawn to him?

He looked at Julia, frustrated by how out of charity he felt with her. It was so opposite what he had hoped to feel. Julia thought that it had all been a game.

"Julia," he said, shaking his head and rubbing his fingers across his mouth as he stared at the ground. "I must ask you to be plain with me. What is the nature of your relationship with Robert Farrow?"

She lifted her chin. "What right have you to ask me such a thing?"

"None," he said. "And yet I do ask you."

"And I," she said with brows raised, "refuse to answer you."

Charles jaw tightened. "So be it. But perhaps it will interest you to know more about Mr. Farrow. He is a depraved man, Ju; one who will stoop to any level to achieve his selfish ends."

Julia's eyes glittered. "You are unjust in your jealousy, Charles."

Charles shook his head, noting her crossed arms and overbright eyes. "It is true that I never liked to see you with him, Ju. But it wasn't just jealousy. And time has proven my suspicions correct."

"If you are still harping on Farrow's indiscretions, please have done, Charles. You are so very stiff." She raised a brow as she noted his rigid posture. "Perhaps it would do you good to follow in Farrow's footsteps a little. You take everything—including yourself—far too seriously."

He grimaced, remembering what she had said to him before his fateful card playing at the Cosgroves. "Surely you can't blame me for preferring the company of Mr. Farrow or Lord Nolan. You've become so preachy and dull of late that it is little wonder, I'm sure."

Would he always be made to feel inferior now that Julia had experienced more of the world? He had little desire to seek the type of female company she referenced, and it was not a good omen that she encouraged it. What woman whose heart was engaged would suggest such a thing to the man she loved?

"It is not Farrow's indiscretions that I speak of, Ju," he said. "It's the young woman whose naivety he took advantage of and then abandoned, refusing to acknowledge his responsibility or her claims upon him." He put up a hand as he saw a retort on her lips. "But we have spoken of that before and must simply part ways on that matter. What I want you to know is that that incident is far from the extent of Farrow's misdeeds. He has made and broken other promises—to his father, most importantly. And again, instead of facing the consequences or striving to rectify his wrongs, he chooses the coward's way out. Julia, he has even resorted to violence against innocents as an attempt to save his inheritance from the consequences of his broken promises and reckless lifestyle."

Julia's nostrils flared, her cheeks pink with emotion. "It is wrong to deprive a man of his rightful inheritance, Charles. Surely you would fight for your own fortune if the caprices of your dying father threatened to dispossess you of it? If a will truly exists which affects Farrow so nearly and terribly, he has every right to see it. You are entirely unjust."

Charles reared back. "You knew?"

Julia smiled, but the smile was devoid of either humor or affection. "Of course I know, Charles. Farrow is not the deceitful blackguard you seem to think him, and I do not condemn him for doing what he must to claim that which is rightfully his. You would do the same in his position, as would any man."

Charles took a step back from her, disbelief on his face. "If you truly think that, you don't know me at all."

"Perhaps not," she said, straightening her shoulders and lifting her chin. "Perhaps I don't wish to."

Charles's jaw tightened. "I will relieve you of my presence." He executed a stiff bow and turned back toward his horse still grazing a few feet away. Miss Burton and Julia's maid looked away awkwardly as his gaze met theirs. He bowed and bid them farewell, too angry to care that they had likely heard his exchange with Julia.

He hopped deftly onto his horse, giving the gelding full rein to canter across the fields of the Park, ignoring the prescribed walkways and the round eyes which followed his progress.

❧ 24 ❧

Isabel stood with a hand on each knob of her opened armoire, staring at the clothes within. She glanced back at the portmanteau laying on her bed. It was nearly full, despite the fact that she had only been able to choose a precious few garments to take with her.

She sighed, grabbing one of the sturdier, dowdier muslins she owned and closing the armoire. It was not a particularly fashionable dress, but it would be much more practical than her other dresses for the life she would be leading. She folded the muslin, placing it in the portmanteau and feeling grateful that she would at least be able to take the clothes on her back as well as what was in the leather case.

Next to the portmanteau on her bed sat a book, open to a listing of Mail Coach routes and timetables. Three sealed letters lay on the nightstand—one addressed to her father, one to the rector, and one to Charles. She eyed them and bit her lip. Once those were opened by their recipients, there was no turning back. There was nowhere to go but forward anyway.

The last item on her list of things to accomplish was a visit to Mary. When she had sat with the quill to a fourth piece of parchment, she hadn't been able to bring herself to write more than the salutation. A letter was simply inadequate to express what she wished to say to her friend. She knew she could rely on Mary's discretion, and she found comfort in the prospect of being able to unburden herself to someone.

She tied the white ribbons of her straw bonnet, stowed the portmanteau and Mail Coach routes under her bed, and went down the stairs to the front door. A servant opened it for her, and she thanked him, looking him in the eye and handing him a shilling. He took it with obvious gratitude in his eyes.

She felt a sudden and new connection with the servants, knowing that she could well be in a similar position soon. Any generosity she could show felt like an act of hope for her own future.

She stepped out into the bustling London air and looked around, feeling strangely free. It was only a temporary feeling. She was in a state of flux, feeling unbound by society's strictures and as yet unbound by weight of the new life she was about to embark on. It was liberating to decide upon a visit to the Holledge's without being obliged to request the company of a servant.

Isabel considered employing the service of a nearby hackney but decided instead to make full use of her freedom by walking to Berkeley Square.

As she walked the streets, she considered the many things she would have occasion to miss when she left the metropolis. The cacophony of sound which permeated life in London would surely be strange to leave behind—perhaps for the better, once she accustomed herself to falling asleep in relative silence. In truth, she preferred life in the country to town life—but life at a country estate was nothing like the life she would be leading as a working woman.

She jumped to the side as something splashed near her feet and looked up to see a woman disappearing from the window above. Isabel wrinkled her nose and picked up her pace. There would also be much she did not miss about London.

At the Holledge residence in Berkeley Square, Isabel was known enough that she instructed the footman not to bother announcing her. Mary was found to be at her needlework in the parlor, and she put it aside with no hesitation on seeing Isabel.

"How is this?" she said, looking down at the dirtied hem of Isabel's dress. "Did you walk here?"

Isabel nodded with a satisfied smile. "And what's more, I did it alone."

Mary's brows shot up, and she turned her head slightly as she looked at Isabel with squinted eyes. "You wouldn't dare."

Isabel shrugged and untied the strings on her bonnet, setting it on a chair. She took a seat on the sofa, still feeling invigorated from her walk.

Mary looked at her with something nearing concern. "What has come over you, Izzy? I never knew you to disregard such things." She came over and sat down, curling her legs up on the sofa as she kept her eyes on Isabel.

Isabel's smile faded slightly, and she sighed. "I'm leaving, Mary."

She spent the next ten minutes explaining everything to Mary, leaving out nothing, even the feelings for Charles which she hadn't expressed aloud to anyone but Mr. Safford. Even then, one spoke differently to one's rector than to one's dearest friend.

"Well," Mary said slowly, "first, I am not so stupid as to have been ignorant of the state of your heart, Izzy. It has been quite plain to me that you are in love with Mr. Galbraith. Second," she said, overriding Isabel's response with increased volume, "I think you are being excessively silly. Leave to go stay with your Aunt Eliza? A woman who is living the life of a poor villager's wife? Good heavens, Izzy! Where is your sense?"

Isabel shook her head impatiently. "I have no other option, Mary. Aunt Eliza is evidence of how little store my father sets by his family connections. You know that he finds his daughters a great burden and injustice. And I have enough pride to wish to take action on my own before he can throw me out with all the violence of emotion you know he will display."

"Then go to Holledge Place and live! I have always wanted a sister near in age."

Isabel grasped Mary's hand with a look of gratitude. "You are a true friend, Mary. And I promise that I have considered such a path. You were the first person I thought to go to. But it is not possible. Please don't try to dissuade me. I am very much resigned to my course, and I shan't be persuaded, much as it pains me to leave you. I only hope you will still correspond with me?"

Mary said nothing, her lips working and moving in the way that Isabel recognized as evidence of the fast work of Mary's brain.

"Mary," Isabel said suspiciously. "I am in earnest when I say you must not try to dissuade me."

Mary only smiled. "Oh, I shan't. I see that you must do as you say, if only because you are abominably proud. But naturally I will correspond with you as much as you can manage. When do you leave?"

"This evening by the Mail. It will take me as far as Colchester."

"Good heavens, so soon?"

Isabel nodded, and she watched as the same contemplative gleam came into Mary's eyes again. "I think," Isabel said slowly as she watched Mary's cogitations in suspicion, "that I must extract a promise from you before I leave."

Mary looked reluctant. "What kind of promise?"

Isabel regarded her with suspicion. "I know you well enough to recognize the signs of your strategizing, Mary. I don't know what you can possibly have in mind, but you must promise me that you will not try to interfere with my plans."

Mary pursed her lips and folded her arms. "Fine."

"Thank you," Isabel said, standing and brushing her skirts down. "I suppose this must be goodbye, then."

Mary laughed. "Nonsense. I am going to accompany you home. If I can only have but a half hour more of your company, I plan to take full advantage. I will have Budd send the carriage and my maid to convey me home. That way I will be back in time to dress for the Enfield's ball this evening."

Isabel had no objections to such a plan, and they set out for Belport Street, Mary chatting happily, and Isabel struggling against the feeling of loneliness and homesickness that began to creep into her heart as the prospect of leaving her best friend hung over her.

When they were let inside, the sun was lowering on the horizon. Isabel felt a burst of nerves as she realized that she had less than two hours before she would need to set out for Fetter Lane where the Mail Coach would depart. The two of them went up to Isabel's room with Mary prattling on about one of the *on-dits* she had heard from her mother over dinner the prior evening. Isabel only lent half an ear, running through a mental list of all the things she had already packed and the ones she might yet need to pack.

A knock sounded on her door, and she opened it to find Paxton holding a letter.

"This just came for you, Miss. I was told it is to be read urgently."

She thanked him and shut the door, inspecting the parchment with a furrowed brow before opening the seal. The handwriting was sloppy, clearly written in a rush.

Miss Cosgrove,

I plead with you to come without any delay.

Reverend A.R. Safford

Isabel's heart thumped in her chest, and she grabbed the bonnet she had just taken off, fingers fumbling to tie the ribbons.

"What is it?" Mary said as she observed Isabel's strange behavior.

"I must go to the rectory immediately. I am so sorry to leave you so abruptly." She took Mary's hands in hers and looked at her.

"Let me come with you," Mary said.

Isabel shook her head. "Thank you, my dear friend," she said gratefully, "but I must go alone. Besides, I think I must plan to go to Fetter Lane immediately from the church so that I don't risk missing the Mail."

She took the portmanteau and book from underneath her bed, ripping the relevant page out and putting it in her reticule. She glanced at the three letters sitting on the bedside table and took the one addressed to Mr. Safford, hesitating as she eyed the other two. Her father would naturally receive his letter when it was discovered that she was gone.

The letter for Charles, though, was a different matter. She took the letter firmly in her hand and looked at Mary.

"Can I rely on you to make sure this is delivered to Charles, Mary? Tomorrow will do. I need him to understand."

Mary nodded, taking the letter and saying, "I will ensure that he receives it."

Isabel looked at Mary with a large sigh then wrapped her arms around her friend, closing her eyes and brushing away two tears. She pulled away and smiled through her watering eyes. "I will write to you as soon as I arrive at Aunt Eliza's, and then you shall wish you had never been my friend with the constant letters from me for which you are required to pay the post."

Mary laughed. "I shall save all my pin money, then."

Isabel grabbed Mary's hand, squeezed it, and then picked up her things and left.

❧ 25 ❧

Charles slipped on his coat, his brows drawn together. He felt conflicted at the prospect of attending the Enfield's ball. He could hardly stand Mrs. Enfield or the giggling daughter she tried her hardest to thrust upon him. But Julia had begged him to come, saying with a teasing smile that it was the least he could do to atone for neglecting her shamefully all Season long.

That had been before their row yesterday, and he had nearly managed to convince himself that the altercation as good as released him from the promise. But in the end, he felt obligated to go, if not to fulfill the promise to Julia, at least to be as good as his word to Mrs. Enfield. If he didn't attend after assuring her that he would, he would be rebuked and guilted for weeks to come with tales of the many girls wishing for a partner to dance with.

Besides, he had hope that he might see Isabel there—a desire he had been preoccupied with since her departure the day before. It was just the type of gathering Miss Cecilia was likely to attend, so there was a chance that Isabel would accompany her.

When he arrived at the Enfield's, he sighed at the number of coaches and carriages lined up in the street, letting down their passengers and then struggling to turn around to make way for other equipages in the limited space available whilst the regular evening traffic carried on in the dirty streets. Mrs. Enfield was never known for hosting intimate gatherings when she could make grand displays to half the town.

He walked in just behind an elderly couple and eyeballed the crowds of people congregated in the surrounding area as he trailed behind the slow-moving pair. Provided Julia saw him in attendance, he felt no need to approach her in person. It would be much better not to, in fact.

If their interactions over the past weeks were any indication, he was just as likely as she to become frustrated by their conversation. He couldn't remember the last time he had spoken with Julia and come away not feeling discontented or bothered. In any case, Julia was not known to have a firm hold on her temper, and he had no desire to attract the attention which had been occasioned at the Rodwell's rout when they had their first great row.

His heart jumped as he spotted Cecilia Cosgrove ascending the stairs. A throng of people passed in front of him, though, preventing any view of whether Isabel accompanied her. He moved from left to right, attempting to get a better view, when an arm slipped through his. He turned and saw Julia looking up at him with a smile.

He grimaced, and her expression became provoking, one eyebrow arched and her mouth teasing. "I doubted whether you would keep your promise," she said, "but I should have known! I can always rely on my Charles." She guided him forward through the throngs of people, toward the end of the passageway which let out into a garden. As hot as the night was, it felt like a cool breeze in comparison with the heat of the indoors. A few other people sat on benches scattered among the garden's alcoves.

Charles's expression had morphed from one of confused surprise to one of doubtful contemplation. "What is this, Julia?" he said as they walked arm-in-arm around the garden's perimeter.

"What is what?"

He stopped, and she turned to look at him. "Do you truly intend," he said incredulously, "to pretend that nothing has happened between us after yesterday's incident in the park?"

"Oh, pooh!" she said, turning back around and pulling him along. "That is but a distant memory. Let us forget all about it."

He stopped again, disengaging his arm from hers. "It is not a distant memory, though. It was only yesterday. You made it quite clear that you wanted nothing more to do with me. That is not something I am likely to forget. Ever."

Julia heaved a sigh, but the teasing smile still lurked. "Oh, Charles, do you wish me to grovel? It pains me to think of kneeling in this gown, but I shall do it if you insist."

"No," Charles said. "I'm afraid groveling would change nothing. I only wish to understand what precisely has brought about such a change in your demeanor toward me. Perhaps you mistook me for Farrow," he said with a bite to his voice. "Is he not here?"

Julia laughed dismissively. "I'm sure I have no idea."

"Perhaps you should search him out," Charles said. "I don't believe you can have anything further to say to me, and I have someone I need to speak with. Allow me to leave you in the care of the Misses Bailey here." He indicated two young woman just entering the garden together. "I know you hold them in particular affection." He greeted them warmly and then left Julia with them, trying not to betray his amusement at Julia's mixed rage and awkwardness.

She had never liked the Bailey sisters.

His long strides quickly brought him back into the uncomfortably-warm house. He didn't know what Julia was about, but she quite clearly had no intention of explaining what had changed since their last meeting.

He raised up on his tiptoes, trying to locate any one of the Cosgrove family. The sound of violins and a cello wafted down the stairs, and he trotted up the staircase to try his luck there. He needed Isabel to know that he had no desire to relinquish the friendship they had formed over the last few weeks. She had made it abundantly clear that she had no desire to marry him, but, fool that he was, he had never had the courage to ask why. He needed to know the reason.

He spotted the large headdress of Mrs. Holledge and scanned the circle surrounding her. Each member was listening attentively to what she was saying. Sure enough, Miss Mary Holledge was amongst the group. He walked up behind her and gently tapped her on the shoulder.

"Mr. Galbraith," she said, slipping out of the circle. Two of the remaining women eyed him with annoyance and closed ranks, leaning their heads in closer to hear what Mrs. Holledge was saying.

Charles's brows went up. "Your mother certainly has her audience in rapt attention."

Miss Holledge gave him a significant look. "For good reason. It seems that Farrow is quite done up. Word that he may be losing his inheritance has caused many of his creditors to call in his debts—of which he apparently has an overabundance."

"Word from whom?" Charles said.

"I understand," said Mary in a low voice, "that his steward left his employ in an outrage and was quite free with Farrow's private business matters once he left."

Charles rubbed his chin in thought. "Well, perhaps Farrow is finally receiving his comeuppance." Julia's sudden appearance at his side, her energetic attentions to him suddenly made sense. Obviously, she had heard the rumors and was trying to repair the bridges she had burned as a result of her association with Farrow.

"Yes, I think you're right," Miss Holledge said, looking around the room and adding absently, "I'm just glad that Isabel is gone. If anyone were to draw his ire now that the news is out, it would be she."

Charles's brows snapped together. "What do you mean? Gone where? And why should she draw his ire?"

Miss Holledge's hand shot up to her mouth, her eyes wide. "Oh dear," she said. "I gave her my word!" She wrung her hands, and when she spoke, it seemed as though she was talking to herself. "But I didn't *try* to interfere! It was not done intentionally."

"Please explain, Miss Holledge," Charles said with a flash of impatience. "I must know if Isabel is in any danger. If Farrow is indeed under the hatches, he is more dangerous than you can possibly know." His forehead creased. "Though why Isabel should be a target of his anger is beyond me. Particularly if he knows that it was his steward who made his situation known."

Miss Holledge's hand relaxed slightly but still hovered in front of her mouth, her expression conscience-stricken. "He was mad as fire after she threatened him. I can only guess what he might be capable of in such a state."

Charles stiffened. "Threatened him?"

Miss Holledge blinked quickly, seeming to recall the incident. "As good as! We saw him in the Park, and he was being abominable toward Hetty. Isabel told him to stay away from Hetty or else face ruin."

Charles's stomach dropped and he swore softly. "Fool!" he said under his breath. "Where has she gone?"

Miss Holledge hesitated, taking her lips between her teeth. "I suppose I have already broken my word to her, so there's nothing for it but to tell you, besides it being utterly ridiculous of her in the first place." She sighed. "She is leaving for her aunt's in Colchester before her father can throw her out."

"What?" Charles's voice was barely a whisper. "Why should he throw her out?"

Miss Holledge raised up her shoulders. "He is very set on you two marrying."

Charles shook his head and blinked slowly, unable to account for the information from Miss Holledge given what Isabel herself had told him. "But she was confident that her sister's forthcoming engagement to Lord Brockway would satisfy him."

Miss Holledge's lips parted and her brows went up. "Oh," she said, "then she did not tell you." Miss Holledge interlocked her fingers. "Things have been at an end between Cecilia and Lord Brockway since, well, since the visit to the menagerie, I suppose. He is expected to offer for Miss Bernard." She opened her reticle and took out a letter, handing it to him. "Here. This should explain everything."

Charles opened it with fumbling hands as Miss Holledge watched his face. He read it with hungry eyes, his expressions changing rapidly.

When he looked up at the end, he felt an overwhelming mixture of urgency and fear. He looked at Miss Holledge without really seeing her and then turned to leave.

"Wait," she cried out. "Where are you going?"

"To bring Isabel back," he said.

She grabbed his coat sleeve. "She received an urgent call to the rectory shortly before I came here. Perhaps you should go there first. I don't believe the Mail Coach leaves for another hour."

The energy stilled in Charles's body. "To the rectory? Surely not."

Miss Holledge's shoulders went up, a sincere look in her eyes. "I saw the letter myself. He said it was most urgent."

"No, no, no, no," Charles muttered, running a hand through his hair. "It's not possible." He looked at Miss Holledge. "When I came here, the rector's coach was next door at Mr. Ellis'. He is giving him his last rites. Why should he send for Isabel to come urgently when he was not even there to receive her? It couldn't possibly have been from Mr. Safford." His eyes widened, and his heart began to pound. "Unless...." He trailed off. Suddenly he turned on his heel, running down the stairs and to the front door through the throngs of people.

❧ 26 ❧

Isabel walked to the rectory as quickly as she could manage with the heavy portmanteau under her arm. Her heart beat faster than usual, and she wondered what could have happened to merit such an urgent message. And one lacking any information at all.

Was the rector in danger? Did he wish for her to come retrieve the will? If he wished her to also deliver it to the solicitor he had mentioned, her plans might quickly unravel. It would mean missing the Mail Coach which would, in turn, mean having to wait until the following evening. Her father may well have read her letter already, and her only hope for the letter to Charles was that Mary would indeed wait to give it to him until the following day.

She shook her head and drew in a breath, trying not to dwell on the precariousness of her situation.

It was fully dusk when she passed under the stone arch and turned into the churchyard. Her eyes flitted in the direction of the graveyard, wondering if she would be obliged to fetch the will in the dark among the headstones. She was not terribly superstitious, but the thought still made her stomach clench. She hurried up the steps and pulled on the door handle, only to be jarred when the door stuck.

It was locked.

She stepped back and stared at it. It made no sense that the rector would lock the church after asking her to come. The remaining outdoor light was fading fast, and there was no light to be seen within the church. Perhaps Mr. Safford was at the rectory?

A click sounded behind her, and she whipped around, only to be met by the barrel of a pistol.

She froze.

"I'm so glad you could join me, Miss Cosgrove." Mr. Farrow's arm was fully extended, the dark metal of his pistol gleaming in his hand. "I knew I could trust your sense of loyalty to bring you here post-haste."

She pictured the short missive which had brought her, the sloppy handwriting which she had assumed to look different from Mr. Safford's script only due to his haste. "You wrote the letter?"

Mr. Farrow's mouth stretched into a lopsided smile. "Yes. And now you will show me where the good rector has hidden the will."

Isabel swallowed, and her chin came up slightly. "I am at a loss to know what you're referring to, sir."

He bared his teeth and put the pistol up to her temple. "Does this help bring anything to mind?"

Isabel's jaw tightened.

Mr. Farrow smiled. "Yes, I urge you to reconsider. Your admirable but unwise threat in the park confirmed what I had already suspected: Safford confided in you after my last visit to him. I know the will is somewhere on this property. His loyalty to my father would not permit him to let it out of his care. You will show me where it is."

Where was Mr. Safford? She felt sick as she thought on the possibility that Mr. Farrow had already done harm to him. "What have you done with the rector?"

"The rector is safe," he said disinterestedly.

"I don't believe you."

"And yet it is true, despite that," he said. "He is, I believe, engaged in performing the last rites for someone. But I cannot vouch for his safety once he returns, which he may well do at any time. For that reason, haste on your part will ensure the good rector's safety."

Isabel could feel her palms sweating and the leather portmanteau began to slip in her fingers. What would the rector have her do? It was terribly important to him to honor his promise to his brother. But she also didn't feel he would wish for Isabel to sacrifice her life over the matter.

Would Mr. Farrow truly kill her if she refused to comply? She could try to buy time, but that might only ensure that harm would also come to Mr. Safford when he returned. Surely Mr. Farrow wouldn't kill in cold blood the only two people who knew the location of the will? What if it was happened upon by someone else later?

She thought of Hetty, of Farrow's heartless role in consigning her to debtor's prison or possible transportation. Her jaw tightened. Who else would become a victim if she didn't stand up to him? She at least had nothing to lose.

"No," she said.

"Come again?" His teeth were gritted.

She looked him in the eye, feeling a burst of confidence "I will not help you to find and, I assume, destroy the will. And you must know that to kill me would only ensure your own undoing."

"You insist, then, on doing things the hard way?" He kept the pistol trained on her and stooped down to pick up a rope from an open rucksack lying at his feet. "So be it."

Isabel's confidence flickered.

He took the portmanteau from her and then turned her around, commanding her to sit down on one of the steps next to the wrought-iron railing. He set the pistol down next to his foot, watching her as he did it, as if to tell her not to even consider an attempt to wrest it from him. Keeping his eyes on her, he began tying her wrists, first together, then to the railing.

She couldn't help but ask, "How does this advance your cause?"

"Quite effectively, I assure you." He tied a final knot in the rope. "You will not tell me where the will is hidden. Very well, then I shall have to destroy it by some other means. I prefer a less messy ending, but you have forced my hand. And you, my dear Miss Cosgrove, shall be unfortunate collateral damage. Whatever knowledge you have of this dies with you." He stooped down again to pick up a long cloth which he tied around her mouth.

Picking up a flint box and some kindling, Mr. Farrow walked with brisk steps toward a spot near the middle of the length of the church, stooping down.

Isabel's eyes widened, and she gave a tug on the rope. Its rough fibers chafed her wrists.

"Stop!" she cried out, but the sound was muffled, and he made no evidence of hearing her.

He struck the flint toward the kindling, and she saw a small red ember glow and then spread.

❧ 27 ❧

C harles instructed his coachman to take the quickest way to
St. James's. He sat on the edge of his seat, his hands
clenching in impatience and impotence as he waited to
arrive at the church.

Perhaps his suspicions were incorrect, but knowing that Farrow
was at the end of his rope and that Isabel had threatened him, he felt
great anxiety on Isabel's behalf. It was the type of fear that gripped
him and made him feel cold.

The voice of his coachman came through the windows muffled.
"Do you still want me to proceed, sir?"

Charles furrowed his brow and peered out the window,
wondering what obstacle could possibly be in their way. The lighting
outside was peculiar, the darkness moderated by a faint orange glow.

He opened the coach door and leaned his body out. He went
rigid for an instant and then jumped down, sprinting toward the
church with an order to his coachman to stay put.

Flames leapt up around the building, and Charles felt the heat
increasing as he approached. He saw a number of people in the
street, pointing at the building.

222

He flew under the arch, slowing his pace as his eyes frantically scanned the scene. The fire was spreading through the garden, and the pungent smell of greenery burning assailed his nose. The building itself was aflame, but the stone was providing a barrier to the fire's attempts to spread indoors.

He looked toward the door and froze. Collapsed on the steps of the church was Isabel.

"Isabel!" he called out, racing toward her as he coughed from the smoke and swore.

He almost skidded to a stop, kneeling next to her and taking her by the shoulders to sit her up. Her hands were tied to the iron railing, and he could see the bright red marks from where she had perhaps struggled against the ropes. His jaw tightened as he put an ear to Isabel's chest, listening intently amidst the crackling sound of the fire. The thump-thump of her heartbeat was barely discernible, but he felt a gush of relief at the sound. Beads of sweat trailed down his forehead.

Charles looked at Isabel's face, framed by disordered hair and a bonnet which had fallen back. Her mouth was stretched by the tight gag around it, her cheeks red and glistening with sweat.

He glanced around, and his gaze landed on the stones which paved the courtyard. One was cracked, its corner breaking away. Setting Isabel gently back down, he hurried over to the stone, using his boot to break the remaining edge away, then picked it up and returned to Isabel.

He sawed at the rope with the jagged stone, eyeing the flames which were quickly making their way toward the church door. Once the fire reached the wooden door, it would inevitably move to the interior of the church.

He could hear shouts coming from the street. He desperately hoped that the Watch had been alerted and would soon bring in help to combat the fire.

As his sweat dripped onto the stones below and coughs came relentlessly, the final thread broke, and he pulled the loosened ropes from Isabel's wrists. He undid the bonnet ribbon around her neck, letting the straw hat slip onto the ground.

Slipping one hand under her legs and one under her back, he hoisted her limp form into his arms and made his way out of the churchyard. His coachman stood in the street, his feet shuffling anxiously as he awaited instruction.

"Open the door," Charles said breathing heavily. Once the door was open, he instructed his coachman to take Isabel's legs. He supported her upper body and, watching over his shoulder, carefully stepped into the coach. The coachman handed in Isabel's legs, and Charles worked to position her in the limited space on the seat, with her upper body resting in his arms.

He debated where to take her. His lodgings were closest by a matter of minutes, and he felt a great deal of urgency—Isabel needed to be seen to by a doctor without delay. Every minute counted.

But to take her to his own lodgings would be to court gossip, to endanger her reputation.

His jaw clenched. It was all so ridiculous—endangering her very life in order to save her reputation?

What were such considerations when she was lying unconscious in front of him? Besides, how could he entrust Isabel to her father's care when it was clear that her well-being was hardly a concern to him?

It was Charles's fault that any of this mayhem had happened, and he had to ensure Isabel received the care she required, that everything was set right. It was his responsibility.

But he couldn't sacrifice her reputation if there was any way to avoid it. He bit his lip, wishing he were able to call on his mother.

A wry smile appeared on his face in the dark of the carriage. She would have liked Isabel. Certainly it wouldn't have taken Charles so long to come to his senses if he'd had his mother's wise and guiding influence in his life.

He sighed. If nothing else, he could have Isabel's maid sent for— someone who could vouch for the absolute exigency of the situation while safeguarding her mistress against scandal. Between the maid and his own housekeeper, he had to believe it would be enough. There was no time to do anything more.

"To the house," he said curtly, noting the chaos that had begun around them, with people arriving on the scene and others leaving.

The coachman nodded, shut the door, and had the horses put to in a matter of seconds.

The coach ambled along the dirty streets, and Charles worked to still his ragged breathing. He cleared his throat, suppressing the urge to cough which the smoke caused.

It was dark within the coach, and he could hardly see Isabel's features even though her face was right before him. He put a hand under her nose to check for breathing and realized that his hand was trembling. He clenched it. Now that the adrenaline of the fire was dissipating, he was left with his thoughts and emotions.

That Farrow was responsible for it all, Charles had no doubt. Only a man who stood to lose as much as Farrow did could do something so entirely reckless. What if the fire spread further than the church? He had done his level best to kill Isabel, and he may well have succeeded in killing many more if Charles had not gone after Isabel—if Miss Holledge's tongue had not slipped.

His heart raced, and he felt his brow sweating again. He took slow, deep breaths to steady his anger, knowing that underneath it lay fear.

He stared down at Isabel again, his lips forming a tight line at the sight of her, unconscious. If she had sustained any lasting harm or if, heaven forbid, the heat and smoke inhalation proved fatal, he would never forgive himself.

He brushed away a hair which stuck to her damp forehead, and his eyes softened. What if he never had the chance to tell her how he felt? To apologize for how stupid he had been not to recognize it sooner, fool that he was. He swallowed and closed his eyes, laying his head back.

It was only a matter of minutes before the coach stopped altogether in front of Charles's lodgings.

With the coachman's help, he transported Isabel's body inside, placing her on his own bed. Noting her still-flushed cheeks, he removed her pelisse as gently as possible and propped her head up with a pillow, letting his hand trail from her disheveled hair and down her cheek.

The coachman cleared his throat, and Charles turned, hurrying to ring the bell as he instructed his stone-faced coachman to have the doctor sent for immediately.

Once the coachman was gone, he sat on the edge of the bed, watching the rise and fall which evidenced Isabel's steady breathing.

A knock soon sounded on the door, and the maid entered. He gave her swift instructions, and she left as soon as she had come, only to return in a matter of minutes. She carried a basin of water, a towel, and a blue vinaigrette.

"I have sent a footman round to the Cosgrove residence, requesting that the miss's maid be sent here immediately."

Charles thanked her and took the towel from her hands, dipping it in the water and wiping it across Isabel's forehead.

"Isabel," he said softly. "Isabel, can you hear me?"

There was no movement.

He motioned to the maid, and she handed him the smelling salts. He took the blue glass vinaigrette from her and waved it lightly under Isabel's nose.

Isabel's eyelids fluttered, and her shoulders came up as she took a deep breath and went immediately into a fit of coughing.

Charles quickly set the vinaigrette on the bedside table so that he could support her, scooting closer and wrapping an arm around her back as she coughed violently into her hand.

The fit went on for what felt like an eternity to Charles, though it could only have been a couple of minutes. He noted the maid looking on with round eyes and felt impatient with her worry because it increased his own anxiety.

He had no idea how long Isabel had been at the church or how much smoke she must have inhaled before his arrival.

When the coughing finally subsided, Charles guided Isabel back down to a lying position and instructed the maid to have some broth brought up. He dipped the towel in the water again, wiping it gently over Isabel's forehead.

Her eyes opened slowly. They were bloodshot, and the previous warmth of her skin at the church had been replaced by a pallor which worried Charles more than the earlier flush had.

He saw her brows knit in confusion.

"You are safe," he said, smiling down at her with tenderness.

Her eyes began to widen, watering, and she whispered, "No, no." She turned her head away and brought her hand up to wipe at a tear, wincing. "I cannot bear it."

He blinked slowly, unsure what to make of her reaction. "What is it?" He took her hand in his and felt it jolt.

A knock sounded on the door, and he stood, hesitating as he looked down at Isabel. Her head was turned away, but she was still. A tear streamed down her face, and she wore a look of defeat.

"You should not have come," she said softly.

❦ 28 ❦

Isabel listened as Charles spoke in low tones with the doctor. She had no idea what time it was—she only knew that it was dark outside and that her chest and throat burned whenever she breathed. Another tear pooled in her eye, and she tried to blink it away.

She didn't know where she was nor how she had come to be there, but that Charles was there was enough to make her heart and mind feel weighted with lead.

The only way he could have interfered in her plan was through Mary's tampering—confound her well-meaning stratagems. How Isabel could make an escape for Aunt Eliza's with a loud, debilitating cough and limbs that felt so weak as to be almost useless was beyond her ability to think through.

Would Farrow be looking for her? Or had Charles encountered him when he arrived at the Church? She felt the hairs on her arms stand on end.

Too many questions and troubling thoughts buzzed around in the fog of her mind. Which problem needed to be addressed first? In

Charles's company and with his voice sounding in her ears, she found it hard to focus on anything but him.

No doubt his conscience was hanging over him like a dark storm cloud.

She breathed deeply in an effort to calm her anxiety but doubled over in a fit of hacking.

When she emerged, she felt Charles's steadying hand on her back and saw the doctor peering over at her. She avoided Charles's eyes, lying back as the blood from the exertion of coughing drained from her face.

The doctor asked to listen to her heartbeat and her breathing, and Charles politely turned away during the short exam. Isabel tried to breathe in deeply, knowing that to truly do so would result in yet another fit. The doctor pursed his lips as he listened, saying, "You seem to have inhaled a great amount of smoke, but I believe a couple of days in bed and a cupping or two should have you feeling much better."

Isabel agreed to the doctor's words with a polite nod. "May we delay the cupping until tomorrow?" she asked. "I am feeling quite fatigued at the moment." She had a great dislike of doctors and even more so of the practice of cupping, but she knew that if she could but delay it, she would be gone by the time the doctor returned to perform the deed.

The doctor looked less than pleased. "It would be much better to do it now when you are in greatest danger of succumbing to your injuries."

Isabel took her top lip under her teeth, wondering how to refuse the doctor without seeming obstinate or ungrateful.

"Thank you, good doctor," Charles interrupted with a note of finality, "but we will wait until tomorrow all the same." The doctor looked to be offended, and Charles added, "Your services are indispensable, and we rely on your continued care."

The doctor looked slightly mollified and instructed a diet of gruel for the next day before taking his leave.

Isabel's eyes flitted over to Charles, keenly aware that they would be alone.

He shut the door behind the doctor and turned back toward her with a fist covering his mouth. His fist came away, revealing a frown underneath.

"We will decidedly not rely on him for your continued care. The man must cup a score of people every day," he said, shaking his head and approaching the bed. "I sometimes wonder if he truly knows any other treatment."

Isabel heaved a sigh, smiling weakly. "Thank you for intervening. I have the greatest fear of being cupped. I had the treatment as a child and became violently ill for days afterward."

He sat down near the foot of the bed, looking at her with a creased forehead. "How are you feeling, Isabel?"

She swallowed at his use of her name. Now that their pretended courting was at an end, it made more sense to address one another formally. His use of her given name was an unwelcome reminder of what could never be.

"I shall be well enough," she said, "if I can manage to sleep without constant fits of coughing." Even as she said the words, another fit came on, leaving her breathless and red-faced.

The concern on Charles's face was evident—his mouth in a tight line, his black brows drawn together, and his jaw set. "Perhaps some laudanum might help?"

"Thank you, but no," she said with a grateful smile. The thought of deep sleep uninterrupted by coughing or by restless dreams was enticing. But she needed her wits about her if she was to start on her way to Colchester. She had already missed the Mail, but she might well be able to find a hackney to take her to some inn just outside London—anywhere away from Charles—from his ability to stop her. To stay where she was would be to risk losing the opportunity to leave altogether. Where was she, anyway?

"Mr. Galbraith?" She paused, looking around the room. "Am I at your lodgings?"

A look of displeasure crossed his face. "Yes, you are at my lodgings," he said shortly. "Am I reduced then to 'Mr. Galbraith?'"

She colored up as his eyes rested on her. She didn't wish to seem ungrateful.

"Not reduced, surely." She felt suddenly tongue-tied.

He said nothing, and she felt obliged to explain. "It is only that, since we are no longer required to pretend the level of familiarity we had assumed for a time, it seems proper to return to a more formal address." She swallowed uncomfortably, noting the large lump in her throat as she said the words aloud.

"I see," he said, his irritation still visible. "Well, I am sure, Miss Cosgrove—" he said her name deliberately "—that you wish to be left alone. Please know that you need only pull the bell, and a servant or myself will be here in naught but a moment." He bowed with more stiffness than usual and turned to leave.

It was unbearable to feel his displeasure, and Isabel couldn't help but call out to him, saying, "Charles, wait."

He turned toward her, his brows no longer clenched together.

Her mouth hung open as she tried to think what to say to him. She swallowed the persistent lump in her throat. "Was it you who saved me?" Her voice was quiet.

Charles gave only the slightest, most reluctant of nods.

Isabel took her lips between her teeth, and she felt her eyes burn. He had no doubt risked his own life to save hers. "Thank you," she said with a slight crack in her voice.

His shoulders relaxed, and his hand dropped from the door handle.

"I can only assume," she said, "that if it weren't for you, I should not be alive."

He stiffened slightly and closed his eyes for a moment.

She looked down at her hands, noting the red skin on her wrists from the ropes, reminding her of all that had happened. Her head came up quickly as she thought of all the questions she should have been asking. "What of Mr. Safford and the church?"

"I believe the rector was safely engaged in other parish matters all evening—his coach left Mr. Ellis's next door just as ours arrived." Charles grimaced. "As for the church, I don't know. I sincerely hope that they were in time to control it before it entered the building or moved to the nearby houses. I'm afraid there must be much damage."

Isabel nodded, hoping he was right. She shivered. "What of Mr. Farrow? Did you see him?" She tensed. "Did he follow us?" How had she not considered that possibility before?

Charles's brow grew black. The veins in his neck protruded, and Isabel watched his hands ball into white-knuckled fists as he stared at the wall. "No, he did not follow us. If I had caught sight of him, I assure you that he would not have been alive to run like the coward he is." He looked to her, the anger still written across his face. "Are you raving mad? Why did you not tell me you had threatened him?"

She swallowed, knowing that this conversation had been inevitable. But what right did he have to lecture her? He didn't need to protect her. She lifted her chin. "Mary talks far too much for her own good."

"And thank heaven she does," he said with a bite to his voice. "It is to her you owe your life, for I should never have known where to find you if not for her." His jaw shifted. "I never thought that I would come to trust Miss Holledge's confidences and mistrust you."

Isabel's eyes stung.

His voice grew thick, and she saw betrayal and anger in his eyes. "Why would you lie to me about your sister and Lord Brockway?"

Her lip trembled, and she clenched her jaw and shut her eyes to ward off the emotion. How could she explain it all to him without betraying her feelings for him? She suddenly felt tired of it all. Of the pretending. Of the feelings. "Oh, what does it matter?"

"It matters a great deal," he said, running a hand through his hair and walking toward her. His expression softened. "I told you that I wouldn't let ill come to you as a result of my folly. I meant it." He took her hand in his and knelt beside the bed. "I promised your father I would marry you. I am a man of my word, Isabel."

She put a fist in front of her mouth, stifling a frustrated scream. Again, he offered to sacrifice himself and his future with Miss Darling—all to save her. Out of pity, out of honor. Whatever it was, she didn't know if she could bear his martyrdom another second. "I don't want your word. I don't want to marry you. Please," she said, closing her eyes as a quick breath escaped her. "Just let me go."

He blinked quickly, an injured look in his eyes, and released her hand. He rose to his feet stiffly, inclined his head slowly, and then turned on his heel.

The sound of the gentle closing of the door was followed by a few moments of silence.

Isabel sat motionless, her eyes staring at the drawn curtains on the window opposite her bed. Tears slowly began to course down her cheeks, and her eyes burned as the salt and smoke in her eyes combined.

✣ 29 ✣

Anaïs arrived shortly after Charles's departure, all concern and shock at the sight of Isabel. She and Mrs. Crewe, Charles's very matronly housekeeper, had attended to Isabel's needs for close to an hour.

But they had since left her to rest, Anaïs installing herself on the floor of the adjacent sitting room where Isabel hoped fervently that she was sleeping soundly, and Mrs. Crewe reassuring Isabel that the lightest tug on the bell would bring her to the room.

While Isabel had been grateful for Charles's forethought and propriety in sending for Anaïs, it was a wasted effort in the end. Isabel had little need of her reputation any more.

Despite that, it made her cringe to think of the tales Anaïs would bear when she returned to the Cosgrove house the next day.

Isabel had been surprised when, upon questioning the maid about what story she had given for her sudden and urgent departure, Anaïs had assured her that she had pleaded a family emergency. It was uncharacteristically loyal of her, and it granted Isabel the extra hours she needed.

It took time for Isabel to gather the physical strength to stand. She waited until all the sounds of the house had stopped. She had barely the energy to walk, but it didn't matter. She had to find energy, to generate it from sheer willpower if necessary.

The maid lay in the adjacent sitting room, and Isabel fervently hoped that Anaïs was a sound sleeper.

Her lungs burned with each breath, and she had to stop to cough into a pillow more than once. Her pelisse lay on the chair next to the bed, a fact which led her to close her eyes in a silent prayer of gratitude.

She had put her money in the pocket Anaïs had sewn into her pelisse rather than in the portmanteau, which was nowhere to be seen. It would be a burden to earn the money for the clothing the portmanteau had contained, but she hadn't any other option.

SHE LOOKED AROUND THE ROOM, wondering if there was anything of use to take with her. She opened a door that led off from the bedroom, relieved when it proved to be a dressing room. A clothes press stood up against the wall opposite the door, and she stifled a cough in the crook of her elbow as she opened it and scanned its contents. Cravats and shirts were folded neatly inside, and Isabel drew back slightly. Had Charles placed her in his own quarters, then? But where, then, was he sleeping?

She shut the clothes press quickly, feeling as though she had intruded on Charles's private space.

She would have to make do with what she had on her back. Spotting a mirror on the dressing table, she picked it up to take stock of her state. The only available light was the faint light of the moon, shining through a crack in the curtains. She turned so that the light fell on her face as she looked in the mirror. Her eyes widened in horror. Her eyes were puffy and her hair disheveled.

She hadn't the time or means to arrange her hair as she would wish, but she used her fingers to tuck and repin a few of the larger pieces as best she could. She tried not to think of what Charles must have thought seeing her in such a state.

The house was in complete darkness as she opened the bedroom door, none of the pale moonlight reaching beyond the room.

She winced as the door creaked slightly. It would be a challenge to navigate an unknown house in silence, but she could only do her best. She tiptoed down the stairs at a creeping pace, hoping to minimize any possible creaking. Even if she managed to descend both flights of stairs without causing a loose board to creak, the intensity with which her heart was pounding was bound to alert someone.

Three times she was obliged to cough into her elbow, and each time, she emerged from the fit with wide, alert eyes which scanned her surroundings in fear that she had been heard. Would Charles try to stop her? After her outburst, it seemed unlikely.

She ached to set things right with him, to explain why she had deceived him, why she had no choice but to leave.

But she couldn't. It was a selfish thing to wish for anyway. It would only add to his sense of obligation to her.

She stepped onto the landing with a sigh of relief that turned, once again, into a cough, catching her off guard so that the first two barks went unmuffled. Her only consolation was that she had reached the ground floor where there were no sleeping quarters.

The landing was surrounded on three sides by different doors, presenting her with a predicament: which one would lead to the entry hall and front door? She had been in many London houses, and the majority, including her own, seemed to have the same general layout.

She tiptoed around the base of the staircase toward the door behind, cringing at another squeaking floorboard which sounded deafening in the silence of the night. She stood before the door and took in a large breath, putting her fingers on the handle. She pulled it gently, peeking her head around to look through the gap and sighed with relief as her eyes met the unmistakable view of the front door. She slipped through the opening toward it.

She took one backward glance at the entry hall of Charles's home, wondering where he was and whether he was hurt by her words earlier. *"Let me go."*

She glanced at the table next to the entryway where an empty, silver letter tray sat and reached a hand over to brush her fingers over it lightly. She imagined a letter there, written in her own handwriting, conveying everything she had never been able to say to Charles.

But it couldn't be. An imagined letter would have to do.

"Goodbye, Charles," she whispered with a painful swallow.

"Isabel?"

She froze, hoping it was just her imagination, and turned slowly.

Charles stood in the doorway she had just come through. His hair was tousled, his shirt front open, and his eyes narrowed and blinking as though he had just woken.

Isabel's mouth opened wordlessly, her voice suddenly uncooperative. She watched his eyes flit to her hand on the front door handle.

"Where are you going?" he said, taking a step into the entry hall.

Isabel met his gaze, her own clear and direct. There was nothing she could say to deceive him now, to pretend that she wasn't about to walk out the door. "I'm leaving."

He stared for a moment and then shook his head slowly. "I can't let you do that."

"You must," she said. Her heart throbbed inside her. It would have been so much easier to leave without having to face him.

"At this time of night? Unescorted? And all when you should be resting." He shook his head again. "You nearly died tonight, Isabel." His jaw tightened. "Surely your frantic need to put distance between us can wait one more day."

She swallowed, and her eyes brimmed with tears. Was he really so blind that he didn't understand why she couldn't bear to be near him? Tears spilled over, and she turned her head to hide them from him.

His hands reached out as he moved to bridge the distance

between them, but he dropped them suddenly as he stopped in his tracks.

"Please," he said. "Let me fix this. Don't leave."

She shook her head, not trusting her voice.

A weak half-smile appeared on his face. "Didn't I tell you that I would abduct you and marry you if need be?" The smile faded, and he met her eyes with his own determined ones. "Marry me, Isabel. Let me keep you safe. You don't have to do this."

A small sob escaped her, but before she could speak, he continued, his palms up in surrender. "I will leave you be. I will give you whatever space you wish for. Please," he begged again. "Just let me set this right."

She couldn't bear it any longer. "Stop," she cried in a near-shout. She rubbed a hand on her brow, feeling frayed and out of control. "I don't want to marry you, Charles." It was true. And yet so very false.

He stiffened. "Yes," he said, his voice harsh all of a sudden. "You've made it abundantly clear that the prospect of marriage with me is enough to send you running toward a life of penury."

She closed her eyes and shook her head. It seemed impossible that he should be ignorant of her feelings for him. How could he believe that she was running away because she despised him? And yet she thought she saw the hurt hiding under his anger. Her resolution wavered.

"I am only trying to help you," she said. It was a reminder to herself as much as it was an explanation to him.

"Help me?" he said incredulously. "By leaving me?"

"Yes," she said. "From the beginning, everything I've done has had one aim: your happiness, Charles. And that is exactly why I must leave."

He doubled back and blinked rapidly, staring at her with a knit brow.

She swallowed. "It is true. Please believe me."

He began to pace from side to side, one hand stroking his cheek. "I ask you to marry me, and you wish to run for the hills. And yet you say you wish for my happiness?" He stopped, looking at her with his palms facing up in front of him in an uncomprehending gesture.

"You don't understand," she said helplessly.

"Then, by all means, explain! What has given you such a distaste for me that you would do anything to avoid marrying me?"

It was there again—the hurt. She had seen his brow furrow enough times to recognize that there was more than anger there.

Her last shreds of composure frayed. "Oh, Charles! I don't want a martyr for a husband. I don't wish to live my life knowing that you sacrificed your chance at love—all to save the woman you felt duty-bound to marry." She shivered at the thought of the life she described and looked to meet his eyes.

Charles's jaw was slack, his lips parted, and his eyes blinking slowly. "Is that all you think this is? Duty?"

Isabel said nothing, shutting her eyes tightly and pulling her lips between her teeth. Of course it was duty. Entertaining any other idea would reignite unbearable hope. She heard the sound of his soft foot-steps approaching her, and her nostrils flared. She didn't know if she could bear his touch or having him near.

She opened her eyes, and her breath hitched. He was so close, and yet the distance between them felt unbridgeable. His hands hung at his sides, looking as empty as she felt.

"What do you want, Isabel?" he said in a gentle voice, his eyes searching hers. "You. Forget everyone else. What is it that your heart wants?" He let out a shaky laugh. "Have you even considered that through all of this mess?"

She took in a deep breath and let her head fall back. Had she considered it? Only every single day. She had hardly been able to think of anything else. She brought her head forward again and let out her breath.

"Say it," he said softly. His brows were still drawn together, but there was no anger left, only pleading.

And she wanted to say it. She wanted him to know the truth. She couldn't leave him here, thinking she had left because she loathed him. She couldn't leave him here with the distress and pain she had glimpsed.

His eyes watched her, his throat bobbing.

With an impotent shrug, she looked at him with frank, watering eyes and said, "I want you."

He stared at her for a moment—a moment which stretched on and on, building with each second. And then suddenly he closed the remaining gap between them, his arms wrapping around her, his lips meeting hers with an insistence and force which left her lightheaded.

She froze for a moment, shocked by the suddenness, the unexpectedness of it—by the implication of it. And then she softened, letting herself yield to the pull. She wrapped her hands behind his neck, returning the embrace.

It was minutes before Charles pulled back and looked at her. His eyes were soft and warm, and he gently pushed a hair out of her face, letting his hand come to rest on her cheek.

Her shoulders raised up as she pulled in a needed breath. "I don't understand. What about Miss Darling?" She searched his eyes.

He smiled down at her. "What about her?" His hand slid from her cheek down to the arm which rested on his shoulder. He pulled it down and brought her hand to his mouth, kissing it as he kept his eyes locked with hers.

"It has been some time since Julia's company brought me even a fraction of the joy that I find in your company, you know." He let out a puff of air through his nose, his brow knitting. "I couldn't see it, though—I was too blinded by my old assumptions." His half-smile appeared. "Besides, I thought you wanted to put as much distance between us as humanly possible."

Isabel laughed softly, grasping his hand a little tighter. She had been frighteningly close to never experiencing what it was like to have his arm wrapped snugly around her.

"I couldn't bear the thought of you feeling obligated to marry me," she said.

His thumb stroked her hand. "But I do feel obligated to marry you." His eyes teased her. "If only to ensure my own happiness."

She glared at him playfully. "Even if you must forgive all my father's debts?"

Charles chuckled. "A small price to pay for my own happiness, I think." His smile faded as he gazed down at her. "I love you, Isabel. And I will spend the rest of my life endeavoring to comfort you and make you laugh the way I did when we first met."

She looked up into his eyes, her heart fluttering at the thought. "I should like that very much."

He leaned over and pressed his lips to hers yet another time.

EPILOGUE

Walking at a brisk pace across the busy street, Isabel felt her arm tugged, and she looked up at Charles.

He was smiling down at her, eyes alight with amusement. "If only I could get my horses to walk with as much purpose as you do, love." He pulled back on her arm again, bringing them both to a halt once they were clear of traffic. "Why the rush?"

Isabel sighed, trying to relax her posture. "I am terribly impatient to know the result of the trial, Charles. Surely you understand?"

He looked up and down the street before stooping his head and kissing her lightly on the lips. "I do. And yet running to the rectory won't change the outcome. I am sure it all turned out as we expected it would. They could hardly return any verdict but guilty."

Isabel shot him a significant look and determinedly pulled him forward to continue on their way. If Farrow had any connection to the magistrate, it was entirely possible that he would be let free.

They turned the corner into the churchyard, and Isabel slowed, scanning the scene before her with a sudden lump in her throat. There was a stark line on the stone and in the greenery, a soot-colored delineation showing exactly where the fire had been extinguished.

Charles squeezed her arm. "It looks worse than it is. The trees and plants that burned will make way for new life, and the church will be washed and repaired. It could have been much worse."

Isabel turned toward him, wrapping her arms around his waist and looking up at him. "It is only thanks to you that it *isn't* worse." She looked at the place on the steps to the door of the church where she had sat, fearing for her life as the fire grew around her. She swallowed. "And only thanks to you that I am here at all."

He brought her in closer, pulling her tightly against him and placing his mouth firmly on top of her bonnet. "Thank heaven," he murmured softly.

Footsteps sounded, and they pulled apart, their eyes meeting the neatly-dressed figure of Mr. Safford as he entered the churchyard.

Isabel pulled away from Charles, letting her hand slide away from his back and down to clasp his hand. She looked at Mr. Safford with a quick heartbeat and suspenseful eyes.

Mr. Safford stopped, meeting Isabel's gaze. "Guilty," he said on an exhale. "Transportation for life."

Isabel let out a relieved, shaky breath and looked at Charles. His mouth was stretched in a firm line, and he nodded.

"It is you we have to thank," Mr. Safford said to Charles, "that things have turned out as well as they have. Without you, Miss Cosgrove's life and my life might have been forfeit, and the will might have been destroyed, along with the rest of this sacred place." He looked around himself wistfully.

"I am only sorry," Charles said, shaking his head, "that I didn't do something about Farrow sooner. His desperation took him to lengths I never would have thought possible; worse with each action."

"I, too, waited too long," said the rector.

"He shan't hurt anyone anymore, though," Isabel said solemnly.

CHARLES OPENED the door to the Cosgrove residence in Belport Street, and Isabel passed through in front of him.

They had only just stepped into the entry hall when a familiar, boisterous voice assailed Isabel's ears.

"Oh ho!" the voice cried.

Isabel's brother Tobias stepped into the hall from the doorway before them and stopped, raising a brow enigmatically as his gaze landed on Charles. He took two large strides over to Isabel and wrapped her up in his customary, strong embrace.

"I can only assume," Charles said with a touch of humor, "that you are the infamous brother Tobias who has been teaching my fiancée cant expressions."

Tobias pulled back from Isabel, his mouth pulling into an even larger grin as he regarded her with approval. "Ain't at all strait-laced, is she?"

Isabel suppressed a smile. "I had no notion you would be home, Tobias! I am surprised in the very best way. And," she said enigmatically, "I am pleased to introduce you to my affianced husband, Mr. Charles Galbraith."

The two shook hands, and Isabel looked on with a sense of contentment. She had little doubt that Charles and Tobias would get along.

"Never thought I'd see the day when you became a tenant for life, Izz!" Tobias winked at her and leaned in, whispering, "Always believed you'd marry before Cecy."

"Be kind to her, Tobias," Isabel said in a censuring tone. "She has suffered a number of disappointments since you saw her last."

Tobias raised his brows questioningly.

Before Isabel could respond, a footman entered, requesting that Tobias join his father in the library.

Tobias shot Isabel a feigned look of apprehension before winking again, bowing to Charles, and walking back the way he had come.

Isabel turned to Charles.

His brows were raised, his eyes lingering on the doorway Tobias had disappeared through.

Isabel smiled. "Quite a character, isn't he?"

Charles nodded. "He is. But I think I like him."

"Then you must help me to find him a suitable wife, for he is notoriously terrible at making decisions and desperately in need of settling down."

Charles's half-smile appeared. "I think I shall stay well out of that fight, my love." He grabbed her hand and pulled her in toward him. "Your father could use a child who doesn't concede his every wish."

Isabel brushed a hair away from Charles's face. "True. Much as I desired to go against his wishes, I found myself dragged by a myste-rious—" she stood on her tiptoes, punctuating each word with a kiss "—handsome, charming, unstoppable force." She dropped back down off her toes. "So, I have, very regrettably, surrendered. And Cecilia will naturally marry just the sort of titled gentleman my father wishes her to." She sighed dramatically.

"I wouldn't be so sure," Charles said. "Perhaps Cecilia will surprise us all and marry a nobody like your Aunt Eliza."

Isabel only laughed.

"Or," Charles said, looking through the doorway as if to check for witnesses before he swiftly scooped Isabel into his arms.

She suppressed a squeal. "Charles!" she hissed, unable to hide her large grin as she wrapped her arms around his neck.

"Or," he continued, ignoring her protest, "perhaps I don't give a fig what Cecilia does."

And he leaned in, kissing Isabel as soundly as she could ever wish to be kissed.

Join my newsletter to keep in touch and learn more about the Regency era! I try to keep it fun and interesting.

You can also connect with me and eight other authors in the Sweet Regency Romance Fans group on Facebook.

If you'd like to read the first chapter of the next book in the series, go ahead and turn the page.

CECILIA: A REGENCY ROMANCE
CHAPTER ONE

DOVER, ENGLAND 1792

Jacques Levesque hoisted a small, wooden chest from the Comte de Montreuil's ship cabin, hearing a slight tinkering inside as he settled it into his arms and began walking it to the wagon.

The chest was heavy for its size, challenging the nine-year old's strength to its capacity. He knew what was inside—or he could guess, at least. Monsieur le Comte had fit every valuable he could inside the privately-chartered ship they had taken from Calais. And now it was Jacques's job to ensure it was all transported to the nearby inn where they would spend the night.

Jacques's eyes shifted around the port, curious and wary of this new land.

England. He had heard of it time and again, but it was nothing like he had imagined—nothing like the glittering descriptions he had gleaned from Monsieur le Comte's friends in the snippets of conversation he had been able to catch around the Comte's estate.

All Jacques could see was distant green hills on one side and, on the other, flat blue ocean as far as the eye could see.

The chaos of departing from the Comte's home in Montreuil had been acute, a culmination of the growing fear inside the household since the storming of the Tuileries and the anticipated collapse of the monarchy.

Jacques was not sad to leave behind life in France, but he was very anxious and unsure of what to expect with Monsieur le Comte in England. Would he drink less heavily? Would he be less cruel? Or would he become even *more* cruel and demanding?

"Jacques," said his father in an urgent voice. The Comte's arm was draped over the shoulder of Jacques's father, his face pale and lethargic. There was unmistakable worry in his father's eyes.

The journey across the Channel had been a rough one—and the Comte had been not only drunk but violently ill. Jacques's own legs still felt wobbly on the sturdy ground of the port.

"Continue loading Monsieur's things into the wagon," his father continued. "He is unwell, and I am going to accompany him to the inn. This man"— he used his head to indicate a French shipman who nodded and slipped a coin into his pocket —"will assist you and drive you to the inn once you have everything."

Jacques nodded and set the chest down in the wagon with a grunt.

His arms ached by the time everything was loaded and the wagon moving across the cobbled street. But aching or not, he would be obliged to help move everything from the wagon to the inn next.

He sighed, but he knew better than to complain. His father had told him sternly that he was to do whatever was asked of him without a word and to keep perfect track of Monsieur's possessions, for it was only under such a condition that the Comte had agreed for Jacques to join them on the voyage.

Jacques hoisted yet another chest into his arms, pressing forward to the carriage with an extra grunt of determination. He was eager to prove that it had not been a mistake to bring him along. He would ensure the safety of Monsieur's belongings.

The Comte would not trust his valuables anywhere but his own room—he had been clear that everything was to stay with him, and his paranoia would surely continue until they arrived in Dorset where he would be among family and could place it all under lock and key. Though they were relatives, apparently the Comte had never met the Broussards, and yet he seemed to trust them. The ways of the aristocracy were strange to Jacques.

The yard of the inn was loud with animals and voices when the carriage bobbed in, and their arrival seemed hardly to be noticed. Jacques searched for the hired coach his father had accompanied Monsieur in and saw it across the yard.

He peeked into the small, wooden chest he had just transported and quickly snapped it shut, the glinting of a ruby ring lingering in his vision. He lifted the chest into his arms and told the French shipman to remain in place until Jacques could receive instruction from his father and the Comte.

He headed toward the inn door, asking one of the innservants in broken English where he could find the French monsieur.

When Jacques arrived upstairs, it was to the sound of imperative voices speaking within the room he had been directed to. Opening the door slowly with his shoulder, he looked inside to see his father and an unfamiliar young gentleman, kneeling beside the prostrate form of the Comte.

The young man rose quickly and turned for the door, his expression urgent and grave.

"No," Jacques's father said in French, his shoulders slumping as he wiped his sweaty brow with a forearm. "It is too late."

The young man stilled and nodded, eyeing the Comte with a frown. "I am sorry," he said in mediocre French. "We did all that we could. My name is Retsford. I am just two rooms down if you need anything."

Jacques's father offered no response, staring at the body in front of him with a stricken look in his eyes.

The man Retsford opened the door, glancing at Jacques with a grimace before pushing past him.

Jacques's father crossed himself and then let himself fall back into a sitting position, with his back against the wall as he ran his hands through his hair.

"Father?" Jacques said hesitantly, setting down the chest.

His father's head came up, and Jacques felt a flash of fear at the sight of his hopeless expression. His father motioned for him to come, and Jacques walked over, shooting a brief, sidelong glance at the motionless body on the floor. Why wasn't Monsieur on the bed where he could sleep comfortably? It would likely be hours before he awoke, if the amount he had drunk aboard the ship was any indication.

"He is dead," his father said, a catch in his voice.

Jacques's eyes widened, and he looked at the form of the Comte, swallowing. There *was* something different about the Comte; something missing.

But dead? Jacques had never seen death up close. Of course, his mother had died giving birth to him, but he didn't remember that at all. His father was his only family.

He felt mesmerized by the sight of the Comte, and yet he was afraid. How did death look so similar to and yet so different from sleeping?

He looked to his father, fear taking an even greater hold at the sight of the dejection there. What would they do now? They didn't know a soul in all of England. Did this mean they would go back to France?

He shivered. What would they do there without Monsieur le Comte to serve? They would be homeless, penniless. They already *were* penniless. The Comte was not a particularly generous master.

Jacques thought of all the jewels and valuables sitting in the wagon, waiting to be brought upstairs to the Comte's room. He thought of the ruby ring he had just seen. Surely the Comte wouldn't be upset if they had to use one small trinket to buy their passage back to Calais? Or a spot on the Diligence—or whatever it might be called in England—to London? One small trinket out of hundreds.

"I saw a ruby ring, Papa," he said in a miserable voice, looking up at his father, whose face was covered by his hands. "Would that be enough to buy passage on the packet?"

His father shook his head in his hands. "It is not ours, Jacques."

Jacques felt a small stirring of hope. "Shall we stay in England, then?"

His father shook his head again, and Jacques fell into a confused silence.

A knock sounded at the door, and Jacques jumped up, moving to open the door a crack. His father didn't stir.

The French shipman stood outside, a question on his face.

"The Monsieur's things," the man said. "Shall I bring them up?"

Jacques looked at his father, who shook his head and then froze, an arrested expression in his eyes.

Jacques waited. "Papa?"

His father blinked twice and looked at Jacques. He nodded at him. "Have him bring them into the next room."

"Yes, please," said Jacques to the servant. "Into the room next door."

The man nodded and left.

Jacques's father stood and began pacing up and down the room next to the body of the Comte. His hand pulled nervously at his lips.

"It could work," he said, stopping and staring at the papered wall. "No one would know." His gaze moved down to the body beside him, and he shook his head again, resuming his distracted pacing of the room.

"Know what?" Jacques said.

His father came over and kneeled in front of Jacques, putting a hand on each shoulder and looking him in the eye with a strange energy Jacques found disturbing.

"It will not be easy, my son," his father said. "But you know how things work in noble households. Can you imagine yourself to be the son of a Comte instead of the son of a valet? Can you act the part of a noble?"

Jacques swallowed and nodded.

His father put a hand on Jacques's cheek. "God has given us an opportunity for a better life, thanks be to Him." He looked toward the window, his jaw tight and hard. "I will not waste it."

Continue reading *Cecilia* on Amazon or Kindle Unlimited.

OTHER TITLES BY MARTHA KEYES

If you enjoyed this book, make sure to check out my other books:

Families of Dorset Series

Wyndcross: A Regency Romance (Book One)

Isabel: A Regency Romance (Book Two)

Cecilia: A Regency Romance (Book Three)

Hazelhurst: A Regency Romance (Book Four)

Phoebe: A Regency Romance (Series Novelette)

Regency Shakespeare Series

A Foolish Heart (Book One)

My Wild Heart (Book Two)

True of Heart (Book Three)

Other Titles

Of Lands High and Low

The Christmas Foundling (Belles of Christmas: Frost Fair Book Five)

Goodwill for the Gentleman (Belles of Christmas Book Two)

Eleanor: A Regency Romance

The Road through Rushbury (Seasons of Change Book One)

Join my Newsletter to keep in touch and learn more about the Regency era!
I try to keep it fun and interesting.

OR follow me on BookBub to see my recommendations and get alerts about
my new releases.

AFTERWORD

Thank you so much for reading *Isabel*. I had a wonderful time writing this story, and I hope you enjoyed getting to know Isabel and Charles.

I also hope you look forward to reading the upcoming books in the series to learn more in depth about some of the characters you've only heard briefly about so far.

I have done my best to be true to the time period and particulars of the day, so I apologize if I got anything wrong. I continue learning and researching while trying to craft stories that will be enjoyable to readers like you.

If you enjoyed the book, please leave a review and tell your friends! Authors like me rely on readers like you to spread the word about books you've enjoyed.

If you would like to stay in touch, please sign up for my newsletter. If you just want updates on new releases, you can follow me on BookBub or Amazon. You can also connect with me on Facebook and Instagram. I would love to hear from you!

ACKNOWLEDGMENTS

There are always a few key people who are instrumental to the creation of a novel. My mom has rooted for Isabel and Charles from the very beginning and given me valuable feedback.

My husband has given up precious work hours of his own in order for me to write, edit, write, edit, *ad nauseum*. My little boys are almost always good sports about their scatterbrained mom and my constant sneaking away to the computer to get down an idea while it's fresh.

Thank you to my editor, Jenny Proctor, for her wonderful feedback—I'm so glad I have you!

Thank you to my Review Team for your help and support in an often nervewracking business.

And as always, thank you to all my fellow Regency authors and to the wonderful communities of The Writing Gals and LDS Beta Readers. I would be lost without all of your help and trailblazing!

ABOUT THE AUTHOR

Martha Keyes was born, raised, and educated in Utah—a home she loves dearly but also dearly loves to escape whenever she can travel the world. She received a BA in French Studies and a Master of Public Health, both from Brigham Young University.

Word crafting has always fascinated and motivated her, but it wasn't until a few years ago that she considered writing her own stories. When she isn't writing, she is honing her photography skills, looking for travel deals, and spending time with her husband and children. She lives with her husband and twin boys in Vineyard, Utah.